STOLEN BRIDE

M JAMES

Copyright © 2021 by M. James.

All rights reserved.

No part of this book may be reproduced in any form or by any electronic or mechanical means, including information storage and retrieval systems, without written permission from the author, except for the use of brief quotations in a book review.

This is a work of fiction. Names, characters, businesses, places, events and incidents are either the products of the author's imagination or used in a fictitious manner. Any resemblance to actual persons, living or dead, or actual events is purely coincidental.

CATERINA

When I wake up, it's with absolutely no sense of where I am.

It takes me a minute to realize that the voice ringing in my ears isn't actually speaking. It's just the memory of the last thing I heard before I passed out—*we're here for* you, *Caterina*—followed by the rippling of that bone-chilling terror that I'd felt as the needle had slid into my neck.

I've never had a phobia of needles, but if I survive this, I might have one now. I'll never be able to forget the sight of it gleaming above me, the liquid beading from the tip right before it punctured my throat. Then I slipped into a cold dark haze that I'm only just now coming out of.

Whatever they drugged me with, it's slow wearing off. I don't feel as if I can move at first, and for a moment, I'm terrified that I'm going to be alert but unable to move. That sounds more terrifying than just waking up and discovering where I actually am.

Cold. So much cold. As the sensation starts to return to my limbs, that's the next thing I notice. Not just a chill, but a bone-deep cold, as if every bit of heat had been leached out of the room.

Slowly, I try to pry my eyes open, doing my best not to move. I don't know where my kidnappers are, but if they're nearby, I don't want to alert them that I'm awake. I want a minute to try to get my bearings, to make a plan.

Growing up in the Family, I never felt particularly in danger. I felt secure that my father would protect me, and my eventual husband, whoever that was. But there was always the knowledge, deep down, that I could be a target. That my position as Vitto Rossi's daughter made me valuable and that I needed protection. That whoever he married me off to would also need to protect me.

I'd been so concerned these past months with protecting myself from the men I married—first Franco and now my Bratva husband—that I'd forgotten there were other people out there who might have reasons for wanting to catch and hurt Vitto Rossi's daughter, or the *Ussuri*'s wife. That even if I felt secure that Viktor wouldn't ever hurt me the way Franco had, that didn't mean I was safe.

Whoever these men are, they knew about Viktor, so it's safe to say that they're probably after me as his wife, not as my father's daughter. This is a Russian problem, not an Italian one, making the entire situation even more terrifying. The Italian mafia can be cruel, but I've heard stories of what happens to women caught by the Russians. For all his flaws, Viktor seems to be the best of them. I don't think these men are anything like Viktor.

My eyes feel dry, burning, but I manage to get them open and look carefully around through blurry vision as much as I can without moving my head. There's a shaft of sunlight coming through the window to my left, lighting up a grey sky that tells me it's still early, which explains the cold despite it being May. My hands are still bound behind me, which sends another panic-fueled dart of terror through me, but I force myself to breathe, slowly and shallowly.

Think, Caterina. Take stock of the situation, and think.

I press my fingers against the surface beneath me—it's a hard mattress, one that I can feel the springs starting to push through. It feels lumpy, and I don't dare look down—I'm not sure I want to see the rest of the condition that it's in. The curtains on the window are mostly closed, except for the small space between them where I can see the sunlight gleaming through, and I think that I see a glimpse of tree branches.

Did they take me out to the woods? I feel another flutter of panic. If we were back in New York, I might be able to figure out where I am, but I don't know anything about the geography around Moscow. Russia is entirely foreign to me, and the thought of being held captive out somewhere in a Russian forest threatens to overwhelm me with another hopeless wave of fear.

Viktor. I might not know Russia, but my husband does. Will he come for me?

That thought makes me go very still. It hadn't occurred to me before that he might not, only that there might not be time. But if he's decided that I'm more trouble than I'm worth as his wife and the future mother of his child, this would be an easy way to get rid of me. He can let them do what they want, and tell Luca whatever he pleases —that he couldn't get to me in time, that he couldn't find me, that they wanted something in exchange for me that he couldn't give. This might be his way out of a marriage that I suspect I might have made as unpleasant for him so far as it's been for me.

Not entirely unpleasant, though.

The last thing I want to think about right now is the complexities of what Viktor and I have done in bed—or what he's done to me, rather. I don't know if it's enough to overcome the friction between us, the way I've refused to bend to his will, or if he'll choose to simply take a way out that won't have the same consequences as sending me back to Luca.

Or—there's another terrifying possibility that I hadn't yet thought about.

What if this was Viktor?

I still don't know how the first Mrs. Andreyev died. I don't know what part, if any, Viktor played in it. And the realization comes rushing in that there's a very real possibility that after my reaction to seeing his business here, Viktor decided that it was time for his second marriage to come to an end in a very final way.

Fuck. Fuck, fuck, fuck. I squeeze my eyes tight, forcing myself to think through the fear. I've had to do it before, during the worst of the times with Franco, when saving myself meant thinking past my own fear and pain and calming him down.

I've been alone before, and I've saved myself. I can't rely on Viktor, whether or not this is his doing. If this isn't him, I'm still somewhere out in the Russian forest; god knows how far away from him I am. And if it is—then it's even more imperative that I figure this out for myself.

I hear a shift from behind me and go very still. There's a scraping over the floor, like a chair being moved, and then a gruff voice speaking in Russian. I can't understand a word of it, but he sounds angry, his voice clipped and harsh in a way that makes my heart stutter in my chest.

A second voice joins the first, speaking in a deep, rough growl. They don't bother lowering their voices, either because they don't realize I'm awake or because they assume I can't understand them, which is definitely true. And I don't want them to realize that I'm awake yet.

My heart is pounding so hard that I can hear the beat of it in my ears. I grit my teeth, doing my best to keep my breathing even and my hands from clenching. *Be brave, be brave,* I tell myself repeatedly, and I wonder, if I survive this, if this will be the most difficult thing I have to face.

I certainly fucking hope so.

I hear footsteps, heavy on the floorboards, coming closer. *This is it,* I think, and then I feel a hand gripping my shoulder, rolling me onto my back.

"I think she's awake, boss," the man hovering above me says in thickly accented English. My vision is still clearing from the drugs, so I can't make out his features exactly. I can see that he's heavyset and thick-lipped, his sausage-like fingers digging into the hollow of my shoulder as he rolls me over. "Time for some fun."

"You know the rules, Andrei," the man behind him says, his voice equally thick.

"No permanent damage. Don't fuck up her face." Andrei sneers down at me, and I almost wish my vision wasn't clearing because nothing about him is anything I want to see. I can feel some of the sensation returning to my limbs, my muscles twitching as my body comes back to life, and I don't know how I feel about that, either.

On the one hand, if I can't move, I can't fight. On the other, whatever they plan to do to me next, I'm going to feel it.

His hand tightens on my shoulder, and I can't help but try to flinch away. Andrei laughs, a wet drop of spit landing on my face as he does so.

"Ooh, this little *koshka* has claws," he says with a grin, and his hand squeezes, clenching my shoulder so tightly that I cry out in pain.

It burns away what was left of the drugs, though, bringing me fully and abruptly back to my senses. I buck under his hand, twisting and wrenching my hands in the cuffs despite myself, and I hear him growl above me.

"Stepan, get the bitch to be still."

I let out a yelp despite myself as two hands latch onto my ankles, yanking me down the mattress so that I'm flat on my back. There's no way for me to grab on to anything or stop it, not with my hands bound behind my back still and gone numb from how tight the plastic cuffs are. But I refuse to go down without a fight.

Andrei's other hand finds my breast, squeezing through the satin of my half-destroyed evening gown, and I jerk like a fish, kicking at Stepan's grip. As far as I can tell, there are only the two of them, for now, but I know that might not last forever. There might be more outside or on the way, and neither of these two is the cold man who slid the needle into my neck before kidnapping me.

"Christ, she squirms like a worm on a hook," Stepan growls, his fingers digging into my ankles until I yelp with pain again. He jerks my legs apart, leering up the remains of my skirt, and as I get a good look at what remains of my dress, I feel a twist in my stomach.

It's half ripped, torn off, or cut off at my knees, probably because they got tired of wrestling with all of the fabric while they transported me. The bodice is still mostly in place, thank god, but all of the material is filthy. I can feel how tangled my hair is, and I wonder how much time has passed since I was taken out of the apartment. A day? Two? More than that?

"They didn't say we couldn't fuck her," Andrei says, his accent thickening even more. "She's no virgin. No one can tell the fucking difference if we get our dicks wet anyway."

"We weren't told we could, either—" Stepan sounds hesitant. It's very strange to feel a moment's gratitude towards him for something so absolutely ridiculous as a hesitance to actually violate me, but here we are.

"Look at her." Andrei's hand slides down my rib cage, and I feel my muscles tense, my skin shuddering away from his touch. "You want to ask permission or forgiveness? How often do we get a piece like this that isn't off-limits entirely?"

Stepan's gaze slides up my legs again, and I can see him considering it. He lingers on my inner thighs, and his grip on my ankles slackens just a little, enough to let me wrench one foot out of his grasp.

I know it's stupid. I know it's useless. My hands are bound, and I'm still weak from the drugs; there's no way I'm going to overpower them. But I can't just lay here and let them do this.

The moment my foot is free, I twist, kicking as hard as I can and aiming for the side of Stepan's head. He's so busy ogling me that he doesn't see the kick coming. Andrei doesn't either because he's focused on running his hands over my breasts and stomach, chuckling with every twitch of my body as it automatically tries to escape his touch.

The kick isn't hard enough to knock Stepan out or do any real damage, but it *feels* good. I have one single moment of feeling absolute satisfaction at the shocked look on his face before he lurches back towards me with a furious expression.

He comes halfway across the bed in an instant, Andrei jumping out of his way as Stepan's hand fists in the front of my dress, the delicate satin ripping in his rough grip. He yanks me forward, his right hand connecting across my cheek in a slap that makes my ear start ringing and my head go sideways so hard that I can feel a muscle in my neck strain too far.

"Fucking little *bitch*," Stepan snarls, his hand grabbing my jaw in a vice grip as he shoves his thumb between my lips. "Suck on this while I get you something better to suck on, you little mafia whore."

Oh, fuck this.

I know whatever I do, they're going to give it back so much worse, but I can't help it. At that moment, I know I'd rather die than let them use me however they wanted. Maybe they'll do it anyway, but I'm damn sure going to make it hard for them.

I bite down on Stepan's thumb hard, my teeth sinking into the flesh as I taste blood. His sudden screech of pain is even more satisfying than the kick to the side of the head, and I dig my teeth in, wanting to hurt him as much as possible before he retaliates.

The punch comes without warning, a fist in my side that takes the breath right out of me and leaves me gasping, my jaw dropping open and letting Stepan extricate his ragged thumb.

"Hold her," Stepan snarls, his face an evil mask of rage, and I feel my stomach twist with bitter fear. Whatever's coming next, I know it won't be good.

Andrei's thick hand wraps in my hair, pulling my head backward as Stepan hits me again, hard enough that I feel my lip split, starting to swell almost immediately. The blows come fast and furious then, Andrei's grip tightening until it feels as if he might rip my hair from my skull. I can feel myself starting to go limp, the pain blooming through my body like a fresh bruise.

And then I feel Stepan's hand around my throat, squeezing as he looks down at me with a vicious light in his eyes that terrifies me more than anything I've ever experienced.

As my vision goes dark again, all I can think is that I'd give anything for that to not be the last thing I see.

VIKTOR

*I*t's been three days since Caterina went missing.

I came back to the apartment to find her gone, and at first, I'd thought that she might have taken the opportunity to escape me. But the knocked-over side table and broken vase by the door, with one of her high heels lying in the midst of the shattered glass, was enough to suggest that she hadn't left of her own volition.

My first call was to Levin back in New York. The information he'd given me had only served to intensify my certainty that Caterina had been taken rather than running away. He'd told me that there was more unrest among the men, that Alexei had been insubordinate, and that he'd look a little more deeply into that. The threatening tone in his voice had told me that Alexei was in for an—uncomfortable conversation.

A day and a half later, he was on a jet to Moscow to join me here, leaving Mikhail in charge to keep an eye on Alexei and the burgeoning rebellion at home. Deep down, I knew it would be best to leave Levin there to oversee things, but I also need my second in command here with me, helping me to find my wife.

Moscow is a minefield for me, full of those who envy what my family built for ourselves in America and those who simply think that

I don't deserve all I have. My father and his father weren't from any important family. The fact that the Andreyev name has risen so high is a bitter pill for many still here to swallow, and there's no shortage of those who would like to see me brought down.

I suspect that one of them, or more, might have gotten to Alexei, whispered poison in his ear, and planted the seeds of mutiny there. And if that's the case, the place I *should* be right now is Manhattan, purging the infection out of my organization before it can take hold and protecting my family.

But Caterina is here, abducted and held somewhere. Even as my hand hovered over the phone to call and tell the jet to get ready to take me back to New York, I knew I couldn't abandon her.

Now I'm in the cold of Northern Russia, a place where the temperatures hover low even in May, bundled up and camping as we search for her. I feel torn in two directions, between my duty to my wife and my duty to my responsibilities back home, and it's made me irritable and difficult. Levin brought a handful of men with him to aid in the search. They're keeping a bit of a distance from me as we set up camp, a few of them cleaning weapons as they talk quietly among themselves.

"You think it was Igor?" I ask, keeping my voice low as I sit by the fire. "He's had his eye on my stake in the business for a while."

"I think it's likely. He's the other supplier, and you're in direct competition with him—but you do better even though he has the ear of some of the most influential men in Moscow. If he had the opportunity to bring you down from the inside—"

"You suspect Alexei, too." It's not a question. My voice is flat and certain. I know Levin has the same concerns that I do.

"I do," Levin confirms, looking into the fire. "He's been even stranger since you were gone, more withdrawn and restless. I think something is going on. I trust him less than I did before, and that was already eroding."

"There'll be hell to pay when I get back, if he's responsible for doing this to Caterina. And if she's not alive if we find her—"

"When," Levin says sharply, but he still doesn't look at me. "We'll find her, Viktor. This won't be a repeat of Vera."

"I hope not."

I have faith in Levin's abilities to help me track her, and I believe that we'll find her—or at least the ones responsible—eventually. I have less faith in what condition she'll be in once we get there. It's already been three days, and we're a decent bit away from Moscow now into the woods. If the trail goes cold, we might not find her in time.

And there are worse things than finding her dead.

The thought lingers with me as I lay down to try to sleep, which eludes me. It's not the discomfort of being out in the woods—for all the luxuries I've acquired for myself, I'm no stranger to roughing it when need be. There's even a certain peace to being out in the cold night, the trees close and thick around me, and the faint noises of wildlife in the distance. But in the dark, the memories of Vera come crowding back in, her pale, lifeless face and the blood on her wrists, the way my heart had twisted and shattered when I'd seen the absolute, brutal finality of it.

I'd sworn to myself that I'd never feel anything again like what I felt for her, that I'd never open my heart to someone again only to know that we'd disappoint each other in the end. But as I lie there looking up at the ceiling of my tent, the darkness close and cold around me, I can't deny that there's a part of me that wants to do exactly that with Caterina.

And in the end, I'll disappoint her too. I can't be anything other than what I am—I've only ever been this. Vera had wanted me to be something different, and when I couldn't, it had destroyed her. Now I'm very afraid that the life I lead will claim another woman that I've come to care for and that I won't be able to stop it. Or that she won't be dead, but a shell of the woman I married instead.

I'm not sure which would be worse, honestly.

It's her that I finally dream about when I do fall asleep. I dream of her on the balcony outside our hotel room on our wedding night, the breeze ruffling the heavy satin of her skirt, her fingers clenched around the railing. I see her leaning forward the way I had when I walked out of the bathroom, feeling the clenching fear in my stomach again that she might have been thinking of throwing herself off.

Marriage to me can't be worse than death, can it?

Vera had proved that wasn't the case.

In the dream, though, Caterina hears my voice the way she had on our wedding night and turns away from the railing, her hair blowing loosely around her shoulders as she faces me. This time, there's a smile on her face as she looks at me, her eyes soft instead of cold and blank the way they had really been that night.

Her lips part and I know she wants to come to me. I can feel the pulse of desire that passes through me at the look on her face, and I take a breath, setting the drink in my hand aside as I take a step towards her, suddenly very aware of the bed to my left and what I intend to do to her in it in just a few moments—

And then Alexei appears next to her, his hand on her arm, grabbing her roughly. Before I can speak or move or even breathe, he hauls her over the side of the railing, shoving her hard as he throws her over to the concrete all the way down.

I scream, a sound that could be her name or his or something else altogether, and then I jolt awake.

I sit up, gasping, a cold sweat clinging to my forehead and palms. The sound of Caterina's shriek in the dream is still ringing in my ears, the sight of Alexei throwing her off of the balcony so vivid and real that it's almost hard to believe that it was a dream at all. My heart is pounding, and I have to take several deep, full breaths as I remember where I am, that none of it was real.

Vera is gone. I can't change that. I can't fix the mistakes I made with her. But there's still a chance that I can save Caterina.

Part of me has wanted to abandon the search these past twenty-four hours, to accept that she's gone and go back home to my children. I could root out the dissent in my organization, purge it clean and then make sure that Anika and Yelena are safe, the two people in the world who need me the most.

But every time I've come close to saying it aloud, something has stopped me.

The vows I'd made to Caterina hadn't *meant* anything to me—or at least I hadn't thought that they did. I hadn't bought her an engagement ring or said anything beyond the most traditional of vows because it had all been a means to an end, a situation of convenience, and nothing more.

But here, now, I feel a responsibility that I hadn't known I would. She's my *wife*, and that thought makes me feel something intense and primal, a rage at anyone who might touch her that I hadn't expected. However hard I'd tried to keep my distance; clearly, I hadn't done well enough. I feel an ache for her that goes beyond simple duty. As I lie back on my sleeping bag, I feel that pulse of desire from the dream as I remember the last night before she was taken.

She'd wanted me. She might deny it if I said it to her face, and it might never fucking happen again, but she'd wanted me that night. She'd been willing, soft, and yielding, and it had cracked open something in me that I thought I'd vaulted shut forever.

As much as I want to pretend she means nothing to me beyond the bargain that I made with Luca, I know that it's not true.

I hadn't thought I could fear losing someone again other than my children. But tonight, alone in the dark, I allow myself to admit the one thing that I've been avoiding for days.

Caterina has found the chink in my armor, found her way into the spaces I'd locked up tight.

And now, I'm afraid of losing her before I've even really had her.

CATERINA

When I wake up again, there's no part of my body that doesn't hurt.

It's dark again, and I'm freezing cold. It's hard to pry open my eyes—they must have been leaking tears when I was unconscious, and now my lashes feel frosted to my cheeks. My face feels swollen, and I taste blood inside my mouth, my entire body heavy and aching.

It takes a moment for me to realize that I'm outside, lying in a stand of trees, and a fresh horror washes over me as I realize that they must have thrown me out here after they knocked me out. I'm still dressed but barely, the top of my dress clinging to me by a few stubborn seams, and my skirt wrapped around the tops of my thighs.

I know I can't stay out here, but the idea of going back in feels equally horrifying. I lay there in the dirt for a moment, trying to breathe, my hands still bound behind my back. I don't even know how I would get to the door—I'd have to crawl without being able to use my hands, and the utter humiliation of it threatens to rip me apart at the seams.

Viktor, are you out there? I look up at the clear sky, stars swirling overhead, and I wonder where he is. Is he back in Moscow, trying to find out what's happened to me? Is he out here somewhere in these woods, looking for me, staring up at the same sky and trying to follow the stars to wherever I am?

It's such a ridiculous thought that I start to laugh, and then immediately stop with a small cry as a violent pain shoots through my head, sending a wash of red over my vision. I can feel the throbbing ache that follows it, shooting down through my neck and the rest of me, and I slump back down onto the ground, gasping.

Maybe he's not coming. Maybe this is all his doing, and I'm going to die out here, after whatever the two stooges in there decide they want to do to me first.

I don't think I can fight them off. They drugged me and beat me, and I wasn't in the best of shape before this—too thin and still getting back to myself. I can fight back, but it'll only make it worse in the end. That doesn't mean I *won't*—only that I know that it'll be a futile attempt to save myself.

It's a strange feeling, lying there in the cold and the dark, reckoning with the end of my life. Wherever this is going, whether they have someone to deliver me to or if they're just toying with me until they end it themselves, I don't doubt that it ends with a knife at my throat or a gun barrel to my head. I'd been terrified before with Franco, but I'd never really, truly believed I would die. I hadn't thought, deep down, that he'd have the balls to kill me. And besides, I was the thing he needed to keep his power. Without me, he'd have been nothing, and he'd known it.

But now—I'm going to die. The knowledge seeps into my bones, chills my blood in a way that the cold air never could, and I let it settle over me as I try to think about what it means, to come to terms with it.

In the end, what do I have to leave behind exactly? Two children who aren't mine, one who might love me but who are too young to remember me for long if I'm gone, and another who hates my guts. A husband who might be relieved to have me gone, if he hasn't orchestrated my demise himself. No family left, and only one friend, one who I haven't even known all that long.

That makes me sadder than the idea of death itself, the realization that there wouldn't really be all that much for me to leave behind. No one to mourn me really, or miss me. Just a life spent doing the bidding of others, giving up everything I'd ever wanted to do what was expected of me.

It feels like such a waste. I hadn't wanted to cry, but out here with no one to see me, the weight of hopelessness settling on my shoulders, I close my eyes and let a few of the tears drip down my cheeks.

At this point, I almost want it to just be over.

I'm not sure how much time passes before the door to the cabin opens. I'd relinquished any thoughts of trying to crawl back towards it myself—I can't really with my hands bound. Anyway, I'd rather freeze to death than give Andrei or Stepan the pleasure of knowing I'd crawled back in to them. Freezing is better than anything they could have planned for me, anyway.

But eventually, the door does open, letting out a sliver of yellow light into the darkness. I hear the sound of their voices, but it's garbled, which makes me wonder if they've done permanent damage to my eardrums in some way, with how Stepan had struck me. Andrei is the one who comes out to get me, heaving me up like a sack of potatoes without any care for my injuries. I don't want to cry out—I don't want to give him the satisfaction—but I can't help it. Franco beat me badly more than once, but I've never felt anything like the white-hot pain that shoots through every part of my body as he roughly hauls me back into the cabin.

My hope is that they'll toss me back onto the filthy bed and let me sleep. At this point, I'm so exhausted that I think I could sleep anywhere, regardless of the state it's in, but I'm not that lucky.

Andrei sets me down, holding the cuffs around my wrists as a means of keeping me on my feet. Stepan strides towards me with a malicious gleam in his eye that chills my blood even more than it already is.

When I see the massive hunting knife in his hand, I want to throw up.

"Keep her still," Stepan says gruffly to Andrei, stopping close enough in front of me that I can smell the foul onion scent of his breath as he speaks. He presses the point of the knife between my breasts, giving me a vicious smile that makes my stomach flip again, knotting until I nearly gag.

"This dress looks like it's seen better days," he says with a laugh, grunting as he pushes the knife into the fabric, hard enough that I have to force myself not to cry out from the pressure of the point pushing into my ribs. "I think it might as well come off. Don't you, Andrei?"

Andrei shrugs, chuckling lasciviously. "Might as well see if what's under it looks as good as we think it does."

Stepan grabs the fabric above my breast then, using the knife to cut down through the material, splitting it apart as he saws down through the satin. With a jerk of his hand, he rips it sideways as he keeps cutting, down to my navel where he pauses, pushing the point of the knife into my belly again.

"I could gut you like an animal," he growls, twisting the knife until I feel it break the skin ever so slightly, and I bite down on my lower lip, refusing to make a sound. If he does much more, I don't know if I'll be able to keep quiet, but I'll hold out as long as I can.

"Stepan—" Andrei's warning voice comes from behind me, but Stepan just grins, twisting the knife a little harder. I feel something warm and liquid running down my stomach, and I feel the nausea rise up again as I realize that it must be my own blood.

Is this it? Is this where they decide they're done toying with me?

"There's a lot of parts you could probably live without," Stepan says conversationally, as the point of the knife leaves the spot where he dug it in and carries on slicing my dress open. He yanks the fabric again, tearing it open down the middle so that it suddenly hangs on either side of me, leaving my breasts bare. Only the thin black seamless panties I'd worn beneath it clinging to my hips.

"Cut those straps off," he continues, glancing towards Andrei, and there's the *click* of what sounds like a smaller knife. I feel the quick pressure of a blade and the sensation of it cutting through the straps at my shoulders. Then the dress falls in a puddle of ruined fabric to the cabin floor, leaving me with almost nothing left to cover me at all.

I can't even try to use my hands because they're still cuffed behind my back.

I want to let myself start to shake. I want to cry. I want to crumble and fall apart, but I can't. These two men are stripping everything from me—my dignity, my clothing, and soon I'm sure, my life. I won't give them the satisfaction of seeing me tremble and cower and sob. I'll hold out as long as I can before I give them even another single whimper.

"What do you think?' Stepan asks, leering at me. "Does she have some answers for us?" He holds up the knife, and I feel another jolt of nausea as I see my own blood gleaming wetly on the tip.

"She might," Andrei says, shrugging from behind me. "She might know a lot. Or a little. Or nothing."

What am I supposed to know? A new frisson of fear runs down my spine because I don't know much of *anything* that could be worthwhile to men like them. And I'm not entirely sure that they'll believe that.

"Sit her down." Stepan pokes my nipple with the point of the knife, pushing inwards until I have to bite back a scream of fear. I remember him saying *no permanent damage* earlier, but what if that's changed? What if that only lasts until they realize I have nothing for them?

I feel so sick, weak, shivery, and nauseated, either from hunger or fear, or both. I'm struggling to stay upright, and I'm almost relieved when Andrei pushes a chair forward and yanks me down by my shoulders down into it, even when I feel him grab my cuffs and thread something through them, fastening my wrists to the back of the chair so that I can't get out of the chair even if my legs didn't feel like they were made of jelly.

"Now," Stepan says, dragging the tip of the knife across my chest, over to my other nipple. "We have some questions about your husband's business, Mrs. Andreyva."

"I don't know anything about it," I say softly, looking up at him. I hate the sight of him, hate looking into his pale, watery blue eyes, but all I can do is hope that he'll see that I'm telling the truth. "I only found out what my husband's business even *is* a few days ago. I don't have any information for you."

"And if I think you're lying?" Stepan smiles cruelly. "I can make you suffer, Catarina. I can make you wish you'd never married the *Ussuri.*"

Trust me, I don't need you to make me wish that. I'd do anything right now to undo that particular decision, as if I'd ever really had any way out of it. I wonder what Luca would think if he knew where I was right now, that his agreement with Viktor had led to this.

I wonder if he'd still think it was worth it.

I don't know if I still do.

"I'm not lying," I tell him firmly. "I don't know anything about any of it. All I know is that my husband traffics women. And I think it's disgusting," I add for good measure, curling my lip as I look up at him. "So I didn't *want* to know anything about it, even if he'd wanted to tell me. Which he didn't."

Stepan pulls the knife back, tapping it against the fingers of his other hand as he considers. "I'm disappointed," he says finally. "It's not much fun if you really don't know anything." He frowns. "Maybe you'll come up with something."

And that's when it really begins.

That's when it becomes clear that maybe Stepan and Andrei have been tasked with getting any information I might have out of me. Neither of them really care all that much about it themselves; they want the opportunity to hurt me, and the information is just an excuse to do that.

And now he's just going to make up an excuse.

Franco was always your garden-variety abusive husband. He wasn't one to come up with creative ways to cause me pain. A slap, a punch, a fist in the hair. A night where I had to please his every whim, regardless of how I felt about it. But he didn't have the imagination or the inclination to be more intentional about it than that.

Stepan is something else. A sociopath, definitely. A sadist, certainly. And someone who clearly enjoys torture simply for the sake of it.

By the time he's halfway done with me, I've stopped being able to think. My body was already a mass of pain, but now it's one of bruises and shallow cuts too. Stepan's knife is drawing on my flesh as he asks me questions about Viktor's business, about money and ledgers and girls that I couldn't possibly answer even if I wanted to. I don't have the presence of mind to come up with lies, either. So I keep murmuring the same thing miserably over and over, wishing more than anything that this could simply come to an end. Whatever that means.

"I don't know. I don't know. *I don't know.*"

After a while, it seems like Stepan has stopped caring about whether I know anything or not. And a little bit after that, I stop being able to respond at all.

I'm lucky, I guess, that I have all my teeth and all my nails still. Whether it'll stay that way, I don't know. But for tonight, I'm safe at least, because before either of them can resort to those types of tried-and-true torture methods, I'm finally untied from the chair and lifted unceremoniously onto the mattress, where I'm left to lie there curled up on my side.

My hands are still behind my back, numb at this point, and I wonder if it's doing any permanent damage. I wonder what sort of consequences there are to lying on a mattress this dirty, naked, with open wounds. I wonder if they're ever going to feed me or give me water. My stomach feels like an empty pit, and my mouth is so dry that it's nearly unbearable.

I wonder if any of it fucking matters anymore.

Viktor hasn't come for me.

Maybe he isn't going to. Maybe this is all because of him. It doesn't make sense why they would question me about him if he'd set this up, but maybe it was just some elaborate plan. Maybe he told them to make it seem realistic.

Whatever it is, I'm starting to understand the urge to simply want to die. To slip away and have the pain and misery end.

After all, what do I have left to live for?

I shift on the bed, wincing as a bruise on my stomach presses against the mattress. I think of how many times Stepan punched me there, of the cold and the pain and the lack of food and water, and as my stomach clenches with nausea, I have a sudden, horrible thought.

What if I'm pregnant?

Viktor and I have never used any kind of protection. There was also a long space where we didn't have sex—until very recently, too soon to have any sort of symptoms or really for anything to have taken root.

But there was our wedding night.

I know the likelihood that I got pregnant on the first night is slim. I know the possibility that if I were, that the pregnancy could have survived what I've been put through since the kidnapping is even more so.

But just the thought that I could be, that there's even a slight possibility, makes me curl in on myself as if I can protect the potential of that tiny life inside of me. I didn't even want Viktor's baby, but the thought strikes some primal urge in me, a sudden flare of protectiveness that I hadn't known I could feel.

Don't think about it. I can't save myself, let alone the possibility of a baby. But now that the thought has taken root in my head, I can't shake it free. And the thought that it might not only be me that dies here makes my heart feel as if it could shatter.

I squeeze my eyes shut, forcing myself to breathe through the pain, the hunger, the feeling of hopelessness. Whatever happens, I'm not dead yet. There's still a chance.

A small one—but a chance nonetheless.

I fall asleep dreaming of water.

VIKTOR

Can she still be alive?

The further into the woods we go, and the colder it gets, the more I wonder if there's any chance of finding my wife at all, let alone alive. Even Levin has grown quiet and grim as we've continued on, his face settled into harsh lines as we progress forward.

A few times, I'm tempted to give up on the search. I can feel the restlessness from the others, their surety that we're chasing a needle in a haystack or looking for a woman who is already dead. I think if I asked Levin, he would say that we would do better to go back to Moscow and try to find out who was responsible for this. That Caterina herself is already lost.

But every time, I stop just short of it. Even if the outcome seems clear, I can't abandon her, and I don't entirely understand why. Is it guilt left over from Vera's death? A feeling that I'd failed one wife, and I can't fail the second? A lingering sense of duty?

On the fourth day, it's not until the afternoon that we actually find something to go on.

"Here!" Levin waves to me, gesturing for me to come to where he's standing, near a trail that leads into the eastern forest. It's thick with mud, and I see immediately what caught his eye—tire tracks from a heavy vehicle, something capable of traversing this sort of terrain.

I'm hesitant to believe that it will lead me to Caterina. It could be anyone—a hunter maybe, someone camping, although I find it hard to believe anyone would *choose* to camp out in this weather. But it's the first clue we've had to go on, so I nod to him, following as we track the tire marks deeper into the forest.

Several yards in, Levin holds up a hand abruptly, and everyone comes to a halt.

Past the next stand of trees, there's a cabin. I don't see smoke coming from the chimney or much sign of life, but there's a vehicle parked outside that could have made the same sort of tracks that we saw at the trailhead.

"We don't know if she's in there," one of the men mutters, and I stiffen. This kind of questioning is what is poisoning my organization back in New York, and I'd had Levin choose men who specifically weren't close with Alexei. But even these don't seem to be able to entirely follow me without question.

"There's only one way to find out," Levin says flatly. "Be ready for anything."

Slowly, we move in towards the cabin, eagle-eyed for any sign of who might be occupying it. It's not until we reach the edge of the trees just outside of the side door that I see a sprawl mark in the dirt near those trees, as if a body was thrown there at some point.

I motion to it, and Levin nods, his jaw tightening. And then, together, we move towards the cabin door.

From the moment Levin kicks it open, everything happens very quickly. I catch a glimpse of a naked, dark-haired woman passed out on a mattress, her hair covering her face, and although I can't be certain that it's Caterina, the sheer possibility of it is enough to spur an instinctive reaction in me that can likely only end with someone dead.

There are two men in the cabin, one stocky and the other lankier, and both of them recoil as we burst in. "Keep one of them alive to question," I snap at Levin, and instantly their entire demeanor changes. It's clear they can see that they're outmatched and outgunned, and I can see the instance in which they both shift from the offensive to self-preservation.

"I didn't fucking touch her!" the stocky one blurts out, his face paling. "It was all him. He's the one who cut her up—"

"It wasn't just me!" The lankier one reaches for something as if to grab a weapon, and in an instant, Levin fires a shot, hitting the smaller man's kneecap and sending him shrieking to the floor.

"Just fucking take them both if you can," I snarl, my gun leveled at the forehead of the stockier man. "We'll sort it out later."

There's no doubt in my mind now that the woman on the bed is Caterina, and I turn away from the fight, trusting Levin and the others at our back to deal with the two men while I go to collect my wife. I don't see a sign of anyone else at the cabin—clearly, whoever had ordered her abducted had thought two guards would be enough.

They'd clearly underestimated me.

No one fucking touches what's mine and gets away with it.

There's nothing on the bed to wrap her up in. I cast a glance around until I finally see a questionable blanket balled up in one corner of the room, shoved between the wall and a torn armchair. There's no time, and so I grab it anyway, throwing it over her prone, still body and lifting her off of the bed.

"We'll take the truck outside," I shout, seeing that Levin and the others have the two men down on the floor, the stockier one on his knees with his hands up. The other curled on the floor, still moaning from the pain of his shattered kneecap. "Someone fucking hotwire it so we can get out of here."

All of my concern is for Caterina. I can see her breathing shallowly—she's still alive—but I'm not sure how thin the thread is that she's hanging on by. I carry her out into the cold air, my chest constricting as I breathe in, forcing myself to believe that she'll make it.

Levin leaps into the driver's seat the moment the truck is hotwired, the growl of the engine filling the quiet forest air as the others pile in. One man is next to Levin, the others in the open bed with our two prisoners. I sit next to Caterina in the back, looking at her bone-white face as she lies there unconscious.

"We'll go to the safe house," I tell Levin sternly. "I know it's a fair distance, but it's the best option. As quickly as you can get us there."

I've never been a religious man. But watching Caterina as she lies there, I'm almost tempted to pray for the first time in my life.

My wife is in grave danger.

* * *

It's past midnight when Levin gets us to the safe house. It's a cabin tucked well away in the woods, not unlike the one we just rescued Caterina from, with a large shed in the back. "Put both of them in the shed and make sure it's secure," I instruct sternly, jumping out of the truck and carefully reaching for Caterina. She's barely moved for the entirety of the journey, only the very slight movement of her chest letting me know that she's even still breathing. "I'm going to get in her inside."

I take her directly to one of the bedrooms, carrying her up the steps and into the house bridal-style. The irony of it isn't lost on me, but I don't have time to be sentimental. I need to take stock of the situation, and the first part of that is what state Caterina is in.

I kick the door closed behind me as I carry her into the bedroom, laying her down carefully on top of the bed. I'm hesitant to unwrap the blanket around her, almost afraid of what I'll see.

I've seen a lot in my lifetime, things tragic and horrific and vile, but seeing the tortured body of my wife is something else. I hadn't thought anything could be worse than when I'd found Vera, but something about the state Caterina is in exceeds even that. Vera wasn't mangled, but the sight when I pull back the blanket, prying it away from where it's stuck to her body with dried blood as carefully as I'm able, makes my stomach turn over and my blood boil with a primal urge to go outside and rip both men in the shed from limb to limb.

In fact, one of the only reasons I don't is because Caterina deserves to see it happen after what they've done to her.

From shoulders to ankles, her body is a mass of cuts, some shallow and others deeper. There's hardly an inch of her skin that isn't bruised, her body a rainbow of blue and black and purple, broken capillaries fanning out in a grotesque pattern over her skin. Only her face is mostly untouched, and even then, her lip is split and bruised, her jaw swollen and nose bleeding.

She's barely hanging on. I can tell that much. She doesn't make a sound when I touch her, or even move, her chest rising and falling with the most shallow of breaths. She needs a doctor, but I'm very afraid she won't make it long enough for someone to get out here.

A heavy knock comes at the door, and I pull a quilt over her before answering it. The action feels surprisingly tender to me, striking a chord somewhere deep inside of me that I'm not sure I've felt before. Not even with Vera.

I don't give myself a chance to think too hard about it. Instead, I open the door to see Levin standing there, his face set in hard lines. "They're secure in the shed, sir. I have two of the men watching them." He glances over my shoulder, a flicker of worry creasing the lines between his eyes. "How is she?"

"Not well." My jaw tightens as I consider what to do next. "I need you to see how quickly we can get a doctor here that we can trust. And Max."

"Max?" Levin raises an eyebrow, and I frown.

"Where else in Russia would you find a Catholic priest?"

"He's not—"

"It's close enough. Just do it." I shut the door then, turning back to the bed. Levin won't mind the brusque brush-off. He's used to following orders. He and Mikhail are the only two I trust implicitly, and I hope that Mikhail is managing to keep Alexei in line back in New York.

I feel torn impossibly in two. Part of me wants nothing more than to stay in this room, watching Caterina obsessively until she finally opens her eyes again. And part of me knows that I can't do that, that I have my children back home, people depending on me, a duty that goes beyond how I might feel about the woman lying in the bed a few feet away.

But I have a responsibility to her, too.

I don't dare pick her up again, so instead, I leave her alone just long enough to get a bowl from the kitchen and a washcloth from the hall closet, filling it up with the hottest water that I think her damaged flesh will be able to stand.

And then I peel back the quilt, and in the silence of the room, start to wash away the evidence of what those animals did to her.

I feel that pang of tenderness again as I run the washcloth over her skin, skimming it over the cuts and bruises as I start with her face and work my way down, washing away the dirt and blood. My fingers brush her forehead before the cloth does, and I feel how chilled her skin is, almost as if the life has already leached out of her. It makes my chest constrict in a way that I haven't felt since Vera died, and for a brief moment, I want to throw the cloth down and leave the room, to run away from the ache in my chest that I don't know if I can handle again.

But I married this woman. For whatever reason, I promised to care for her.

And just now, I'm not sure if I can handle breaking another vow.

I've never touched Caterina before without sexual intent, but there's nothing sexual about what I'm doing now. In fact, I can't remember *ever* having touched any woman like this, with such gentle care that it feels like handling something fragile and delicate, a glass figure or a baby bird. There's no hint of the spitfire that I married now, only a pale face and paler lips, as if the two men siphoned every ounce of defiance out of her.

I feel a prick of fear at that thought, that Caterina might live, but that they will have destroyed her spirit. I can't imagine what she must have gone through, and the reality of it could be worse than what I've already imagined.

But for now, all I can do is care for her. When I'd stood there at the altar only a short time ago, I hadn't imagined this. I hadn't imagined anything other than a marriage held at a distance. I can feel that distance closing, and at the moment, there's nothing I can do about it.

I'm not entirely sure that I want to if I'm telling the truth.

CATERINA

The next time I wake up, I have no idea where I am.

The stale smell of the cabin and the hard mattress is gone, and I can feel that there's a blanket draped over me, but it takes a moment for me to open my eyes. They feel swollen and heavy, my lashes glued shut, and I have to pry them open blearily. I'm not even sure I should try until I feel a finger touch my forehead, slick like oil, and the scent of something sharp and herbal.

A deep voice murmurs something that I can't quite make out, my ears still ringing a little, and I force myself to pry my eyes open as fear washes over me, my skin tingling with it.

I need to know where I am. However horrible it might be, I need to be aware of whatever is coming next. Part of me wishes that I could have just stayed unconscious—or maybe just not woken up at all. The strength I have to endure this is waning fast.

There's a face hovering over me, blurry at first, then coming into view. I realize with a start that it's an extremely handsome face, a man in his early thirties probably, with a sharp jaw, long nose, and dark hair that's threatening to fall into his eyes. He doesn't look dangerous, and when my vision clears enough for me to see his dark eyes, there's nothing threatening in them that I can see.

There's something purple and silky around his neck, hanging over his black t-shirt, and it takes a second for me to realize what it is—a priest's stole.

Nothing else about him looks priestly, though.

I realize what the scent is then—I've smelled that oil plenty of times before, during every rite of passage as a child in the church. As an adult, in the state I'm in and where I am, it can only mean one thing.

He was performing last rites.

The thought sends a cold wave of fear over me, so intense that it takes a moment for the next to come through—why on earth would my kidnappers bother giving me last rites? It's a considerate thing to do for a woman they'd abducted and tortured for information I don't have.

I blink as he pulls his hand back, and I see a small smile at the corners of his mouth, twitching with what looks like relief. "Oh, thank God, you're awake," he says, and his Italian accent is unmistakable.

"You're Italian," I blurt out in a voice that cracks immediately, but he just laughs.

"I am." He smiles down at me, and I feel that sense of reassurance again, which is strange because nothing about this situation makes sense.

"How—why are you here?" Why would the Russians have an Italian priest with them—especially a man who looks so unlike a priest at all?

"Your husband called me to perform the last rites for you. I'm not exactly qualified anymore, but I could do it in a pinch." His smile seems genuine, his relief that I've woken up palpable. "I'm Max."

"I'm—" I can still barely speak, and he shakes his head.

"Caterina, I know. Don't try to speak. You've been very badly hurt. A doctor is on the way, but I got here first. Your husband thought I should perform the rites, just in case. He said he was sure it was what you would want."

I nod slowly, still trying to process exactly what is going on. *Is Viktor here?* I shift a little in the bed, ignoring the pain that blooms through me at the slightest motion, and I realize with a wave of my own relief that my hands are unbound. I'm afraid to look at them, but they're free.

Maybe I am too.

"Viktor is here?" I ask in a small and creaky voice, feeling my throat tighten and hurt with every word.

Max nods. "I'll send him in. But please don't speak much, Caterina. The doctor will know more, but you were strangled at some point. Your throat is damaged."

Damaged. The word rings through my head. *Damaged, damaged, damaged.* How damaged am I, body and soul? A vision of Ana on the sofa in Sofia and Luca's apartment springs into my head, her feet bandaged, destroyed because of my first husband's treachery. Ana is damaged now, inside and out, her career gone and her spirit broken. Sofia has been trying to heal her ever since, but I don't know if she'll ever be the same.

Is that going to be me now? Irreparably broken because of the treachery of men?

I turn my head to the side, closing my eyes against the sudden sting of tears. My whole life has been a series of events controlled by the men in my life. It's come to this—me lying in a strange bed, my body nothing but pain, hurt beyond anything I'd allowed myself to imagine could ever happen to me.

And I'm still not sure if I think my husband could be responsible for it or not.

Clearly, he came for me, but a small, insidious voice in my head whispers that this could have been to teach me a lesson. Maybe he wanted me broken and didn't want to have to do it himself.

Maybe his first wife died because it went too far. Or perhaps he tried this first with her, and she didn't break.

I'm not sure if I have it in me to hold it together much longer.

The door opens slowly, and I steel myself for who will be on the other side of it. It's Viktor, as I'd expected it probably would be, but everything about him seems strange to me.

I've never seen him wearing anything other than a suit or what he wears to bed. Now he's wearing what appear to be hiking clothes in muted colors and boots, his usually carefully styled dark hair loose and messy. His handsome face is a mixture of relief and worry, and that throws me off most of all because I've never seen my husband look at me like that before.

I also don't want to trust it. I can't.

It'll hurt too much if I'm wrong.

I don't let myself think about the last night we spent together as I look at my husband's face. I don't think about how I let myself enjoy him, *feel* something for him, just for a little while. Whether he had a hand in this or not, he's still a man who buys and sells others. Who traffics women, whose family has always done it, and who thinks he's justified.

I can't love a man like that.

Not ever.

"A doctor is coming," Viktor says quietly, stepping into the room and shutting the door behind him. "You're very badly hurt, but the fact that you're awake is good, I think. Max was as worried that it was the end as I was."

Worried? Are you sure that's what it was? I don't say it aloud, though. The state of my throat gives me a good excuse not to have to speak, and I plan to use it as long as possible. It will let me get my thoughts in order before I have to actually talk to my husband again.

He slowly walks towards the foot of the bed, and I watch him warily, trying to gather my thoughts. Is he capable of what I suspect him of? Would he do that, or has the life I've lived made me paranoid?

Am I even happy that I'm still alive?

"I thought you were gone," Viktor says quietly. "It's going to take… time for you to heal."

Inside or out? Another question that I bite back, tearing my gaze away from my husband's and looking towards the wall. The room I'm in is very different from the one I was held in before; I can see that now. Besides the bed being more comfortable, the room is clean, with a rough hardwood floor covered in a thick sheepskin rug, a dresser on one wall, and a soft-looking armchair by the other wall. There's a nightstand and lamp next to my bed, and it all makes a perfect, cozy picture of a cabin to hide away in. It could even be romantic, under different circumstances.

Right now, nothing could be further from those circumstances.

Viktor hesitates, clearing his throat. "You should rest," he says finally, and I can *feel* the awkwardness as he shifts his weight from one foot to the other, unable to quite meet my eyes. "The doctor will be here soon."

I study his face for a long moment, trying to decide if I want to try to vocalize any of the thoughts tumbling around my head, if I even would know how to begin. But in the end, I just nod, my fingers curling under the blanket as my heart pounds in my chest.

I don't have the energy to ask any of those questions, and I don't know if it would matter even if I did. I don't know if I'm safe now or simply in a different kind of danger.

I don't even know if I'm going to survive this anyway.

The thought doesn't inspire as much fear as I would have thought. I feel cold despite the blanket, every inch of my body hurting, and all I want is for it to stop.

All I want is to sleep.

So instead of fighting as I might once have or demanding answers, I simply close my eyes and let myself slip away.

* * *

THE NEXT TIME I open my eyes, there are hands on me again, but this time the man hovering over me is much older and much less handsome. I realize as his face swims into focus that I'm naked on the bed again, but I can't quite summon the embarrassment that I feel like I should have. At this point, what does it matter? Nothing about my body could possibly be attractive now, and nothing about the hands on me feel anything but clinical. *He must be the doctor,* I think dimly, letting my eyes slide closed again as I feel a cold chill wash over me.

"She's burning up with fever," I hear the doctor say to someone— Viktor, maybe?— I want to protest that I don't know how that could be, not when I'm so cold. "These wounds were left open to infection for too long."

"I cleaned them as soon as I was able to get her here." Viktor's deep voice rumbles from somewhere beside the bed, and I feel a small flicker of surprise. *Did he clean me up? Did he take care of me?* Somehow I can't quite imagine Viktor sitting at my bedside, tending to me. It sounds like something he would pass off to someone else, to Olga maybe, if she were here. She's not, of course, but somehow I'm still surprised that he would take the time to tend to me that carefully.

It softens something inside of me, makes me question again if I should suspect him at all. *He could be lying,* I think, and I squeeze my eyes shut, hating every second of this. I feel like I'm losing my mind.

I have no one I can trust anymore, except for Luca and Sofia, and they're so far away that they might as well be on another planet.

I'm somewhere out in the Russian wilderness with my husband, and he's the last person I should trust right now.

But that might be my only chance at surviving this.

I turn my head to one side, trying not to think about the doctor's hands moving over my body. "How bad is it?" I hear Viktor ask quietly, and I feel the doctor hesitate.

"The fever is dangerous," he says after a moment. "She's far from being on the other side of this. There are possibilities that I can't check for here—internal bleeding or injuries, for example." His hand presses against my lower ribs, and I cry out before I can stop myself, biting the inside of my cheek at the startled pain.

"A cracked or broken rib," the doctor says. "There could be much worse."

"Was she—did they—" Viktor seems to be having a hard time asking the question that's on the tip of his tongue. "Was she violated?"

I feel myself tense at the question, my heart stuttering in my chest. Even I don't know the answer to that. Not while I was awake—but I wouldn't have put it past Andrei or Stepan to enjoy me while I was unconscious and unable to fight back. With so much pain everywhere, I can't even isolate it enough to determine if any part of my body has been hurt.

"It's impossible to tell for certain," the doctor says carefully. "But I don't see any sign of it." He hesitates then, his hand resting on my lower stomach. "Is there any chance that she could have been pregnant?"

There's a sudden, heavy silence in the room, and I feel my chest constrict. I feel that sudden flash of protectiveness again, the need to keep that slight possibility safe, even if it's nothing but a figment of my imagination, something that's already gone or maybe never existed at all.

"I'm not sure if it's been long enough," Viktor says finally. "But it's possible. We were married a little over a month ago."

There's another thick silence, and then the papery fingers leave my stomach.

"If she was, I don't see how the pregnancy could have survived what she's been through," the doctor says with a finality that feels as if it pierces straight to my heart. "A pregnancy that early is fragile, and she's been through extreme stress. I would expect that she might have some trouble conceiving after she heals for a while, as well. She'll have considerable healing to do."

"I understand," Viktor says, and I can't quite parse out what the tone of his voice means. "It's her that I'm worried about, not a pregnancy." He says the last with emphasis, as if it's the last thing in the world on his mind, and that sends another jolt of uncertainty through me.

"She'll need close, round the clock care if she's going to survive this—"

"You'll stay," Viktor says, with authority and finality to his voice that would have terrified me if it were in my direction. "You'll stay, and you'll make sure she lives."

"*Ussuri*—" There's a tremor of fear in the doctor's voice, and I almost want to open my eyes, just so I can see the look on his face. But they feel too heavy again, glued down with exhaustion and fever. "*Ussuri*, I can't promise—"

"You'll make sure she lives," Viktor repeats, the threat clear in his voice. "And whatever care she needs, I'll see to it myself. But you won't leave this cabin until she's well."

There's that threat again, the undercurrent that says if I don't get well, he might not leave at all. It makes me feel a small flutter of guilt because I can't be responsible for someone else getting hurt just because I can't beat the things that were done to me.

Does he even care that much? I'd never envisioned Viktor flying into a rage because I died, taking out his anger and grief on the person who might have been able to save me. It doesn't make any sense to me, because Viktor doesn't feel the kinds of things for me that lead to anger or grief.

Right?

They're saying something else now, the doctor insisting that he'll do his best, but he can't make promises, and Viktor's rumbling voice replying that his "best" will mean that I live.

I want to say that I can't make any promises either, but the fever is pulling at me, dragging me back into the dark depths that I'm honestly glad to return to.

At least there, it's warm, and nothing hurts.

* * *

I DON'T KNOW how much time passes. I don't know how much of what I see and hear is real or a dream either, a product of my fevered imagination and burning mind, or what's really happening. Every time my eyes flutter open, it seems as if Viktor is there, but I don't know if that's true. It seems unimaginable that he would sit by my bedside, hovering there like some kind of guardian angel. Once I think that I wake up to see Max there too, his hand on Viktor's shoulder as if they're watching over me together.

There's the doctor, too, his dry and cool hands moving over my fevered body, and I try to mark time by how often I notice him there, but it's hard to keep track. It could have been hours or days or weeks since Viktor brought me here; I can't figure out which.

The pain ebbs and flows, and I can only imagine that the doctor is giving me something to help with it. It could be part of what is keeping me in a half-dream state, too, but I'm not entirely sure I want to come out of it.

When I do, I have to face the reality of everything that's happened and figure out what will come next.

The next time I wake up, it feels like I'm floating in cool water. It takes me a moment to open my eyes partway and realize that I *am* in the water, in a bathtub, and there are hands on me, holding me down in it.

The panic that washes over me is frantic and instantaneous, chilling me straight to the bone and making my body jackknife instinctively, fighting the pressure that's keeping me in the water.

"Caterina!" I hear Viktor's voice calling my name hazily, but it can't quite break through the fog of terror. Some small part of me knows that it's him that's there, that he's the one holding me in the bath, but I can't get it to break through. All I can think about are other hands on me, other hands holding me down, hurting me, choking me, and my brain is screaming that this is it, that I'm going to die. That I'm going to drown in a bathtub, held down by strangers, in a cabin somewhere in Russia.

That I'm back in that other awful place where they kept me for god knows how long.

"Caterina, it's me. Caterina!" I feel the hands let go as I writhe in the tub, water splashing as I struggle to get away. My vision is hazy, and I squeeze my eyes shut tight, my hand gripping the side of the tub as I try to heave myself out.

It's no good. I'm not strong enough. I jerk again, twisting as if to bite the hand on my shoulder, and then my eyes snap open as that hand tightens, shaking me just a little.

"Caterina." Viktor's deep, rough, and pained voice cuts through the fear just a little. "Caterina, it's me. Come on, baby. Snap out of it. Please."

Baby. That yanks me back as his face comes into view, and I see the fearful expression there as if what's happening to me is scaring him, too.

Baby. A pet name. He's never called me anything like that. I could hear the emotion behind it when it slipped out of his mouth, and that stopped me in my tracks too. He'd sounded afraid *for* me. As if seeing me like this hurt him.

Slowly, I can feel myself starting to breathe again, although I'm still trembling. Viktor's other hand goes to my waist, steadying me in the sloshing water, and I gasp, forcing myself to relax inch by inch.

It's hard. My heart is pounding in my chest, my skin tingling with the urge to run, to fight, to get out. But it's Viktor.

A man that I'm not sure I can trust, but right now, isn't hurting me. Who has me all the more confused because the look on his face just now wasn't one of a man who would hurt me.

It looked like a man who is terrified to lose me.

And that makes no fucking sense at all.

VIKTOR

I've never witnessed a panic attack before. The way Caterina started to flail in the bathtub, shaking and trembling, sent a burst of fear and rage through me all at once. Fear for her, and rage directed squarely at the two men locked outside in the shed, who had done this to her.

She looked as if she were out of her mind, and in some way, she probably was. Something had transported her back to the days she'd spent in their custody, and the terror in her face had been painful to witness. It made me want to kill them in many slow and painful ways, but at the same time, nothing could have torn me away from her side at that moment.

She's mine. The possessive, protective urge that has been growing steadily since I married her has taken even deeper root in the past days, and the thought that anyone could have hurt her so badly makes me nearly incandescent with fury.

I'm going to kill every last person who had a hand in taking her from me. And no one ever will again.

I don't care how hurt she is or how broken. I'm going to piece her back together, one way or another. But from the look in her eyes when she realizes it's me holding her, I can see that she doesn't trust me. That I'm a lesser evil, not someone she feels safe with.

I can't exactly blame her. But I'm also unsure of exactly why she's so afraid of me when just the night before she was kidnapped, we'd shared a night together unlike anything we'd done before.

I'd thought that would be a turning point in our marriage. Not love, I've never been interested in that. But an understanding. An appreciation for what we can offer each other.

Not love, but maybe passion.

What I feel in this moment, though, holding her in the bathtub as her breathing slows fractionally and her eyes dart around like a frightened deer's, is something deeper than just physical attraction. The body that I'm holding is barely one I recognize right now, but the person inside of it is still Caterina. A woman I swore to protect.

That vow must have gone deeper than I realized.

"I won't let anything happen to you," I murmur, reaching up with one hand to stroke her damp hair away from her face when she's stopped struggling long enough for me to feel certain she won't flail in the tub again and hurt herself. "I'm here, Caterina. It's me. You're safe."

She looks at me uncomprehendingly, as if she can't imagine that. And maybe she can't, with it all so fresh. Carefully, I touch her cheek, avoiding the bruise near her jaw. "No one will hurt you while I'm here," I tell her quietly, wanting more than anything to help take the frightened look off of her face. "No one."

Caterina's eyes drop, her breathing slowing a fraction more. She turns her head away, and I can feel her retreating into herself, her body still tense under my hands.

I know I've never entirely had her trust, but I can see that for some reason I've lost what little I might have had, and I'm not sure why. It might have been when she saw the girls at the hangar, or maybe it goes deeper than that, but I thought we'd made progress.

I'm not sure where we, specifically, went wrong again. And I know now isn't the time to try and figure it out.

I'm not even entirely sure where we go from here, besides my keeping her safe.

I don't know what our marriage looks like, on the other side of this. But I know that it's not going to end with me looking down at her pale, lifeless face, and wondering what I could have done differently.

Gently, I pick up the washcloth that I'd dropped in the water when Caterina started to panic and run it slowly over her skin. I'm not even bathing her at this point so much as soothing her, squeezing the cloth so that the water runs over her flushed skin in warm rivulets. She shivers, and I know she's still feverish, her skin hot to the touch without the warmth of the water. It must feel cold to her, but the doctor had warned not to heat up the bath too much. He'd cautioned against even letting her soak in it too long, worried about the wounds that had needed stitches, but her temperature also needs to come down.

I've never been in a position to care for anyone like this, not even my children. Anika and Yelena have been sick in the past, of course, but Vera cared for them when she was alive, and then Olga afterward. As attentive of a father as I've tried to be, the role of caregiver isn't one I was raised to inhabit. It's strange to be doing it now.

But Caterina has no one else.

"Lay back," I tell her gently, pressing back on her shoulder so that she's leaning back in the tub. It's not large—this cabin was built to be functional, not luxurious. It's a world away from my home back in New York, but at least here, we're as safe as possible.

She obeys, her head tilting back, and I run the cloth down between her breasts, being excruciatingly careful. She lets out a small sigh as I touch her, and when I glance up, I see that the skin beneath her eyes is damp.

There's no way to tell if it's water or tears, but I think I can guess which. And although she won't look at me, I reach up gently, rubbing my thumb over her cheekbone to wipe away the moisture.

"I'll never hurt you," I tell her, keeping my voice as low and soothing as I can make it. I don't know if that's a lie or not—the afternoon that I bent her over her bed and applied my belt to her ass is still fresh in my memory and likely hers—but as far as I'm concerned, I hadn't *hurt* her. I'd punished her, made her aware of the consequences of a choice she'd made, laid out the rules for our future together. But I hadn't hurt her egregiously. I can't lie and say that I hadn't taken some—or a great deal—of pleasure in seeing her gorgeous pale ass turn red under the lash of my belt, but I hadn't harmed her. I'd been careful not to do exactly that.

As for the rest of what we'd done together—she'd enjoyed that. She'd even been aroused by the spanking, as much as I know, she'd never admit it.

This is different. What *they* did to her is different. And as I gently run the cloth over her body, I have to fight back that primal, angry urge to go out and copy the same marks that those animals left on her on their own flesh. They deserve every ounce of pain I can mete out to them and more.

They won't make it out of this in one piece. I can guarantee that.

She's still too warm when I lift her out of the bath and half-asleep again. I dry her off carefully and carry her back to the bed, laying her naked on the clean sheets. The doctor gave me an ointment to put on the shallowest of the wounds, to hopefully help keep them from scarring and help with the infection. I gently apply it bit by bit as she lays there, her breathing soft and shallow again as she slips back into sleep.

The fever has lasted too long, I know that. She was thin before, but I can see her almost wasting away in front of me, and I know that if this goes on too much longer, I'll lose her.

I'm not sure if I'd actually follow through on my threat to the good doctor if Caterina dies. I can guarantee that the men outside will suffer. And I'll enjoy every second of it.

When her bandages are changed, she's fast asleep and there's nothing else I can do. I pull the blanket back over her, looking at her delicate face. It's the only part of her that looks almost the same, only slightly bruised with the split and swollen lip that's slowly healing. Her face reminds me that Caterina is still in the battered body lying there and that there's a chance she'll come back to me.

That they didn't destroy her entirely.

"Viktor." Levin's voice comes from outside the door, and I jerk back from where my hand is resting on the blanket, as if I feel guilty for touching my wife, looking at her with affection. I take a step back, my jaw tensing as I turn towards the door. I can't forget about my other responsibilities, simply because of her. I can't lose sight of the bigger picture.

Sometimes, I think I'm very much in danger of doing that.

The expression on Levin's face when I step out into the hall outside of Caterina's room is far grimmer than what I'd hoped to see. "What happened?" I ask tightly, stepping away from the door and motioning for him to follow me down to another of the rooms, where we can talk privately.

"I got a call from Mikhail," Levin says, his voice low and angry. "Alexei has staged a coup, back in New York. He's killed several of the men who tried to stand up to him and nearly Mikhail as well. Mikhail said he's injured but alive. He's going to try to get back to the house and get the girls, Olga, and the others out of there before Alexei can get to them."

Fuck. I clench my fists at the mention of my daughters, the building rage I'd felt earlier threatening to burn out of control. I've always considered myself a levelheaded man, without much of a temper.

But it's been sorely tested lately.

"Call Luca," I say sharply. "We have an accord, and that means that he should be ready to help defend my territory if need be. Beyond that, Alexei might strike at him. And Liam—"

"Alexei has already moved against the Irish," Levin says quietly. "He invited a few of Liam's men to the warehouse under the guise of you asking and shot them. Mikhail said that he plans to try to use the instability of the Irish right now after Conor's death to take the Boston territory."

"Is Luca aware?"

"Not yet, that I know of. I wanted to tell you first and find out your orders, *pakhan*."

Levin is rarely so formal with me—he's been my right hand since we were young men. The fact that he is now is just another nod to the seriousness of the situation, and I straighten, squaring my shoulders.

"I know you need to worry about your wife right now, but—"

"I have other responsibilities, too." I cut him off, nodding. "Keep me informed. I'm going to call Luca now and have him send men to the house to watch the girls."

What I want to do is go back down the hall and sit at Caterina's bedside, holding her hand and watching her breathe until I'm certain that she'll keep breathing. But she's not all that I have, and she's not all that I'm responsible for.

The time difference is considerable, but Luca answers the phone on the third ring. "Yes?" he asks sharply, as if he's suspicious of why I've called. "I haven't heard from you, Viktor, but I know you've taken Caterina to Russia with you. I expect that you have your reasons?"

My jaw tenses. "I don't need your permission to take my *wife* anywhere. I've called you about a more serious matter."

He pauses for a moment on the other end, as if considering debating the first point, but finally lets out a breath. "Go ahead."

I'd been hesitant to tell Luca about Caterina's kidnapping, but if I need him to hold up his end of our bargain, he'll need to be fully in the loop. I explain everything in as little detail as possible, from the business trip I'd insisted Caterina accompany me on to her kidnapping and Alexei's mutiny.

"You're in Russia, still?"

"In a safe house with Caterina until I can extract the information about who abducted her. I can't come back to New York just now, and Levin is with me. Mikhail is headed to my home to protect my children and household, but he'll need help. Alexei killed several of my remaining loyal men." I pause, taking a breath. "We have a bargain, Luca—"

"I don't need you to remind me of our bargain," he cuts me off. "I'll go there myself with some of my men as soon as I make sure that Sofia and Ana have protection."

Shit. I hadn't thought of Ana, who I know Alexei hates deeply for what she did on behalf of Sofia. I've been willing to overlook it in the interest of the truce I'd formed with Luca, but Alexei will have no such intentions.

"Let me know as soon as the girls are safe," I say sharply. "Levin is trying to get ahold of Mikhail again now."

I curse aloud as soon as I hang up, my hand clenching around the phone. It takes everything in me not to throw it against the wall, but instead, I set it down, clenching my fist so tightly that I can feel my short nails biting into my palm.

And then I leave the room, heading back down to the bedroom where Caterina is sleeping.

Right now, the only place I want to be is at her side.

Tomorrow, I'll get answers.

CATERINA

The first time I wake up feeling more like myself, Viktor is sitting at my bedside.

It's almost unbelievable. I open my eyes slowly, feeling for the first time in I don't know how long like I'm not freezing to the bone, my skin a mass of pain with every touch and movement. I can feel that I'm sore in every inch, exhausted despite how much sleep I've had, but the pain is the least it's been. I don't know if that's because I'm healing or because I'm medicated, but there's no bolt of pain through my skull when I turn my head towards Viktor, and my throat doesn't scream at me when I part my lips and murmur his name.

His head shoots up the moment he hears the sound, and I see that relief again, as if my waking up mattered to him. He's on his feet in a second, moving to sit on the edge of my bed as he reaches for my hand.

"You're awake," he says, looking down at me with those blue eyes that I've seen in so many different moods, despite how briefly we've been married. I've seen them carefully blank, I've seen them burning with anger, I've seen them dark with passion, frustrated and happy, and everything in between. But right now, all I can see in them is worry.

Worry for me?

"I am," I say slowly, hearing my voice creak. "I think—I don't feel like I have a fever now?"

Viktor reaches out, touching my forehead, and the gentleness of the touch startles me. "I think it's broken," he says, relief coloring his tone.

The sheets around me feel clammy, which is a good enough indication that he's right. "I'll call the doctor in," he says quickly, standing up. "He should look at you. Try not to talk too much. You don't want to strain your throat."

The old me might have made a comment about how men like him prefer it when women like me don't talk too much, but I can't seem to manage it just now. Even those few words felt difficult, and I just nod, closing my eyes again briefly while I wait for the doctor to come in.

I get a better look at him this time—a man easily in his fifties or older, with a lined and craggy face and deep blue eyes set well back in his head. He gives me a reassuring smile as he approaches the bed, reaching out to touch my forehead with a more practiced motion than Viktor as he slips a thermometer into my mouth.

"The fever has broken," he confirms, looking down at me and then over at Viktor. "I think the worst of it is over. You're going to make it, Mrs. Andreyva. It'll be a long road until you're fully healed, but you've survived the most dangerous part."

He pulls back the blanket then, examining my wounds clinically, before covering me up again and motioning for Viktor to join him outside of the room. Before he goes, he pats my hand, giving me that reassuring look again. "You'll heal," he says, and then he and Viktor both stride out.

I take the moment alone to take stock of myself. It's been the first time I've been aware enough to really look at the state I'm in, and as scared as I am, I also know that I need to do exactly that.

Slowly, I raise my hands, looking at my wrists where they were cuffed. There are deep lacerations all the way around, like two grotesque bracelets, bruised around the edges. My hands still hurt, probably from the lack of circulation, and I reach up to touch my throat where I can feel the bruises from where Stepan strangled me.

Taking a deep breath, I reach for the blanket, lifting it enough for me to look down the length of my naked body.

What I see makes me gasp and drop the blanket, horrified.

My body looks like a patchwork, a mass of cuts, some shallow and others bandaged, ostensibly because they were so deep. There's hardly an inch of my skin that isn't purple and yellow with healing bruises, and when I shift my weight in the bed, I feel the bone-deep ache of my injuries.

I'd always sympathized with Ana, felt a deep guilt for what my husband had done to her. But now, for the first time, I *understand* her. I haven't lost something so deeply important as the ability to dance and a career, but I know now what it feels like to have something taken from you.

To no longer feel at home in your own body.

I can feel myself starting to shake. I can't look at myself again, and I press the blanket down tightly around me as if that could somehow erase it. A dozen different fears spring up at once, mingled with grief for something I'd never known was so important to me—my looks.

I've never been vain, but I've also always known I was beautiful. Even after the grief and pain of the last several months, when I'd lost too much weight, I'd still looked at myself in the mirror and felt that way. I'd been a little self-conscious, but not more than any other girl would have been.

Now, I feel horrified. I can't imagine looking in the mirror, and when I think of how Viktor has seen me like this—what he'll see every time he looks at me—I feel sick. Even if he had no part in this, what will happen to me? How could he want a wife who will inevitably be scarred, who won't be the beautiful woman that he'd married?

Our marriage wasn't one of love. It was one based on convenience and attraction and nothing else. Without the attraction, will the convenience be enough? And how will I give him the son he's demanded if he doesn't want to fuck me?

We could always go back to the fertility clinic, I think with a burst of grim humor. Then I reach down under the blanket, touching my stomach gingerly as a fresh wave of grief replaces it.

I remember all too clearly the doctor saying that there was no way a baby could have survived all that I've been through. I know that wasn't a product of the fever. It's too clear and vivid.

I don't even know if I was. There's no way I'll ever know, but the possibility was there. And in this particular moment, whether it's because of how torn apart I feel in every other way or simply because of the fact itself, I feel as if I'll wonder for the rest of my life if that was true.

If I'd been pregnant and lost my baby.

I press my hand harder against the concave flat of my belly, ignoring the pain from the bruises and cuts there. I don't know why I'm so sad about it. I didn't even want a baby with Viktor. I didn't want to bring a son or a daughter into the world he's created for his family. But now, knowing that might have existed—

I feel as if my heart is breaking.

For myself. For the possibility of a baby that no longer exists. For Ana. For every woman who has ever endured the things that I'm lying here suffering through because of the machinations of men.

At that moment, I almost hate Viktor.

The door opens as if my thoughts summoned him, and he walks back into the room, alone this time. Carefully, Viktor sits down on the edge of the bed, his eyes roving over my face as if worried.

"What did the doctor say that he didn't want me to hear?" The words come out raspy, my voice sounding strange from disuse. As strange as the way my body looks to me now.

"He wanted to discuss with me, that's all."

"Shouldn't I know?"

Viktor hesitates. "He's concerned about your healing. We'll have to move soon, we can't stay in one safe house for long. We've already stayed here longer than we should, but you couldn't be moved in your condition. Now that the fever has broken, we can, although the doctor is hesitant."

"Why?"

"Your wounds are still healing. He said light movement is good, but the strain of moving to a new location altogether might make things worse. I don't know that we have much of a choice, though."

"Was there anything else?"

Viktor lets out a breath. "He's concerned that there might have been internal damage we can't know about without taking you to a hospital. Damage that could cause issues later, including—" he hesitates. "Including your ability to conceive."

I turn my face away at that, trying to hide the sudden pang of grief. "That must make me nearly useless to you then, outside of the bargain you have with Luca."

"What?" Viktor reaches for my hand, startling me. "Caterina, no. I —" he stops, his broad, rough palm encircling my smaller hand. It feels very fragile just then, in his grasp. "I'm not concerned with that right now," he says finally. "I'm concerned with keeping you safe. With making sure my daughters are safe, and my household."

That catches my attention. "What about Yelena and Anika?" I ask, hearing a thread of fear winding through my voice. "Are they okay? Has something happened?"

"There's—difficulty back home," Viktor says carefully. "I don't tell you too much, Caterina, precisely because of what happened to you. I don't want you to have information for anyone to pry out of you."

That didn't stop them from carving me up like a turkey, I think bitterly. *Just because I didn't have answers. It didn't save me.* But I don't say it out loud. I think Viktor knows that as well as I do, and there's no point in letting it hover in the air between us, thick with resentment.

"The girls may be in danger," he says finally. "Luca is going to them. And what's happening back in New York may be connected to your abduction. Levin has been—questioning the two men we found keeping you prisoner. I'll take a more personal approach to it myself tomorrow. I'll find out if that's true."

His gaze meets mine, and I find myself staring at him, trying to make sense of it all. My husband just bluntly told me of his intent to torture Andrei and Stepan, who likely have already received rough treatment at Levin's hands, a man whose bad side I wouldn't prefer to be on. I should be appalled—but I'm not. In fact, I don't feel anything other than a faint satisfaction at the idea that they might feel some of the same pain and fear that they'd subjected me to.

What is happening to me?

I've never had to face the realities of the life I live so clearly before. I'd grown up sheltered, insulated from it all, a pampered mafia princess without any real understanding of the machinations in the shadows. I'd gotten a peek at that darkness when I was married to Franco and seen it all too clearly towards the end. I'd thought I'd been exposed to some of the worst of it. But now I'm seeing that I'd only scratched the surface.

I wonder what kind of woman this will turn me into in the end.

If I'll ever heal completely, inside or out.

"You'll have another day to rest," Viktor says. "And then we'll move to the next safe house. The doctor will come with us."

I nod, unsure of what to say. Everything I've heard in the last few minutes seems to point towards Viktor not having had anything to do with my abduction. He seems furious about it, worried about whatever is happening back home, and concerned for me. But after everything that's happened, I don't know how to trust that.

My first husband was an abusive traitor. My father was a man different from the one I'd always believed him to be. Luca asked things of me that I'd never thought he would. Viktor has always been cold with me except in the bedroom, and now I've been destroyed, body and soul, by men who did it for nothing but their own pleasure.

I don't know how to trust any longer. I don't know who to believe, how to know for certain. I can think of reasons why Viktor might still have been behind it, how he could be manipulating me right now. I don't know if that makes me paranoid or if I've finally come to my senses.

It's exhausting. And all I want is to rewind to the moment Luca asked me to marry Viktor and tell him that I can't. No matter the consequences. To stop shouldering the responsibilities of a life that I never asked to lead and take mine into my own hands.

To be free.

"Alright," I say softly, looking away. "I'm not exactly in a position to do anything other than what you think is best."

"Caterina—" Viktor hesitates. "Do you remember anything? Anything at all about the men who took you?"

I close my eyes, not wanting to remember. I can still feel the cold sting of that needle, if I let myself think about it for even a moment. But I know that Viktor needs this. That it might help catch the men who wanted me hurt, even dead, before they can do worse.

Before they can get to Viktor's daughters.

"Not much," I admit. "There were several of them. Most of them just looked like goons. But the one who drugged me was tall, wearing a black coat, with very light blond hair and blue eyes. He had a square jaw and looked—" I pause, trying to think of how to explain it. "He was dressed like he was someone important. But it wasn't just that. There was—an air that he had."

Viktor's jaw tightens. "I have an idea of who it could have been. Thank you," he adds, his hand tightening around mine. "I know you don't want to remember these things. If I could—" he hesitates. "If I could take it away from you somehow, Caterina, I would. If I could make the memories go away."

I nod, feeling a sudden lump of emotion well up in my throat. I don't know what to do with this new, gentler Viktor. This man, who holds my hand and looks as if he's worried for me, who may have stayed at my bedside and tended my wounds and bathed me. I still don't know what was a dream and what wasn't, but those two men—the one I knew and the one he seems to be now—don't add up. And I don't know which one to believe or what to trust.

"I won't let anyone else harm you," Viktor says, letting go of my hand and standing up. "I'll extract all the information I can from those two men, and I'll make sure that whoever is behind this is punished. They won't get away with it, Caterina."

I nod, still unable to speak from the lump in my throat. He can punish them all he wants, but it doesn't change what happened. It doesn't take away the memories or the nightmares I had while trapped in the clutches of the fever, nightmares that I suspect will come back again and again. It won't repair my body, give me back my looks, or take away the physical pain.

I'm not even sure it can heal the emotional pain.

"I should rest," I say quietly, and I see his jaw tighten as if he wants to say something. But he simply nods, and then to my surprise, bends down to kiss me softly on the forehead.

"Rest well," he says softly. And then he turns and leaves me there, staring after him as I clutch the blankets and wonder if I'm still caught in a fever dream, after all.

VIKTOR

It's been a long time since I've been this covered in blood.

The screams have stopped. The stockier one, whose name I know now is Andrei, is sitting in front of me, slack-jawed and tied to a chair. The other, Stepan, is on the other side of the shed, kneeling with one of my men standing over him, ready to react at the slightest sign of resistance.

The shed smells like blood and piss. Both men soiled themselves at some point, Stepan first. For all that, he's apparently the one who is responsible for most of Caterina's condition; he's a sniveling coward when it comes to his own pain. Which is why I chose to question him second.

I'm enjoying forcing him to watch while I question Andrei. I'm enjoying giving him the extra time to think about exactly what I'm going to do to him when it's his turn, and not just because I want information from him.

Because I want him to hurt, the way he hurt my wife.

Andrei, unsurprisingly, didn't know much. He'd tried to act tough, told me to fuck off at first, but once I'd liberated a few of his teeth, he'd started to sing a different tune. A fingernail or two later, and he was screaming that they'd been hired by a third party, just a job to watch an asset for someone important in Moscow and get a little information out of her. He didn't know who the boss was or who was behind it, and he'd stuck to that story well enough through a solid beating and a couple more teeth being pried out of his mouth that I was convinced.

That didn't stop me from breaking every finger on his right hand when I discovered he'd held Caterina down for Stepan to beat her after she tried to fight back.

This isn't an ideal situation by any stretch of the word. I've tortured men before, of course, these days I tend to leave it to someone else I trust when such methods are necessary, like Mikhail or Alexei, when Alexei was still someone I could trust. And when I have been the one to apply the heavy hand, it's been with a cool head and a detachment that enables me to get the information I need and then let it go.

But there's no keeping a cool head in this situation. I can't look at either of these two men without seeing Caterina and everything they did to her. It's all I can do just to stick to extracting information from them and not simply tearing them limb from limb for my own revenge.

"Don't kill me, please—" Andrei starts to blubber, the words coming out strangely through his missing teeth, blood and saliva dripping down his chin. "Please, I'll tell you anything else I know, I know it's not much—"

"I've heard all I need from you. You're lucky I don't take your tongue for the pleasure of it." I jerk my head towards one of my men. "Cuff him again. It's the other one's turn."

Stepan lets out a high, keening noise, like a trapped animal, and the man holding him cuffs him in the side of the head hard. "Shut up," he snarls in Russian as Stepan rocks sideways on his knees. "You talk when the *Ussuri* tells you to talk, and no sooner."

It's gratifying to hear loyalty from one of my men at this point. I think that I can trust everyone here with me, but there's no way to know for certain. Alexei's poison has run deeper than I'd expected, and I know that it's wise to keep one eye open until every last bit of it can be rooted out.

Stepan's cowardice makes my job easy, but it doesn't help him in the slightest. I have no intention of showing him mercy, especially after how thoroughly Andrei blurted out that Stepan was responsible for most of Caterina's injuries while I was working his thumbnail free. Stepan had done his best to argue his case, but no one was listening to him at that point.

The only thing that saved Andrei more pain was his assurance that they hadn't violated Caterina at any point and his blubbering over and over again that Stepan was the one who had taken the most pleasure in hurting her, that he'd kept going long after Andrei had suggested that there was no point to it anymore. I hadn't believed him at first, thinking that he might simply have been trying to save his own skin. When a man repeats the same story over and over under such duress, it's usually the truth.

Stepan, it turns out, doesn't know any more than Andrei does about their shadowy employer. Neither of them was there when Caterina was kidnapped to hear them tell the story. She was dropped off and drugged at the cabin, and watched until Stepan and Andrei arrived for their guard duty. Then the kidnappers left, without ever speaking to either man or showing their faces. The payment was left in a cupboard inside the cabin, and strict instructions on a burner phone voicemail about what they were to do with Caterina.

Andrei had laid those instructions out for me, quite clearly for a man who'd had pliers locked around one of his molars a few moments before.

1. Hurt her only as much as necessary to get information.
2. Question her about her husband, a man named Viktor Andreyev, and get information about his business.
3. Keep her alive, to be transported to the next location when instructions were given.
4. Not to rape her, do permanent damage, or harm her face.

I'd been moderately impressed at how well Andrei had managed to recall all of that, enough that I'd given him a few moments respite from the torture before starting back in again. It's also frustratingly clear that neither man will be able to provide me with anything that will tell me if this is Igor or someone else who is behind all of this, let alone if Alexei is connected to it.

Which makes it even harder to contain the furious rage that makes me want to rip Stepan apart and scatter the bits of him across the Russian wilderness.

I ask him, again and again, why he continued to torture Caterina when it was clear that there was no more information he could get out of her.

At first, he insists that it was his instructions. But I already know that's a lie.

There are few things in this world that I hate more than a liar.

By the time he starts to beg, I can feel myself on the verge of losing my cool. I'm already in a fog of rage, my shirtsleeves rolled up above my elbows, my forearms spattered with blood. I feel as if I'm slipping into some kind of daze, an out-of-body experience where I no longer really care about what comes out of Stepan's mouth.

I know the truth. He enjoyed hurting Caterina. He enjoyed inflicting pain, finding all the ways he could take her apart at the seams without technically breaking the rules, and maybe he even got off on it. Who fucking knows. But what *I* know is that nothing on earth will stop me from inflicting that same pain on him for my own brutal revenge. Not the truth, not his pleas, not anything he can say or tell me. He could lay out every secret in Moscow for me on a silver platter, and I would still carve lines in his body to match the ones on Caterina's flesh.

At some point, I think he realizes that—that his fate is sealed, no matter what he says. That I don't give a shit what comes out of his mouth. And that's when his cowardice shifts to something approaching bravery—or really, just defiance.

"I fucking liked hearing her scream, what about that?" he spits through a bloody mouth, sneering at me. "I wanted to fuck her until she screamed some more, but Andrei wouldn't let me. He wanted to stick to the *rules*. Well, the rules don't fucking matter now, do they? We're here, and you're going to fucking kill us once you're satisfied. So I might as well have gotten to put a load of my own in that pretty Italian bride of yours." He spits, blood spattering across the floor. "I bet she would have felt so fucking tight and sweet around my—"

He doesn't manage to finish the sentence before my fist connects with his face.

That's when I lose it. Whatever veneer of control I'd had, whatever pretending I'd been doing to try to maintain some semblance of a cool head, it's all gone. All I can feel is the burning, visceral rage that had bubbled up in me when I'd first seen Caterina's broken body curled on that filthy mattress, an anger that's been boiling steadily ever since, waiting to erupt.

And now, this is it. This is the moment when I can no longer hold it in.

It feels so fucking good to beat the shit out of him.

It's only through the barest of self-control that I manage to stop before I beat him to death. It would have felt good to feel his life drain out underneath the pummeling of my fists. My knuckles are bruised, bleeding in spots, but I don't care. I've never wanted to take a man's life as badly as I want to take Stepan's at this moment.

There's only one thing that stops me.

His life isn't mine to take.

"You're going to regret saying every single word of that," I snarl as I pull him upright by his hair, leaning down so that I'm only inches away from his battered and swollen face. "Mark my words."

And then I really get to work.

When I leave the shed, my shirt clinging to me with blood and sweat, Stepan has felt every ounce of the pain he's inflicted on Caterina and more. And yet, I still don't feel as if it's enough.

I stalk past Levin and back into the cabin, going directly to my room. The blood is still pounding through my veins, my pulse beating hard in my throat, and I realize dimly that I'm fucking hard, my cock pressing against the tight confines of my jeans as if it's going to burst through my fly. If I had more presence of mind, I might have found it alarming—I've never been sexually aroused by torturing a man. There might be something to unpack there when I have the capacity for it.

But it's not Stepan that I'm thinking about when I slam the bedroom door behind me and lean back against the door, yanking at my zipper and dragging my cock out into my fist desperately, as if I can't go another minute without touching it. It's been days since I've fucked, but it's not just that. It's a primal, almost instinctual urge, the need to rut after a fight, the adrenaline and rush of power all concentrating in my veins and shooting straight down to my rock-hard length.

If I could, I'd go to Caterina this second and fuck her. There's nothing I want more than to sink into her pussy, to feel her tight, wet heat clenching around me as I drive myself into her again and again, filling her so completely that no other cock could ever satisfy her again. But I know that I can't do that. She's in no condition for me to touch her in any way, let alone fuck her.

But the moment my hand wraps around my cock, all I can think about is how desperately I need to come.

It throbs in my fist as I start to stroke it, my hand moving in quick, fast jerks that are nearly a blur as my hips thrust into my hand again and again. I brace myself against the door, biting back a groan as I feel myself throb, imagining the soft, slender curve of Caterina's waist, the way her small breast felt in my hand, the hard peak of her nipple against my palm. I rub that same palm over the head of my cock, sliding my own arousal down the length of it to slicken it. It feels so fucking good, and I can't stop thinking about her, about the sound of her moan or the way her thighs tightened around me when I'd knelt down on the floor in the Moscow apartment and gone down on her, devouring her pussy the way I'd hungered to since our wedding night.

It's so easy to imagine her as my hand slides over my rigid length— the way she looks up at me in bed, that fiery defiance softening to a hungry need that she won't admit out loud but is plain in her face whenever I take her, in the way she moans, the way she comes for me. It's easy to imagine the way her skin feels against mine, the way it feels to slide my cockhead against the velvet softness of her folds, teasing her before I finally slip inside—

"*Bladya!*" I curse aloud, squeezing my cock as I stroke harder. I want to fuck her more than I want any fucking thing on earth right now. Yet, I can't do anything other than lean back against the door, alone in my room, as I stroke myself to an orgasm that feels as if it's about to come at any moment. A flurry of images runs through my head—Caterina in her wedding night lingerie, Caterina's body tightening around me as she came without warning that night, her pale ass striped red from my belt, her eyes looking up at me as I fed her my cock, demanding her submission on her knees after she'd come back home. Her body around mine, her mouth, her sweet tight pussy, her ass that I'd taken so thoroughly.

She's mine. Mine, mine, mine. The word thunders through my head like another pulse, beating in my ears as I feel the orgasm come up from my very toes, exploding through my length with a rush of pleasure so strong I have to grind my teeth to keep from making a sound.

I squeeze my cock as I come hard, the waves of pleasure rolling through me as my hips jerk, my palm rubbing over the sensitive tip as I cup my hand over it, my cum filling my fist as I hunch forward, shuddering with the final throes of the climax.

For a moment, I can't breathe. And my erection won't seem to subside. Usually, after I come, I start to soften fairly quickly. However, my cock is still pulsing, pressing into my hand as if it plans to stay hard even after that fast, rough orgasm. I still feel that aching need, the rush of adrenaline and desire, and just the thought that my cock might decide to stay hard is enough to make me feel a throb from root to tip, my hips rocking forward at the idea.

What the fuck is going on with me? I swallow hard, squeezing my still-aching length as I try to pull myself together. I can't stay in this room and jerk myself raw. I have things to do, business to attend to. I shouldn't even be stopping to do this in the first place, but the tide of arousal that had washed over me had been too strong to ignore.

Even after everything, I still want my wife. In some ways, I feel as if I might want her more than ever. She's proven to be everything I ever thought she was—strong, intelligent, resilient, and brave. All of those things and more, the perfect wife for a man like me. Beautiful and capable.

But deep down, even as I stride to the bathroom to clean up and tell myself that that's all it is—that I'm impressed by her beauty and moxie all in one person—I feel that tightness in my chest that tells me it's more than that. That she's someone I want for reasons beyond just her beauty and value as a wife.

That I'm beginning to feel things for her that I'd sworn I would never feel again.

CATERINA

We're back in the bed in Moscow.

Viktor is lying next to me, his fingers trailing down between my breasts, curving around the swell of each one as if he's tracing the lines of my body, committing it to memory. As if he wants to be here, wants to be here with me, and not just any woman who could salve his desire.

He pinches my nipples. "Do friends not do this?"

"None of my friends have ever done that."

I'd wanted to laugh at that thought. I've never been interested in women, but I can't imagine shy and innocent Sofia ever touching me that way. Not even some of the girls I went to college with, girls who were more experimental, who teased me about being virginal and innocent and planning to stay that way. Who didn't understand the burden of responsibility on my shoulders.

Maybe I should have played around with them, just a little. Found a pleasure that was all my own and not dependent on the whims of a man.

"What about this?" His fingers roll over my nipples, pinching and pulling, not hard but enough to send shocks of desire down between my legs, my clit pulsing with each tug as if there's a direct line between his fingers and my most sensitive spot. I can feel him hardening against my leg, steel covered in velvet, the heat of it burning into my skin as I shake my head.

I didn't have that many friends, anyway. Definitely no boyfriends. No one to make out with, to tease, to play, to explore. I was sold off to the man who suited my father best, and all of my firsts were with him. A man who didn't deserve them.

Well, not all my firsts.

Viktor took the last one of those that I had to give just before we came to Moscow. How do I feel about that? Do I resent him for taking away the only thing I had left that I hadn't let a man use for his pleasure? Do I care? Does it matter at all?

Do I wish I'd offered it up, instead of having him demand it?

I'd come, so maybe not. His demanding, his dominance, the way it had made me feel dirty and small and reckless and wanton all at once, had made my body light up with pleasure. So maybe I don't wish it had happened differently.

His tongue is on my nipple now, circling, sending those sparks of pleasure across my skin. I can't speak, I can't think, and I know deep down that nothing has changed, that I'm not supposed to be enjoying this. But I can't deny that I am, that it feels good, that I don't want it to stop. That electric tether from my nipples to my clit pulses again, throbbing with every flick and swirl of his tongue, and when he tightens his lips and sucks at my sensitive flesh, I can't stop myself from moaning, crying out as my fingers run through his soft dark hair.

I don't stop him when his hand skims over my ribs, down my flat belly, down to where I'm wet and aching for him, dying for his touch. I don't stop him when his fingers brush over my clit, circling the same way his tongue is still making circles around my other nipple now, working in such perfect tandem that I feel as if my head might explode from the sheer pleasure of it. When his teeth scrape against my nipple as his fingers press down on my clit, rubbing now, pushing, I think I might come on the spot. I'm so close, dizzy with pleasure, and when he pulls away, I let out a small cry of protest.

He moves over me, nudging my legs apart with his knee, and I get a good look at my husband before his mouth comes crashing down on mine.

If I'm being honest, my husband is the most handsome man I've ever seen. He's fit and muscular, but not overly so, every line of his body lean and elegant and graceful in a way that not all men can achieve. His dark stubble and chest hair are flecked with grey here and there, reminding me that he's considerably older than me, in his late-thirties, nearing forty. A thing I might have cringed away from, given a choice, but find inexplicably sexy in him. There's something about his commanding demeanor, the dominance that comes with his age, and those flecks of grey hair that turn me on despite myself.

He growls above me, his lips brushing over mine, cursing in Russian as need overcomes him. That turns me on too, despite myself—I shouldn't be turned on by his vulgarities, aroused by his Russian-ness, Though, the brutality of it is somehow arousing, the danger inherent with the fact that he's not only Bratva, but their leader.

Their Ussuri.

"I need to feel you."

The words startle me, thrill me, my disciplined husband losing control as he nudges between my thighs, his huge cock thick and swollen and pushing at my slick, wet folds. But more than that, the intensity behind his words, a need that I hadn't known my husband could feel for me.

A need that I'm unsure about how I feel.

He parts me roughly as he thrusts inside, his movements sharp and almost desperate as those first inches slip inside. I tighten around him immediately, my body eager for him, much to my chagrin. The pleasure is overwhelming as he slides in as deeply as he can go in one long thrust, pressed against me when there's nowhere left for him to go.

I gasp with pleasure, a sharp intake of breath that only deepens when he cups my face with his hand, lowering his mouth to mine again.

The kiss is deep and intimate, his tongue sliding against mine, eager and hungry. It's a lover's kiss, the kind of kiss a husband gives his wife. One that says that I'm his, that every inch of my body is his to explore. One that tugs at something deep inside me, something that I'm afraid to examine too closely.

When he rocks his hips, his cock rubbing at that spot deep inside of me, I moan aloud. When he whispers dirty things to me, telling me how much he loves to fuck me, how he loves feeling me still full of him from last night, that he can't wait to fill me again—I feel a thrill I never knew I could experience. I didn't realize I wanted things like that, to have a husband whisper something so depraved in my ear, to be bent over and spanked, forced to my knees, taken in the ass. But all those things have made me wet, over and over again, turned me on when I would have sworn they never could.

I want him. At this moment, overcome by pleasure, I let myself admit it. I want this, the way he uses me for his own pleasure, spreading me apart so he can watch himself thrust into me. Pulling out and then sinking back in inch by slow inch while he watches his cock pierce my tight, clenching body.

"Feel your tight little pussy being fucked by that thick cock—"

The words shock me, thrill me, turn me on. When he reaches down to flick his finger over my swollen clit in response to my pleas, when he makes me beg to come, I think I'll dissolve from the pleasure and humiliation of it all at once.

"That's right, princess. Beg for it."

He doesn't call me the Russian word for it, just princess. As if he knows I'll like that better. As if he knows it'll send a flush of arousal through me for reasons even I don't understand, until I'm gasping, arching, begging. Feeling on the verge of tears when he tells me to wait, that I have to wait for him, wait for his permission.

Feeling as if that's right somehow, as if that's what I wanted anyway. Needed, even.

"You get off when I do—"

I'm so far gone that it doesn't even occur to me to argue when he tells me to play with myself, when he says that I can't come if I don't, when his blue eyes burn into mine. I know it's that or stay like this forever, hovering on the edge of some brutal ecstasy that I feel as if I'll die without.

"Don't come yet, or I'll punish you."

Is it wrong that I almost want that? That I almost want to let the orgasm crash over me before I'm allowed, breathe in the scent of his skin and soak in the sensation of his thick length stretching me, let his groans ripple over my skin and my mouth and explode with pleasure before he comes, just so that I can feel the sting of his belt or his hand against my ass again?

What kind of girl, what kind of wife wants that?

I feel as if I'm going to shatter, come apart at the seams.

My face flushes with the memory—all of me flushes, my skin burning with need. I tease my clit as he speeds up, holding on to my pleasure by a thread, my thighs trembling as his hips jerk against me. As he groans out more encouragement, the words slipping from his lips in a torrent as he starts to shudder, his cock hard and swollen and throbbing inside of me. Then he's coming and I can too. His body arched as he shoves into me hard, and I can feel the hot rush of him inside of me as I start to convulse, clawing at the blankets as the tidal wave of pleasure crashes over me.

I can feel him dripping out of me, sliding down my thighs, and he hasn't even pulled out yet. How much did he come to make it feel like that? He's still thrusting, still arched against me, his fingers digging into my hips, his face contorted with the same pleasure that's still pulsing through me.

At that moment, I don't want this to end. I don't want to stop. I want to pretend that I don't know what kind of man he is or what he's done, only that in certain moments, in bed together with the sun shining over us just right, after a night of passion, I feel a connection between us that I can't deny.

One that I'm not entirely certain I want to.

* * *

My eyes fly open, and I realize with a start that I'm not really in the apartment back in Moscow. I'm in bed at the cabin, and I'm acutely aware of what I was just dreaming of.

Viktor. Viktor and *me*, the way we were that last morning before I was reminded of who he was and before I was abducted.

Before my whole life fractured.

The cabin is quiet, and I turn my head carefully, looking to see what time it is. It's early morning, about six, and I need to go to the bathroom.

I'll be damned if I'm not going to make it there on my own.

I push back the blanket slowly—very slowly. It's an effort to get up, every part of my body aching, throbbing, burning. It hurts so much, but I refuse to give in. I refuse to let it keep me here, pinned to a bed, unable to do something as simple as getting myself up to go pee.

I couldn't fight them off, but I'm going to fight this.

Each step is excruciating. It feels as if it takes forever just to swing my legs over the edge of the bed, just to push myself up from the mattress and stand up. Each step feels like a massive effort, but it feels like a small win, too.

Each step is one that I wasn't sure if I was going to take again.

My toes press against the hardwood floor, and it feels cold. It feels *good*, though, like being alive. Another bolt of pain shoots through me, and just as quickly, I want to sit back down. *I can't do this,* I think, my toes curling against the hardwood floor, and then out of nowhere, I think about Ana.

Ana, who hasn't managed to walk since Franco attacked her. She can't even stand up, and at least I'm doing that. I can't give up now.

I have to keep going.

Thankfully, there's a bathroom attached to my room, so I don't have to worry about covering up to go out into the hall. It's all I can do just to get out of bed. I don't have the energy to wrap a blanket around myself on top of that. I try not to think about the fact that I'm naked, tottering to the bathroom like a wounded deer. I try not to think about what that would look like if anyone saw me right now.

It's too embarrassing to think about, honestly.

By the time I make it to the doorway of the bathroom, it feels like an hour has passed, although it's probably only a couple of minutes. I have to grab ahold of the door for a moment to steady myself, taking long, deep breaths that feel as if they take all of the energy I have left in my body.

I hate that it feels like a victory that I managed to go to the bathroom on my own, but at this point, I know I'm lucky to be alive.

Everything changed so quickly.

I know better than to stop and look in the mirror. I don't want to see what will be reflected back at me. But at some point, I won't be able to avoid it. It might as well be when I can do it alone, for the first time. When no one can see my reaction but me.

There's a large oval mirror above the sink in the bathroom, big enough for me to see my body down to my hips. It's enough—too much, really. I can see all the cuts and bruises, patchworking their way across my flesh in a grotesque pattern that looks nothing like the body I'm used to inhabiting.

I don't feel like myself. I've never felt so distant from it, not even after my parents died, and I was mired in grief, not even on the morning of Franco's funeral when I had no idea what the future would hold.

I feel numb, broken, and entirely unsure of who I'm supposed to be after this. How I'm supposed to be Viktor's wife, or anyone's mother, or anything else, when I don't even feel like a person.

When I feel like an empty shell.

I can still feel the echoes of the dream clinging to me, but it feels like it happened to a different woman. Like it's a story that someone told me that I can't quite fathom actually happening.

It all feels like everything that happened before the cabin was a dream. A life that didn't belong to me, and that I'm someone else now.

Slowly, I trace the outline of the marks on my body, and I wonder how many of them will scar. How many will stay with me for the rest of my life, making it impossible to ever forget what happened? How many of them will continue to be an outward reminder of my inward pain? Thin white lines crisscrossing my body and making it so that I can't ever erase it.

I'm going to look at myself forever and always think of this. That thought makes me feel so despondent that I have to grab on to the edge of the sink for a moment, my knees feeling weak and watery again. I've never felt so alone.

I need someone here with me, and all I have is Viktor. The thought would make me laugh if it wasn't so bleak.

Carefully, I make my way back to the bed, inching along until I can lower myself back down onto the mattress. When I'm horizontal again, under the blanket that has come to feel like the only safe space left for me in the world, I close my eyes and hope that I can fall asleep again.

If I'm lucky, I won't have any more dreams.

All it does is make me long for a past that I hadn't even known I wanted until it was gone, and remind me that my future is now one that I can't even picture.

I'd rather not think about it at all.

CATERINA

I'm woken up by the sound of footsteps coming into the room. I grab for the blanket immediately, clutching at it as my eyes fly open, and I scoot backward in the bed, ignoring the jolt of pain that shoots through me at the sudden movement. It takes me a moment to realize that it's Viktor—holding a tray with what looks like food on it, which is something I'd never thought I would see.

My cold Bratva husband of convenience, bringing me breakfast in bed. Maybe I did die after all and woke up in—well, this isn't heaven exactly, but maybe it's whatever is in between. Not quite bad enough to be hell, but not good enough to be paradise.

"You're awake." Viktor sounds genuinely happy about it, which surprises me. He comes around to the side of the bed, setting down the tray to one side. He leans over as if to help me up, moving another pillow behind me so that I can sit upright. His touch is gentle, and he holds me there for a second while I fight the throb of pain that shoots through me at sitting upright for the first time in days, as if he knows. As if he's aware of me in a way that I had no idea he could be.

Once I'm settled in the bed, he sets the tray over my lap, and I get a glimpse at what's actually on it. It's nothing fancy, just some scrambled eggs and what looks like a piece of ham and a glass of milk. My stomach rumbles suddenly, cramping with a hunger that I hadn't felt until exactly that second, that reminds me that I don't even know how long it's been since I've eaten. I feel a wave of dizziness and close my eyes for a moment. I can feel Viktor's gaze on me.

"Go slowly," he instructs as I pick up the fork by the chipped china plate. I can't help but notice the stark difference between this and the way breakfast would have been served back at Viktor's home—on fine china, in the elegant dining room. And yet, he seems at ease here in the rustic cabin, with chipped plates and woodsman clothing. It's a side of Viktor I wouldn't have pictured and one that I'd almost like to investigate further if I had the energy.

"You haven't eaten in several days," he continues, nodding towards the food. "It could make you very sick, even kill you, if you go too fast."

I want to laugh at that. That *would* be irony, to survive Stepan and Andrei and be killed by the first real meal I eat after that. My instinct is to devour everything, especially as my stomach cramps again with an even more intense hunger. But I force myself to go slowly, forking up the tiniest bit of the eggs that I can manage. I think Viktor knows what he's talking about, and the last thing I want to do is make myself feel worse than I already do.

"Drink a little in between bites," he instructs. "But not too fast for that, either."

I can't remember the last time I drank actual milk. It tastes incredible, whether because of the thing itself or just because I'm so hungry, and it's all I can do not to start shoving the food into my mouth faster than I can chew.

"Where on earth did you find all this?" I ask, glancing sideways at him. I'm too overcome from the food and hunger to keep my distance from him, or think too much about what I'm saying.

"I sent some of the men out to find supplies. They bought some food from a nearby farm and brought it back." Viktor says it casually, as if that doesn't sound like the most insane thing my Manhattan-dwelling self has ever heard.

"A farm?"

"Yes," he says patiently, with a crinkle of humor around his eyes. "Don't worry, they were very polite about the whole thing. We compensated the farmers well."

Well, it's good to know they didn't just steal it or kill them and take it, I think wryly. The idea of Viktor's men asking politely for anything feels like a bit of an oxymoron.

"So this is like—fresh." I eye the glass of milk. Maybe the taste isn't just because I'm so hungry. All the food must be, and I slowly bring a forkful of the eggs to my lips, closing my eyes in ecstasy at how good they are. There's cheese in them somewhere, and some kind of spice and all I want to do is eat until I'm completely stuffed.

"Very," Viktor agrees. He's watching me intently, as if he wants to be sure that I'm going to eat. He watches me take a bite of food and then another, and when I set the fork down after the third, suddenly exhausted, he leans forward.

"Here," he says gently. "Let me."

Before I can say anything to stop him, he reaches over, cutting off a piece of the ham and lifting it to my lips. "Here," he says gently. "Just eat. I'll help you."

How is this real? I watch him with surprise in my face that I can't hide because I've never been able to picture Viktor doing any of the things that he's done for me so far. Bathing me, helping me up, feeding me—all of those gentle, caregiver sort of things that feel so out of character for him. But maybe they're not. Just like the ease with which he seems to move around the cabin, just like how he seems at home in his hiking gear as a bespoke suit, maybe there's something I haven't seen before.

Maybe there's a different side to the man I've married that I've never known about before. That I could never have imagined.

It's so hard to fathom. This is a man who oversees a business I feel is deplorable, who bargained for my hand in marriage, who threatened war if he wasn't given what he wanted. A man with power that frightens me sometimes, a man who other men are afraid of. A man that I hadn't wanted.

A man I *shouldn't* want.

A man who is right now feeding me ham and eggs and looking at me as if my well-being is the only thing on his mind right now.

"Did you stay here?" I blurt out suddenly after eating another bite. "I woke up a few times, partway, and I thought I saw you here. Sitting by my bed."

"Of course." Viktor stabs another piece of ham with the fork. "You're my wife, Caterina. Someone hurt you. We weren't sure if you would live for a little while there. There's no way I would have ever left your side, except when strictly necessary."

The words take a moment to sink in. The seriousness in his words strikes a chord somewhere deep inside of me, and the lingering paranoia that I've felt since I was abducted, the worry that Viktor had a hand in this somehow, falters. That it was a way to punish me or teach me a lesson. A means to break me, so I would be easier to handle in the future.

But that doesn't match up with how he's looking at me right now. It doesn't match up with anything he's doing.

Or how he's making me feel.

"I didn't think you cared." I regret saying it almost as soon as it's out of my mouth. I don't want Viktor to think *I* care, or that I really even think that much about him at all. I don't want him to think that it matters to me.

"You're my wife," he repeats, as if it should make perfect sense. "Of course I care."

That's not quite what I meant, I think as I eat the last bite of food, but I let it go. I'm not ready to have this conversation, not when I can't even picture what tomorrow will look like.

He stands up then, reaching for a duffel bag by the door that I hadn't seen before. "We managed to get some clothes for you, too. It's nothing fancy, and they might not fit perfectly, but at least you can get dressed. The doctor said that as long as you don't wear anything too tight yet, and keep the bandages clean, it would be good for you to be able to walk around the cabin."

He moves the tray away then, and I get a glimpse as he unzips the bag, handing me a pair of loose men's sweatpants and a t-shirt that will definitely be too big on me. "It's a long way from being couture," Viktor says with a laugh. "But it should be comfortable, at least."

I honestly couldn't care less. I'm just glad to have clothes on again. It feels like another step in the right direction, another step towards normalcy. A step, just like the ones I took from my bed this morning, no matter how few or how difficult.

"Here," Viktor says gently—more gently than I would have imagined. "I'll help you."

He touches me, and I go very still, unsure of what to expect. His hands are soft on my arms as he reaches for me, pushing back the blanket and turning me slowly in the bed. I stifle a gasp as his arm slides around my back, steadying me as he pulls me towards the edge of the bed, and it all feels as if it happens in slow motion. His hand is gentle, pressing against my spine, holding me up. *Supporting me*, I think, and the idea of it seems so ridiculous that I almost laugh.

"Can you sit up on your own?" he asks, his voice faintly rough, and something about it sends a shiver down my spine. It twines with the hot flicker of pain that shoots through me every time I move, making my skin feel hot and cold all at once, and I let out a small sound that could have been a gasp or a moan; I'm not sure which.

Viktor's eyes flick up to mine, and for a second, I see a glimmer of heat in them that makes my breath catch again.

"I think so," I manage, pressing my hands into the mattress to brace myself. The healing lacerations around my wrists burn, but I manage to keep myself upright. With Viktor sitting in front of me, so close that I can almost feel his breath on my skin along with the pressure of his hand on my back, I'm suddenly so much more aware of being naked.

However, with that awareness comes the reminder of how I look now.

I'm not the woman he married anymore. My slender, smooth, olive-hued body doesn't look like the one he unwrapped on our wedding night, the one he lusted after, the one he punished and turned into a sobbing, melted mess of pleasure on his bed. I'm skinny to the point of scrawniness now, my body littered with wounds, my hair lank, my skin sallow. I saw myself in the mirror this morning, and I'm nothing that could be called desirable anymore.

But for some reason, Viktor is looking at me with a heat in his eyes that makes me want to believe he doesn't see any of that.

Don't let yourself think that. You'll only get hurt in the end. The only way you survive this marriage is by remaining as cold as he is.

Nothing about his expression looks cold right now, though. My husband should be as icy as the Russian wilderness beyond this cabin, but I can feel his gaze on me, licking over my skin the way—

His hands smooth over my legs, down the sides of my bare thighs. It's not a sexual caress, but it *feels* like it. I can feel the rough tips of his fingers, sliding over the unmarred spots of skin, skating around the cuts on my thighs. There's one on my inner thigh, a deep one that I know will scar, that he'll never not be able to see if his lips make their way up my flesh ever again.

Just as quickly as the thought enters my mind, I try to push it away. There's no reason for Viktor to ever touch me like that again. I can't imagine why he would want to. *I* shouldn't want him to. Even if his hands feel warm on my thighs, sending a flush through me as if I've been starved for touch. Which makes no sense—why would I want to be touched? I've been touched far too often in the past days, and for all the wrong reasons. But for some reason, I don't want Viktor to move his hands.

But he does, of course. He wasn't caressing me. He was moving my legs gently into place so that he can slide the sweatpants on, the fleece material brushing over my skin where his fingers were before, and it was stupid of me to think that there was any meaning to that light brush of his hands other than something purely practical.

It doesn't mean anything that his hands linger on my waist as he tugs the sweatpants up into place. It doesn't mean anything that when he pulls the oversized men's t-shirt over my head and arms, his hands skim lightly past my breasts as if he wants to touch them. As if he wishes he could touch me the way he used to, without so much skin that's too hurt to really run his hands over.

"There." Viktor pulls the fabric down around my hips, looking up at me with those fathomless blue eyes. I can't tell what he's really thinking. The heat I saw a few moments ago is gone, making me wonder if I imagined it. Surely, I must have. There's no way he could feel anything like desire for me.

Not now. Not ever again.

As he stands up, stepping back a fraction to give me room to try to get up, I tell myself that should be a relief. After all, I'd started this marriage bargaining to keep myself out of Viktor's bed. Any reason for him to want that, too, should put us on the same page.

I'll be free of his demands. Free of the need to lie down and spread my legs for him to give him his heir. Free of his depraved desires and pleasures, free of the confusing way that he makes me feel. Free of everything except for the most basic duties required of me as the *Ussuri's* wife.

In a way, I should be thanking Andrei and Stepan. They've given my husband a reason not to want me, and me a way out of the demands of my marriage bed.

So why do I feel so miserable?

I stand up slowly, pushing myself up from the mattress, and I see Viktor hovering at my elbow as if waiting to see if he'll need to catch me. Every movement hurts, my breath sticking in my lungs, but I force myself to keep going. I don't want to be weak. I don't want to be a burden.

I want to be myself again. The woman who has made it through every, single, thing thrown at her so far. I refuse to let two Russian thugs and their penchant for hurting women be my downfall.

"I've got it," I say quietly, reaching out to hold onto the bedpost to steady myself. I'm not sure that I do, in fact, have it—but I don't want to rely on Viktor any more than I have to. If I have my way, this is the beginning of a distance between us that will be wider and colder than the Russian tundra. I'll have my life, and he'll have his, and the two shall meet only when strictly necessary. I have every reason I need now for it to be that way, and he should too.

Viktor presses his lips together tightly as if my insistence that I can

M JAMES

do it myself frustrates him, but I ignore it. When I'm sure that I won't fall down again, I take a step away from the bed, and then another, and another. Every wasted muscle in my body protests, but I clench my teeth, fighting through the pain.

I won't be weak. I won't be helpless. With Viktor being the man he is and my marriage to him indissoluble without breaking the peace accord with Luca, I need to be prepared for someone to try to use me against him in the future. This is a dangerous life, and I've always known it.

I just hadn't realized exactly how strong I would need to be.

That stops now. I have to be able to take care of myself.

I can't trust anyone else.

I can feel his presence at my back as I make my way to the door, one step at a time, the hardwood floor cold against my bare feet. "I want some sunlight," I say softly as my hand goes to the doorknob. "Is there somewhere I can get that without going outside?"

Viktor hesitates behind me. "There's an enclosed porch on the back of the cabin," he says finally. "Most of the windows are boarded up to ensure the safety of anyone staying here. But I can have the men pull a few down, just for a little while, so you can get some sunlight."

My heart skips in my chest despite myself. I'd expected him to say no, to remind me of the danger, to tell me that wanting to bask in the sun for a little while was a needless, selfish whim. But he hadn't done that. He'd simply found a way to give me what I want—what I *need* right now.

It might be the kindest thing my Bratva husband has ever done for me.

"Thank you," I say softly, turning the knob and opening the door. "It doesn't have to be for long if it's dangerous. Just a few minutes."

"Wait here," Viktor says sternly, stepping around me. "I don't want to risk you falling with no one to catch you." He turns down the hall, disappearing from sight for a few moments and then abruptly returning with Levin. "Levin will help you get to the porch," he tells me, glancing between the two of us. "I'll have the men remove the boarding."

STOLEN BRIDE

I'm even less comfortable with Levin at my arm. He hovers even more than Viktor did, probably because he knows it's his ass if anything happens to me. I know babysitting me as I creep down the hallway one slow, halting step at a time is probably the last thing in the world he wants to do, and I glance up at him apologetically. I don't have any reason to dislike Levin beyond his involvement in Viktor's detestable business.

"I'm sorry," I tell him hoarsely, words still feeling odd and sticky in my unused throat. "I know this isn't your idea of a good time, walking me down the hall like an injured puppy."

"Whatever you or the *Ussuri* requires, I do," Levin says formally, glancing towards me but not meeting my eyes. I wonder if it would be some broach of protocol for him to look at me directly, if meeting the gaze of the *pakhan*'s wife is a violation of some Bratva law. I wouldn't be surprised if it was. "It is my duty to see that you're well when Mr. Andreyev cannot."

His formality tells me all I need to know. I don't push the topic further, just nod as we make our way down, one painstakingly slow step at a time until finally, we go through the kitchen and out to the enclosed porch on the back of the cabin that Viktor had told me about.

A few of his men are still standing there, pulling down a handful of the boards, and not a single one of them will look me in the eye. They all avert their gazes, whether because they're required to or because they can't bear to look at me, I don't know.

What I *do* know is that the sunshine streaming in through the windows is exactly what I needed. The sky outside is mostly grey and cloudy, but some rays are piercing through, enough to warm my pale sallow skin and make me feel a flicker of life again. After the filthy cabin I'd been held prisoner in and the days in bed in that dim room, just seeing the sky and trees and the outside world, in general, stretching out in front of me is enough to send my heart fluttering in my chest.

It feels like freedom. Like I still have a life, and a future, despite all of this. Like we'll leave here at some point, and I can start to piece it all back together.

Right now, that means more to me than anything else.

I'm alive.

And I plan to keep it that way.

VIKTOR

The cabin is quiet when night falls. There's a tentative sense that we're safe for now, although I know I need to move Caterina as soon as possible. There are guards at every possible window and door and a heavy guard on Andrei and Stepan. However, they're hardly in any condition to try to escape.

I made sure to see to that.

What I want is to sleep next to my wife, but *she's* not in a condition for me to do that yet. The doctor cautioned against anything that might jostle her or disturb her healing process, and the last thing I want to do is make this harder for her. She needs to heal as quickly and efficiently as possible, especially because we can't stay in this cabin for much longer. There are still people after her and us, and the longer we stay in one place, the more dangerous it becomes.

It takes a long time for me to fall asleep. When I finally do, my sleep is restless and broken, punctuated by dreams that I haven't had in a long time.

Vera, on our wedding day, resplendent in silk and lace, her blonde hair cascading down her shoulders and her delicate heart-shaped face alight with joy. Her cheeks flushed, her hands gripping mine at the altar, both of us young and full of joy that we were allowed to do this at all, to make a love match when so many in our positions married for status, wealth, or power instead. Me, unable to believe that I had been lucky enough to win her love, this shining example of Russian grace and beauty, a wife that any man could be proud of.

Her body in our wedding bed, hands everywhere, too much of a rush to get her dress off. Hands, pushing it up above her hips, a tangle of lace, her head thrown back, her pretty rose-colored lips parted on a gasp as I thrust into her, groaning with satisfaction. My hand on her face, eyes locked together, bodies tangled in a passion that naively, youthfully, we had believed would never fade.

That nothing could ever come between us. We were young and in love.

We were invincible.

Vera, her smooth flat stomach beginning to swell with the child that would be Anika, her face alight with happiness, swearing she was going to give me a son. An heir, a child to carry on the Andreyev name. To carry on a business that she didn't fully understand because I'd kept her in the dark. Because I didn't know how to tell the woman I loved that I bought and sold other women, that it was what my family had always done, despite how I tried to justify it in my own mind.

Even then, I knew that my justifications were not enough.

But it was what we had always done.

I knew no other way.

My wife, radiant as a goddess in her pregnancy, though she hardly thought so. The images swirl past, the two of us not realizing what we were on the cusp of, rattling around my too-large house, making promises to fill it with children. Vera nesting, decorating. A new piece of furniture, art, or antique every day when I came home.

Anika, coming screaming into the world. The memory I despise, how my wife turned away from our daughter when she saw that she hadn't given me a son, and how she refused to listen when I told her that it didn't matter, that she could give me sons later, that our daughter was as beautiful as her mother.

The beginning of the end.

These are not the things I want to dream about. Not the things I want to remember. But caught in a restless sleep, they all come back to me anyway.

The first divide between us. The way Vera loved Anika, but from a distance, as if the girl was a sign of her own failure. The way sex changed between us, a dogged race to get pregnant again, instead of the passionate lovemaking that it was before. Vera, turning her face away from me when I try to kiss her as I hold her naked body in my hands. Vera, telling me that I can't possibly forgive her that my firstborn was not a son. Vera, who won't listen, no matter how often I coo over and spoil my daughter, no matter how often I tell her that I adore Anika because she is in every way a tiny replica of my lovely wife.

Vera, who can only think about one thing now, and that's giving me a son.

The second pregnancy, and a lukewarm bed. My wife, cradling her belly protectively as if she could change the sex of the child simply by wishing hard enough.

My wife, who refuses to nurse the second daughter she gives me.

Our first real fight. Screaming, shouting, insults that I will carry with me to my grave. Things I said in fear for my children, worry that they would grow up without a loving mother. The night I dragged her to my bed and told her that if she wanted to give me a son so badly, she could take my cock again before she was ready for it.

A night that I will regret for the rest of my life.

My wife, a different woman from the one I married. Sadder, more selfish, materialistic, obsessed with her body and her beauty and keeping it despite her insistence on giving me more children. The son that even I would admit that I needed, no matter how much I loved my daughters.

Her love for me, fading even as she learned to love the children she hadn't meant to give me. What little joy she still had, fading with each passing month that didn't bring a new child. Her horror when some of the other Bratva women, Russian wives visiting from Moscow, slipped and told her more than I ever wanted her to know about my business.

The tears she had cried, the way she'd turned her face away when I'd asked, livid with fury, if she planned to give up the house and designer dresses and the jewelry dripping from every inch of her, since she hated all that I did so much.

The last time I ever took her to bed, and the way the light caught the jewels on her ring finger, the huge diamond that I had asked her to marry me with, and the two bands that I'd given her for our daughters' births.

They'd made me angry. I'd held her hand down, wanting to rip the diamonds off of her finger. The roughness had fueled something in her, too, some emotion that I hadn't felt from her in a long time, and she'd fucked me back in a way that she hadn't before.

Grateful just to feel something besides languid sorrow or pouting fits from my wife again, I'd thought nothing of it.

I'd held her in my hands and reveled in the feeling of her body the way I used to. The sweet, hot clutch of her, the softness of her full breasts and lush hips, the curves that she hated so much and that I loved to feel beneath me, wrapped around me.

When we were done, she'd whispered sleepily beside me that perhaps we'd made a son.

And then I left for a month, on a business trip to Russia.

The next time I saw her, it was in the bathtub upstairs, bloody water spilling out onto the marble floor, her face pale and still, her arms laid open.

In the dream, I hear myself scream her name again. I see myself rushing across the bathroom, slipping in the water on the floor, and falling hard to my knees, reaching for my wife.

I am in my own body again, dragging her out of the tub into my arms, kissing her, trying to breathe for her, calling her name.

Trying to bring her back to me.

In the dream, I don't see the box on the countertop or the oblong plastic shape next to it. I don't find it the next morning. After Vera's body is removed from the house, hold it in my hand and see the thing that turned my heart to stone.

I see nothing except my wife, bloodied and dead in my arms. I feel nothing except for the vast certainty that someone must have killed her, that this is someone else's fault.

That my wife cannot have taken her own life.

In the dream, no one comes rushing in to the sound of my screams. No one tries to pull Vera from my arms, or comforts me or tells me that it must have been suicide, that there's been no break-in, no sign of anyone else, that there's no possible way even the best of assassins could have left absolutely no trace at all.

In the dream, I'm left alone, tears running down my face for the first time in my adult life as I cradle my wife's body in my arms, my eyes tightly shut, whispering her name. Begging for her to come back to me. Telling her that I'll make it up to her, that I'll change everything, that I'll be whatever she needs me to be.

If only she'll come back to me.

For a brief moment, I think I feel her stir. I think I hear her whisper my name, but it isn't Vera's voice that I hear.

I open my eyes, and it's Caterina's bloodless body and pale face that I see, her body limp in my arms, scattered with a thousand cuts.

My second wife, as dead as the first.

Another woman that I've failed.

She opens her cold, dead eyes and whispers my name.

VIKTOR

I sit bolt upright in bed, gasping.

It's been a long time since I've had a nightmare like that. The waking life of a *pakhan* has enough fodder for nightmares. I rarely have them when I sleep. In fact, with the exception of the first months after Vera's death, I haven't been known to have them at all.

But things are different now, I suppose.

I run my hand over my forehead, wiping away a cold sweat. The room feels dark and close and hot despite the chill, and I throw the covers back, sliding out of bed and heading for the door without even really knowing where I'm going. I tell myself that I'm going to the kitchen for a glass of water, but my feet lead me in a different direction instead.

Down the hall, to Caterina's room.

To my wife's room.

I tell myself that I'm only going in to check on her, that I want to see for myself that the dream was only that—a dream. That she's alive, sleeping soundly and safely in the room she was given, that tomorrow I'll begin the process of figuring out how to move us to a new safe house, and all will be well.

It takes a moment for my eyes to adjust to the darkness in her bedroom. I can see the slender shape of her under the quilt, so different from Vera. A difference that I like because it means that I rarely think about my first wife when I'm in bed with the second.

When I do, it's not to compare body types.

I like how delicate Caterina feels in my hands, how fragile. I like her small breasts and small stiff nipples, the narrow curve of her waist, the way I can squeeze all of her hips in my hands. The angles of her face, her wide eyes. Everything about her turns me on, makes me wildly aroused in a way that I hadn't known I could feel any longer.

She might not have thawed my heart, but she's awakened a heat in me that I thought was equally dead.

The former is so long frozen that nothing could ever change it. Not after what I've seen. Not after what happened.

I can't go through that again.

I won't.

Slowly, I step closer to the bed, so that I can see the outline of her face in the cool darkness. She makes a small sound in her sleep, and I stop in place, feeling myself grow even harder. My cock had stiffened just from looking at the shape of her in the bed, aching after so many days away from her. That small sleepy moan sends a fresh pulse of blood to my groin, the aching sweeping through me as I look down at my wife.

I want her. I know that she finds herself less beautiful now; I can see it in her eyes, in the way she withdraws and won't meet mine when I look at her naked body. I can see her thinking about the scars that will linger, the way that those two monsters held out in the shed has changed her, that she'll never again be the same woman that I married.

But nothing about those injuries has changed how much I want her. I see nothing when I look at her other than the same beautiful woman who has driven me close to madness with desire, frustration, and need.

They tried to take her away from me.

I won't let them succeed.

I know I should leave her in peace, go back to my room and try to get some more sleep myself, hopefully, dreamless this time. But I feel rooted to the spot, unable to look away from her face, coming even more into focus as my eyes adjust to the darkness. She looks so beautiful, so peaceful, her soft lips parted as she breathes, and I feel that aching, maddening throb in my cock again as I look down at her.

Without meaning to, my hand slides downward, brushing over the soft cotton covering my cock, feeling it lurch into my palm at the slight touch. I haven't had a release in days, too focused on what was needed of me, too worried about Caterina, too concerned with the future of my family and my business.

But now, in the dark silence of the night, standing next to my wife's bedside, all of that seems to slip away.

There is only the two of us and my need for her, like a third being in the room. Present and palpable, aching, throbbing. *Wanting.*

I can't fuck her. Even I'm not that much of a monster. She's still too injured, and I know she wouldn't want me. Not now, not yet, and I won't force myself on her, not after what she's been through.

But I need something. Some kind of relief.

I feel almost like I'm in a dream again as I slip my cock out, the instantaneous pleasure of feeling the velvet skin of it against my palm, rock-hard and burning hot, making me suck in a breath through my teeth. It's been too long since I've come, and I start to stroke slowly, forgetting what this is, what I'm doing, what it would look like if anyone saw this.

No one will. No one else would dare come into my wife's bedroom in the middle of the night.

No one but me.

I look down at her parted lips, aching to push my cock against them, to feel the warm wet heat of her mouth. She looked so beautiful on her knees, so lovely when she opened that mouth to take me in, her eyes wide and pleading, her hair wrapped around my fist. Her throat had felt so good when I fucked it, and I squeeze my hand around my shaft, wanting to feel that again. Wanting to feel the clench of her hot throat around my length, trying to squeeze the cum out of me, to drink it down.

I should do this quickly, stroke hard and fast, come as efficiently as possible, take the edge off and go back to my room. But now that I've begun, I want to make it last. If I can't fuck my wife, I want to look down at her face as I jerk myself off, imagine my cum painting those rosy lips.

God, I want so much more than that.

I want all of her again, her tight hot pussy and the clenching squeeze of her ass around me, the reminder that all of her body is mine, that I own it. That she is *my* wife, my bride, mine to fuck as I please. To take, to possess, to—

I grit my teeth, biting back a groan that could wake Caterina and give me away as a bolt of pure pleasure shoots from my shaft to my toes, curling them against the hardwood floor as I stroke from balls to tip, rubbing my palm over the damp cockhead as I lube myself with my own arousal, dripping now from the strength of my need.

Fuck. The desire to rip back the quilt and look at every inch of her naked body is almost uncontrollable, to roll her onto her back and part her thighs, and sink into her even more so. I crave her heat, her wetness, the way I feel her squeeze around me when I take her despite herself, and my cock throbs again in my fist, hard and eager and wanting. It takes every bit of self-control that I have to stay rooted to the spot, my strokes quick and fast now, my gaze on my wife's lips as I feel my balls tighten with the impending orgasm that I know I can't stave off much longer. It doesn't matter how much I want this to last. I need to come.

And I will, with the memory of my wife's mouth wrapped around me, her throat convulsing as she swallows down every drop—

Bladya! I curse in my head in Russian, my native language, all I can remember as the pleasure shoots through me, white-hot and racing across every nerve, lighting up my body as I curl my palm over my cockhead and feel myself shoot, hot and thick, into my hand. I squeeze my left hand over it, thrusting into my palm like a shallow pussy, still stroking with my right as I clench my jaw so hard that it feels as if my teeth could crack in the effort to stay silent. I don't want to wake her and frighten her, but by god, I can't say I would regret this even if I did. Next to being inside of her, this orgasm is one of the best I've had.

I come for longer than I ever have on my own, my cock pumping cum into my fist until I can *feel* my balls hanging lower, entirely drained. I rip my shirt off with one hand, balling it up in my left as I squeeze my still-hard erection with the other. I take a step closer to the bed, feeling my cock still pulsing with the last aftershocks of my release.

I shouldn't do it. I could wake her, and besides, she's asleep. She has no idea what I've done. But I can see the last drop of my cum pearling at the tip. I take another step closer until I can brush the velvet of my cockhead over her slightly parted lips, leaving that last drop of cum clinging to the full shape of her lower lip, glistening wetly in the darkness.

When I step back, my erection finally beginning to soften, she lets out another small, soft moan—and licks her lips in her sleep.

Fuck. My cock throbs, on the verge of hardening again, and I can feel it swell a little in my fist as I tuck myself away. I stare at her for a moment, almost unable to believe what I just saw.

The sight of her pink tongue running over her lower lip, licking up that droplet of my cum unaware in her sleep, will be something I remember as I jerk off for a long fucking time.

It's almost enough to make me need to come again, here and now.

Instead, I retreat to my own room, telling myself not to push my luck. The hallway of the cabin is thankfully empty, though no one would dare question me anyway, not even Levin. I'd hoped that the release would make it easier for me to sleep, but instead, when I lie down, I'm wide awake, my body still pulsing with adrenaline. I stare up at the ceiling in the darkness, forcing myself to think of Caterina and her tongue running over her lips instead of all of the other thoughts that threaten to crowd in.

There will be plenty of time in the morning to solve those problems. For now, what I need is sleep so I can function with a clear head.

Unfortunately, sleep is hard to come by for me tonight.

I get perhaps a few more broken hours and rise heavy and

exhausted the next morning. My first call is to Luca to make arrangements. We need to move our families to the next safe house, and that includes his, thanks to our bargain. Sofia is in as much danger as anyone else on account of my alliance with her husband.

"Russia?" The disbelief in Luca's voice is plain when I tell him. "You want me to bring my family to a safe house in Russia?"

"It's not just a safe house," I tell him flatly. "It's a goddamned fortress. Sofia will be protected there. And you and I and Liam will hold our own meeting there to decide how to proceed with Alexei."

There's a moment of silence on the other end. "He's taken over it all," Luca says finally. "The men loyal to you have either escaped with Mikhail or are dead. Mikhail is at your home now, guarding your household with what is left of your men, but from what I know, Alexei will make a move soon. You're right to get them out of there. I'll take as many soldiers as I can and extract them before Alexei can mobilize, but your business—"

"I'll worry about the business later," I grind out, and I mean it. "I want my children safe." I pause, remembering something else, something that no doubt will endear my wife to me, no matter how she's feeling these days. "Bring Anastasia Ivanova too," I tell him firmly. "Alexei has a particular grudge against her for her infiltration of my ranks. She's in just as much danger as anyone else."

I can hear the surprise in Luca's voice as he agrees, and I know why. I've made it clear that I'm not fond of the former ballerina that my wife befriended either—for the same reasons. She seduced my men, extracted information, and spied on my ranks—if she were a man, or if I'd been entirely free to do with her as I pleased, I might have had her killed or sold for her crime. I know who her father was, and I can't help but think that traitor's blood runs deep in the Ivanov family. I don't trust her.

But part of Luca's bargain for peace, after Franco Bianchi and Colin Macgregor's deaths, was that Anastasia not be punished. He'd insisted that what she'd done, she'd done for the love of her best friend and that he was as much to blame as anyone else for her actions since he'd kept Sofia in the dark.

Whether I agreed with his estimation or not wasn't the question at hand, it was whether or not I'd agree to leave Anastasia be. I had agreed since the life of one traitorous little ballerina wasn't worth the blood that would be shed if I'd continued to fight Luca. Once I'd heard what Franco had done to her, I'd been even less inclined to punish her further. His cruelty had far outstripped anything I might have done to punish any woman.

This is exactly why I can't, in any conscience, leave her to Alexei's mercies. I know how deeply his resentment and hatred towards her runs, and I know that what he would do to her if he got his hands on her, is the stuff of nightmares.

Nothing I would willingly allow to be visited on any woman, much less one of my wife's friends.

Caterina would never forgive me.

And for some reason, these days, my wife's forgiveness matters very much to me.

It's something that I can't get out of my head as I finish the arrangements with Luca and hang up. I shouldn't care about her forgiveness, emotions, or desires. She's my wife, a wife of convenience, one that was never meant to do more than give me the heir that Vera couldn't. The heir that Vera stole from me.

But somehow, over the brief time we've been married, she's gotten under my skin. Made me feel things beyond desire, something that I'd thought I could no longer feel.

The man who stood in her room last night, feverishly stroking himself to a climax while staring at her mouth, the man who brushed his cum over her lips while she slept, is not a man I recognize.

It's not a man I've ever been before.

Caterina is turning me into a man obsessed.

And if there's one thing I know above all else, it's this—

Obsessions are dangerous.

CATERINA

I have a limited amount of time to heal.

When Viktor brought me breakfast this morning, he let me know that we'd be moving to another safe house in two days. He looked almost apologetic when he said it, as he set the breakfast tray over me as if he felt bad. As if he wanted to give me more time here, to heal on my own without having to worry about being moved.

I wanted to tell him about the strange dream I'd had last night—about him coming into my room and watching me as I slept, about the odd salty taste on my lips this morning, as if the things I'd dreamed about had really happened. But just thinking about saying it out loud, telling Viktor about the things he'd done in that dream, made my cheeks flush and burn until I knew there was no way I could tell him.

Besides, there's no reason for me to want to share those fantasies with my husband. Our marriage was never meant to be like that, and now that he can't possibly want me anymore, it won't be like that ever again. That's a *good* thing, I tell myself as I look down at the bowl of oatmeal and small plate of eggs in front of me, with another glass of milk. "To help you regain your strength," Viktor says firmly. "I know it's difficult, but you need to eat it all, Caterina. Today is going to be a hard day for you, but it's necessary."

There's a seriousness to his voice that I haven't heard since waking up here, and it sends a tremor of nervousness through me. I might not trust Viktor entirely, but I do believe from the tone of his voice that whatever he's talking about, must be important.

I just don't know how much more "difficult" I have in me. Every waking moment since I was drugged in that apartment has been difficult. Just hearing that there's something more makes me feel drained, tired in a way that I've never experienced before, even with everything I've already endured.

Hearing that makes any thoughts of what I dreamed about last night fly straight out of my head. I poke at the food, dutifully forking it into my mouth as Viktor watches, and I glance sideways at him as I eat, narrowing my eyes.

"Do you have to watch me the entire time?"

"I want to make sure you're taking care of yourself," he says firmly. "It's important that you get well."

There's nothing in his expression or tone to indicate it, but I feel a small flare of my old defiance come back, partially in response to the way his stern tone makes me feel. Something about the commanding way he's spoken to me this morning sends a flare of heat through me with each statement, reminding me of the way I felt when he bent me over the bed and took his belt to my backside, or the way I'd felt the night before we left for Moscow, when he'd fucked me more thoroughly than Franco could have ever dared try.

"Why?" I ask coolly, stabbing the eggs with my fork again. "So I can start working as your own personal broodmare again?"

Viktor's expression changes in an instant, his face darkening. I see his jaw tighten, and he takes a sudden step closer to the bed, his entire body tensing as his heated blue eyes lock with mine.

I can't help it. For all my defiance, I flinch back. The memory of Andrei and Stepan is still too close. And I'm still not entirely sure that Viktor wasn't behind it.

He stops in an instant, the moment he sees me flinch, suddenly rooted in place as his mouth twitches. "That's my Caterina," he says, his voice a low, soft growl, and the shudder that it sends down my spine and over my body isn't one of fear.

It's a shudder that I'd hoped to never feel again. Not for him. Maybe not for anyone.

A deep, trembling shudder of desire.

His gaze holds mine, and I can feel the air between us thicken, crackling with that old electricity, the way it did before Moscow. It wasn't all that long ago, two weeks perhaps or even less, but it feels like a lifetime. As if I were an entirely different person back then.

"Eat," Viktor says, his voice still that soft growl. "I'll be back to get you in a little while after you're done."

And then he turns away, and I feel the tension release when his gaze lets go of mine, like a rubber band snapping back into place. It sends another shiver through me, and it's not until he walks out of the room, the door closing behind him, that I realize I was holding my breath the entire time.

Slowly, I let go of where I'd been gripping the quilt and pick up my fork again.

It sounds like I really am going to need my strength.

* * *

True to his word, Viktor comes back about an hour later, casting a glance at the breakfast tray I set aside. A look of satisfaction crosses his face, presumably at seeing it empty, and then he looks back towards me. "Levin is waiting for us out back," he says. "I'll help you up if you need it, but it would be good to see if you can stand on your own."

"Why?" I narrow my eyes, although I go ahead and push back the quilt. I want to get out of the bed anyway—as painful as walking around was, it *had* felt good to get my blood moving, to stretch my wasted muscles, and feel as if I were somewhat human again, and not just an invalid. But the look on Viktor's face is slightly alarming.

"You'll see." He nods towards me. "We don't have a lot of time, though. We need the afternoon, so go ahead and get up."

The flicker of heat that I feel at his commanding tone immediately wars with my inner desire to tell him to go fuck himself every time he tells me what to do. Still, I only have so much energy right now, and I suspect that I need to conserve it for whatever it is that he's planned. So instead of snapping back, I simply start the process of getting my legs over the side of the bed, moving slowly and waiting for any hint of pain or pulling at the bandages that would tell me that I need to stop.

Surprisingly, I manage to get my feet on the floor and push myself upright in less amount of time than usual. I still feel sore and achy in every part of me, I already feel more capable than I did before, and that sends a rush of adrenaline through me that makes me wobble just a little, grabbing onto the bed frame for support.

"Easy," Viktor says quietly. "Take it slow."

"You said we didn't have a lot of time." I press my hand against my side, where I can feel one of the deeper, bandaged wounds starting to throb, and try to find my breath again.

"We won't have *any* time if you pass out," Viktor points out. "We don't have all day, but don't kill yourself either, Caterina."

"I'll do my best," I mutter, closing my eyes until I feel the deep throb in my side start to fade, and then I take a short, shallow breath, stepping away from the bed.

It takes longer than I would have liked to make it outside. When we finally do get there, I see Levin standing in the open area behind the cabin, dressed in loose-fitting pants and a long-sleeved, tight t-shirt that shows off his impressive muscles. He's built like a wrestler, or a bodybuilder, with broad shoulders and chest that taper down to a narrow waist and thickly muscled arms. Although he's handsome enough, he's not my type, with a strong, stubbled jaw and those bright blue eyes that so many Russian men seem to have. He's dark-haired too, like Viktor, his cut close to his head. His face is set in a stern expression that mirrors the one on Viktor's, and I feel another tremor of anxiety ripple through me.

"Okay." I glance between the two men. "What's going on?"

Viktor turns to face me. "Have you ever learned any kind of self-defense, Caterina? Or how to shoot a gun?"

I stare at him for a moment, taken aback. That's the last thing I'd expected him to say, and it takes me a moment to formulate a response. "No," I say finally. "I haven't. My father had security so that I wouldn't need to."

Viktor's jaw tenses and I realize immediately how that sounded, as if I blame his lack of ability to protect me for what happened. *Do I?* I hadn't really allowed myself to think about who or what I might blame for what had happened, if anything at all—only that it *had*, and now I have to deal with it. Survive it, endure it, heal from it if I can.

I wonder if this new thing will be something to endure or something that can help me heal.

"We're all in danger," Viktor says tightly. "And though I fully intend to have heavy security on you at all times, I want to make sure you have the ability to protect yourself too, or at least some knowledge of it. So that's what we'll be doing today. Nothing too strenuous since you're still healing, but the basics. Enough to get you started and know how to handle a weapon. Levin is going to help."

His voice is hard now, rougher than before, and I know that my comment about my father cut deep. Part of me doesn't care—how many times has he said things that have hurt me? But another part of me, the small part that refuses to remember that Viktor should mean nothing to me, wishes I'd phrased it differently. That I hadn't hurt him.

This might be all his fault, I remind myself. *He might have done all of this just to break you. You don't know for certain.* Even his tender care of me since coming to the cabin could be a trick, a way to make me feel grateful to him after breaking me down, to tighten his grip on me. It sounds paranoid even in my head, but I don't know who or what to trust anymore. Nothing feels right.

Everything about my own life feels strange to me again.

And I don't know if I'll ever again have anything that feels like home.

CATERINA

Viktor nods towards Levin. "He'll begin with the self-defense. I'll assist you with the weapons portion."

It's on the tip of my tongue to say something biting, and I can't quite stop myself. I cast a dark glance towards Viktor, suddenly resentful all over again that I'm having to deal with this at all. "Why Levin? Don't you know how to fight?"

I see Levin's mouth twitch, with irritation or humor, I'm not sure, but the look on Viktor's face is anything but humorous. "I've trained often with Levin," Viktor says tightly. "And I—" he breaks off, his expression hardening. "Do as I say, Caterina. Levin is the better of the two of us to teach you this."

I almost argue, but Levin is already moving towards me, clearing his throat as he levels his expressionless blue gaze at me. "We're going to take this slow," he promises me. "I know you don't have any prior knowledge, so we're going to work with the basics." He takes a firm stance in front of me, letting out a breath. "Breathe out, like I just did, and relax your body as much as you're able. If you're tense and stiff, you're more prone to taking injuries from hits, and you can't move as fluidly. The goal should always be to keep your body soft and malleable and rely on the muscle memory that you build up to get you through the fight. You'll move faster and be harder to hit if you do those things."

It sounds overwhelming just from that, but I nod, swallowing hard. It's the most words Levin has ever said to me at once, and I find myself wondering what his story is, how he came to work for Viktor and his family, and what's kept him there all this time. If he has a wife, or a family of his own, if there's a person behind that expressionless shell.

Or if he's just a brute, like so many other Bratva men.

"For this," Levin says, breaking me out of my thoughts, "I want you to stand normally. You're not familiar with a boxer's stance, so we're not going to try to teach you that right now. If you need any of this, it's not going to be a formal fight anyway; you're going to need to move quickly and efficiently without all the extras. You're probably not going to be prepared anyway if an attack happens, so you should be able to block and strike if need be from your normal stance." He pauses. "And if you are attacked, you're better off if they have no idea that you have any knowledge of how to defend yourself. You want to catch them off-guard as much as you can."

I can feel Viktor's eyes on me, watching us both. "Okay, that makes sense," I say slowly, trying to relax and just stand how I normally would, without thinking too much about it. My heart feels like it's pounding in my chest, and I'm suddenly aware of every ache and pain throughout my entire body, large and small. I'm afraid to do this, afraid for him to touch me, fearful of getting hurt even more. But facing him, I suddenly also realize that I *want* to learn this. I'd never thought about learning self-defense or how to shoot a gun for a single second. My entire life, I was raised with a security detail never far away, and I'd grown up with the certainty that whoever I married would provide the same thing. I was *protected*. I didn't need to know how to defend myself.

But now I see that's not true. Regardless of how good Viktor's security might be, I do need to know. It's not a dig at him so much as a realization that *I'll* feel stronger, better, more capable if I'm not always reliant on others to keep me safe.

If I can fight back too.

I hadn't realized that until I'd looked up at Levin and considered telling him and Viktor to go fuck themselves, that I'm not ready for this, that I don't want to do it, and going back inside.

But I *do*. I might not be ready, but the events of the past days have taught me that I might not get the opportunity to wait until I'm ready. The danger is *now*, and I'm tired of relying on others to face it for me.

I want to stop hiding and taking the abuse of everyone around me.

"Block this," Levin says suddenly, breaking my train of thought again, and almost before I can react, his hand strikes out towards my side. He aims below the bandages—a realization that sends a flush of embarrassment through me because that means that he's seen my wounds and my carved-up body—but I'm glad that he does because although I reflexively reach out to stop him, I don't make it in time. I miss, and his hand connects with my waist.

I let out a small gasp, and he pulls back.

"Did I hurt you?" His voice is business-like, efficient. Less a matter of caring for me and more of simply wondering if we can continue.

I swallow hard, shaking my head. "No, I'm fine," I say quickly. "I'll be fine. It just surprised me, that's all."

"These strikes will be easy at first," Levin says brusquely. "Viktor wants me to continue training you as you heal, so later, when your injuries are mended enough, and you've learned the basics, we'll do this with more intensity. You may be sore or receive blows that may hurt, and you may want to flinch back or stop because of what you've endured. But over time, this will make you mentally stronger, as well as physically."

I look up at him, startled. I'd been thinking just that, but to hear him vocalize it makes me wonder if Viktor told him to say that or expressed it as a goal. It doesn't sound like something Levin would offer up on his own—especially when it comes to me, he's nothing if not simply Viktor's mouthpiece. But what possible reason would Viktor have for wanting me to be mentally stronger? If anything, I would be easier to manage broken. It's my entire reason for thinking that he might have been behind my kidnapping.

Maybe I'm wrong. Maybe he had nothing to do with it at all.

"In time, there may be some full-contact training, although Viktor may want to take that over himself. But you don't need to worry about that right now. For now, all you should concern yourself with is learning the basics that I'll show you today."

He pauses, looking down at me with something that almost looks like a flicker of concern in his eyes. "Are you alright?"

Even that most basic kindness makes my chest constrict, a sudden lump appearing in my throat. I clear it, nodding and forcing myself to speak clearly. "Yeah, I'm fine," I tell him firmly, even though right now I'm feeling anything but fine. I want to go inside, I want to lie down, I want to go to sleep. I want to go back to before all this happened and somehow keep from having to endure any of it.

That's impossible, though. All I can do now is try to keep it from happening again.

Which is why I'm out circling a bodyguard four times my size in the sparse Russian forest, shivering from the cold.

"Alright," Levin says, squaring his shoulders. "Let's try it again."

For the next half hour, the two of us trade minor blows, with Levin striking at each of my arms, then each of my sides, and then each of my hips lightly as I try to block. My forearms are sore, but I force myself to keep going. Towards the end of the half-hour, I find myself being able to block him more often than not, anticipating his movement. He starts to alternate then, mixing up the directions in which he goes for my arms, sides or hips, and even then, I manage to do a decent job of blocking at least half of them, although I'm considerably slower.

"Take a break," Levin says, his voice pleased. "You're doing well. Perhaps we should go in?"

I glance over at Viktor, hoping he'll agree. I'm out of breath and tired, but he shakes his head, his arms crossed over his chest and his face hard. "No," he says firmly. "Continue until you've gone through all of the moves that I instructed you to show her preliminarily."

"I'm not sure—" Levin starts to say, and Viktor's blue gaze turns dangerous.

"As you wish, *Ussuri*." Levin's tone changes instantly, and I look at Viktor, seeing again the man that I'm used to, the one who inspires fear and obedience even in a man like Levin. A man who even the strongest of other men fear.

I don't know how to reconcile that man with the one who bathed me tenderly, who fed me eggs and insisted I take care of myself.

I don't know how they can exist within the same person.

"Alright," Levin says, turning back to me, his tone hinting at veiled reluctance. "We're going to try escaping a headlock. Gently, but I want you to learn the motion."

I look at his arms, uncertainty flooding me. I don't see how I could ever escape anything that strong, gentle or not—and anyone attacking me certainly isn't going to be gentle. But I haven't exactly been given an option, so I take a deep breath, nodding as I face him.

"I'll do my best."

Levin gives me a look that could almost be described as kind, though I can't be sure. "I'm going to put my arm around your neck and pull you back, not quite up against me but close, and move your other arm behind your back. I'll be careful of your injuries. This is less about truly breaking free of a real grip and more about learning the movements."

I nod, unsure of what to say. I brace myself, and when he moves towards me, I think I'm ready for it. But when he grabs my shoulders, turning me and encircling my neck with his arm, I feel a cold burst of terror that leaves me frozen in place, my heart pounding in my chest so hard that it hurts. It feels like it's going to burst out of my ribs. I only barely register him reaching for my arm, moving it behind my back in a careful motion that's anything but rough, but only serves to compound the terror.

He's holding me lightly, keeping my body away from his—certainly because he knows as well as I do that if any man but Viktor pulled me up against him that there would be hell to pay. I can't imagine Viktor standing by and letting any man touch me that intimately, no matter the purpose.

I almost wish it was sexual. Up until now, Levin has only barely touched my arms or sides with his hand, and that wasn't enough to trigger the panic from what I'd been through with Andrei and Stepan. But this is something else, something that reminds me of being held, bound, choked, and I can't breathe past the fear, the soul-numbing, paralyzing fear.

Dimly, I look at Viktor, and I see his hard face, his set expression. But behind the dark look in his eyes—I think I see something else.

Maybe I'm imagining it. But I think I see worry, concern, as if he's waiting to see what will happen. If I'll be able to snap out of it.

Or if I'm too broken, too crippled to fight back.

That thought sends a hot flush of anger through me that thaws the panic just a little. I don't *want* to be broken. I don't want them to have made it so that I can't ever fight my own fear again, so that something as simple as training with a man who I know wouldn't hurt me, who answers to my husband, one of the most feared men in the Bratva, can paralyze me like this.

Levin hasn't let go of me yet. He's holding me in place, not tightening his grasp but not loosening it either, and I know I'm supposed to be trying to get out. I try to push past the fear, to remind myself that Levin wouldn't hurt me.

Viktor would kill him if he did.

Right?

It doesn't help that this reminds me that Viktor has someone who *could* hurt me if he ever decided he wanted to be rid of me. Would Levin do that? I think Levin would follow any order Viktor gave him, no matter what. But if Viktor were going to do that, wouldn't he have already?

Unless, once again, the kidnapping had been a way to break me, a trick to make me think that Viktor had nothing to do with it.

I've got to stop thinking like this. It's tying me up in knots, making my mind feel as if I'm going insane. I need to focus on one thing right now, getting well.

The rest I can untangle later.

I wriggle in his grasp, trying to break the hold, and I can feel him exerting the tiniest bit of pressure to hold me still. It sends another chill of fear through me, but I grit my teeth, forcing myself to think through it. To keep pushing, keep going. To try.

I twist again, not so hard that I might hurt myself, but hard enough to show that I'm making an effort.

Levin lets go, stepping back, and I gasp, my heart still pounding as I turn to face him.

"That's an example of a move we'll work on," Levin says calmly. "We need to teach your body to ignore that fear reaction. Suppose you're attacked again and need to defend yourself. In that case, your muscle memory needs to work apart from your body's natural reaction to run. *Everyone* is afraid," he stresses. "You have more reason to react fearfully than others, but anyone put in that situation will feel a fear response. The purpose of this is to teach you to overcome it."

Something about the way he says it makes me feel as if he's trying to reassure me, to make me feel as if I'm not alone in having that cold, panicked reaction. When I glance at Viktor, his face is still set in hard lines, and I can't tell if he's pleased with me or not.

"I'll show you some tactics that an attacker might use," Levin continues, and I look up at him, wondering why I care so much if Viktor is impressed, or happy, or anything else. He's making me do this, so he should be pleased no matter what.

"We'll go over levels of difficulty and ways to escape. Can you handle that, do you think?"

I take a breath, not giving myself too much time to think before I answer. "Yes," I say quickly, swallowing hard. "I can do it."

"Continue," Viktor barks out. "You're not finished."

Levin goes very still, his face impassive, but I look over at Viktor with shock. "Viktor, I'm tired—"

"Are you in pain?" His jaw clenches. "Are your injuries bleeding again or too painful?"

"I—" I hesitate, trying to measure whether they are or not. I'm sore, but it's not excruciating. "I think I can keep going."

"Then do."

I don't understand the sudden shift in Viktor's attitude. Did my comment about his security really cut that deeply? I can't figure it out, but I see his eyes flick towards Levin, and then Viktor nods.

Levin's hand shoots out, grabbing my wrist and pulling it behind me. It's not a terribly hard grip, but it's enough to catch me off guard and make me gasp as he twists it behind my back, that cold panic flooding me again.

"Ow!" I yelp, stiffening. It's exactly what Levin told me not to do, and I hear him bark that out, his words cutting through the fog of fear.

"Relax, Caterina!"

"You're twisting my arm!" I snap, and I hear Levin laugh. It's not a cruel laugh, but something about it sparks a memory, Stepan laughing as he leans over me, and the pain in my wrist where Levin's fingers are pressing against the laceration suddenly seems to amplify every other pain in my body. I jerk myself free of it suddenly, ripping my wrist out of his hand despite the sharp, burning pain that follows, and stumble backward, feeling myself go pale.

"Just breathe," Levin says, and I glare up at him, gripping my wrist.

"I'm trying," I hiss, and his mouth twitches, possibly the closest thing to the beginning of a smile that I've ever seen on his face.

"You're angry. Anger is good, Caterina. It's better than fear. Anger will get you through. If you're ever in a situation where you have to defend yourself, let yourself be angry. Let yourself feel that rage that anyone would try to hurt you, to take advantage of you. Use it, and push back the fear."

"Have you ever had to do that?" The question slips out before I mean for it to, and Levin tenses instantly, his face shutting down.

"That's not relevant to your training," he says pointedly, and I have to fight not to roll my eyes.

Of course, he's not going to tell me. We're not friends, not even as close as a real trainer and student might be. I need to remember that. As much as I want someone to rely on, I have no guarantees of that. Not here.

"Breathe," I hear Levin instruct again, and I force myself to focus on that, on the mechanics of breathing, in and out, in and out. *I'm safe,*

I tell myself, forcing myself to let go of my wrist. *This isn't real.* Levin isn't going to hurt me. He's teaching me how to protect myself. There's nothing to be afraid of. Nothing here, anyway.

Am I sure about that?

I tell myself that if I learn this, it doesn't matter. I'll be able to protect myself no matter what.

I'm not sure quite how much I believe that, though.

"Not all of this will be so easy," Levin says, his mouth set in a firm line. He doesn't look like he's enjoying this all that much, but I don't think that matters either. Whatever Viktor says, he'll do.

"An attacker would be much, much more forceful than I was just now," he says, his voice taking on that stern tone that I know so well from Viktor. "You need to be prepared for that."

"Do I need to be prepared for all of it today?" I retort, glaring at him. "Because I don't think I'm in any shape to go ten rounds with anyone right now."

"No." Levin's mouth twitches again as if I've said something funny. "But we do need to continue for a little longer. Are you ready to try again?"

I hesitate, but I know that I don't really have a choice. I don't need to look at Viktor to know what the expression on his face will be or ask to know that he's not going to let me leave until we've gone through everything he instructed Levin to show me today. I might as well get it over with.

I give Levin a quick nod, and I see the tension in his shoulders relax a little.

"We're going to do this again, but the other way. I want you to put me into an armlock, and then I'll show you the process to escape. We'll try it with you again after that."

I swallow hard, nodding again. I don't really want to touch him or be so close to him, but it's better than Viktor, I suppose. At least I'm not attracted to Levin. I'm just a little afraid of him.

"Grab my arm and twist it behind my back," Levin instructs. "Go ahead."

It feels ridiculous to even try, but I know that stalling isn't going to get me out of it. So I step closer, reaching out to grab his thick forearm.

"Exactly," he says encouragingly. "Now twist it behind my back. Once you've done that, kick at my lower leg as if you're trying to sweep it out from under me."

I frown, my fingers still loosely encircling his arm. "This is ridiculous. I couldn't take down someone your size if I tried. There's just no way."

"You can when you're trained correctly," Levin insists. "And that's what your husband has instructed me to do." There's an emphasis on the word *husband*, as if he's reminding me of my duty to Viktor, or perhaps Viktor's control over me. The fact that really, at the end of the day, I don't have a choice about anything. I'm just here to be ordered around.

I can feel the resentment bubbling up in me again, and my hand tightens around Levin's arm.

"Good." Levin pauses. "Remember, Catarina, winning a fight is not always about size. Catching your opponent off-guard matters too, and you have the advantage in that because they won't expect you to have training."

"I just don't see how someone my size and someone yours could ever be evenly matched."

"It's not about even matching," Levin explains patiently—more patiently than I'd expected, if I'm being honest. "Winning a fight is a mixture of technique and simply having the advantage. In a planned bout, no, of course not. There's a reason there are weight levels in boxing and MMA. But in real violent combat, things don't always go as planned. Your attacker might not be well-trained; they might simply be a violent brute. Mob thugs often are. Most of all, they'll expect you not to know what to do, to be an easy target. The goal here is to make you a more difficult target. Your goal is to escape, not to win a fight. Do you understand?"

It seems unbelievable to me, even with his explanation, that someone like me could ever hope to even escape someone like him in an attack. But some of what he's saying *does* make sense. And if it's possible that I *could* learn to escape even against someone like him, then I do want to learn that.

I tighten my grip on his arm, twisting it behind his back as instructed. I feel Levin's hand ball into a fist, his muscles flexing against my palm, and I follow his command to kick at the back of his leg, my foot connecting with his knee.

"It's possible to bring me down if you can get me off balance, get a leg out from under me and use my size and weight against me," Levin says. "And if you're on my side of this, the one being held, then you'll want to try something like this."

His other hand comes around suddenly, grabbing the hand holding his arm as he twists his arm in my grasp, reaching with his other hand to push at my fingers. He doesn't do it as roughly as I'm sure he would in the real situation, but even pushing my fingers back the way he does makes me gasp. He breaks my hold on him without much effort at all, sidestepping as he does to avoid the kick. And then, just as neatly, he twists my arm back again, his foot connecting with my calf as he sweeps my legs out from under me.

I go down, face first. His arm is there supporting me, so I don't crash to the ground, but with only one hand to catch myself, it's a shock nonetheless.

"Fuck you!" I yell, twisting in his grasp, feeling pain shoot through me despite Levin's carefulness. I feel breathless, the panic starting to curl through me again.

"You can still get out of this," Levin says from above me. His hand is pressing my arm to my back, and he's barely touching me otherwise, although I can feel him kneeling on either side of my hips. He's being very, very careful to keep this PG-rated—probably because his boss and my husband is an actual murderer.

"What is your first instinct? What should you try to do?" Levin's voice is calm, and it makes me want to hurt him for real.

Maybe that's the point.

"I could headbutt you," I tell him darkly. "Or kick you in the balls. Or use my free hand to throw dirt in your face."

"I don't recommend kicking an attacker in the balls when you're on the ground," Levin says wryly. "That usually pitches your opponent forward, in which case you'll just be trapped, and they'll be angry. You could try throwing dirt in their eyes, but you may not always be outside, and you can't aim well. Which leaves—"

"A headbutt. Should I try that now?" I don't bother hiding the irritation in my voice. I'm tired, in pain, and ready to quit. I don't know why Viktor has chosen today to push me again, but I'm thoroughly over it.

"That won't be necessary." Levin's hand is still on my arm, holding it down. "But in the right circumstances, I would agree that would be the best choice. It could startle your attacker and possibly hurt them to the point where their grip will loosen. That's the point at which you would try to scramble out from under them to escape." He pauses. "Remember, unless they have a gun, your goal is to escape. Don't worry about disabling them or "winning." Just run."

"Running I can do."

"If they're too far back for a headbutt," Levin continues, "use your own weight to try to get them off of you. They won't necessarily be all that braced or stable, so use whatever leverage you can."

He helps me up then, letting go of my arm, and I turn to face him as I let out a long breath. "Just a couple more things," he assures me. "We'll practice more kicks and strikes another day. I'll teach you how to knee an opponent in the gut or groin as a means of getting space so that you can try to escape. We'll go through more headlocks, and I'll teach you how to get out of a grappling move. There's plenty to learn, but we'll have more opportunity at the next safe house once you're better healed."

Levin walks me through the moves again then, skipping the one where I end up on the ground, and then he glances towards Viktor. "I'll pass her over to you."

CATERINA

Viktor smiles tightly, stepping towards me as he accepts a gun from one of the other men, some kind of pistol. My stomach knots the instant I see it—I have absolutely no desire to learn how to shoot a gun; it doesn't appear that I'm going to be given a choice, just like I wasn't when it came to the fighting.

Despite having grown up around violence, I've never liked it. And there was no expectation that I should. I was a mafia princess, protected and coddled. There was no need for me to protect myself.

No need to pick up a pistol and learn how to shoot it.

"There are targets set up over there for you," Levin says, nodding towards a fence line just past a large shed with several men posted in front of it. "Good luck."

I'll need it, I think as I follow Viktor towards the fence, my eyes glued to the dark metal of the gun in his hand.

Viktor stops several paces from the fence, his face cool and expressionless as he holds up the gun. "This is what you'll learn to use," he says, letting me look at it. "The safety is still on for now, but I'll teach you how to take it off quickly and shoot. You'll need muscle memory for this just as much as hand-to-hand combat. As Levin said, you need to be able to act despite fear."

STOLEN BRIDE

I try to focus on what he's saying, but for some reason, him standing this close to me sends a flush over my skin, reminding me of the dream I'd had, all of the other things that have happened between us. I hadn't felt this way when Levin was close to me, but now that Viktor is the one standing so near that I could touch him if I wanted to, my heart is racing for reasons that have nothing to do with my anxiety over using the gun.

"I've never done this before," I tell him quietly, although, of course, he already knows. "I don't know if I'll be any good at it."

"You'll need to learn to be," Viktor says matter-of-factly, sliding a clip into the gun to load it. "It could mean the difference between life and death."

It's on the tip of my tongue to say something short and bitter about how he's my husband, how he's meant to protect me, but I don't. Partially because something about watching my Bratva husband handling the gun so casually, his handsome face set in stern hard lines, is arousing in a way I wouldn't have possibly thought it could be.

"This will have some kick to it," Viktor tells me, moving closer to hand me the gun. He places it in my palm, wrapping my fingers around it, and a shudder runs through me. It feels cold and heavy and deadly in my hand, and I want to hand it back. Just the feeling of it in my hand makes my knees go weak, and I take a deep breath, trying to steady myself.

I can't get out of this, so I have to get through it. Somehow.

"You'll need to brace yourself," he continues, "so it doesn't come back and hit you in the face. We'll take this slowly at first."

"Okay." I lick my dry lips nervously, my heart still racing in my chest. I don't think I'm going to be good at this. I don't know if I *want* to be good at this, except for the fact that both Viktor and Levin seem to think that I might *need* to be.

Viktor moves behind me suddenly, and my breath catches in my throat. In the space of a second, I stop thinking about how terrible the gun feels in my hand, how much I want to drop it and wipe my hand off as if I can somehow get the cold feeling to leave my palm. Instead, I'm viscerally aware of how close Viktor is, of his leanly muscled body angled behind me, the warmth of him in the cold air. His hands cover mine, moving the gun, showing me how to hold it, where to put my fingers, and I feel him move closer still, his body touching me. Chest to hips, brushing against my back, my ass, and I can smell him. I can smell the scent of his skin, clean, brisk soap, and some kind of herbal scent in his hair, and it sends a shiver through me that has nothing to do with the gun in my hands.

"Are you alright?" Viktor asks suddenly, his voice a low rumble next to my ear, and I swallow hard, my heart leaping in my chest at the sudden change in his tone.

"I'm fine," I manage, my voice shaking a little. "I just—"

"You can do this, Caterina. You're stronger than you believe."

I go very still at that. Of all the things I'd expected him to say, it wasn't that. He'd gone in an instant from pushing me past my limits to making me feel cared for again. Supported, even. As if he really were doing this to look out for me and not out of some strange power trip.

"Okay," I whisper. Another shiver runs through me as his hand leaves mine, brushing past my arm. He doesn't move away from my body, the heat of him still so close to me that it's distracting, and part of me hopes that he doesn't realize how he's affecting me, how much I want him.

And then there's another, smaller part of me that wants him to know. That wants him to make me feel beautiful again, desired, the way he did even when I told myself that I didn't want it.

He can't possibly want you that way anymore. Not the way you look now, not after all of this.

But the way he's still standing so close to me, the way his body is touching mine, tells me something different.

It makes my skin feel flushed and hot, making it even harder for me to concentrate on the gun in my hand, on what I'm supposed to do with it next.

"Keep it steady," Viktor instructs, as if my hand were shaky by choice. "Focus on the target. You'll inhale and then exhale on the shot as you squeeze the trigger. Brace your feet apart, shoulder-width, that's right." For some reason, the approval in his voice makes me feel warm, a small flush of happiness momentarily replacing my anxiety, and when he takes a step back away from me to give me space to take the shot, I instantly miss the feeling of him so close to me, the solidity of it.

My pulse races again as I look at one of the bottles propped up, waiting for me to take the shot. *I can do this,* I think, even if I don't really want to. It's not a matter of if I want to anymore.

Breathe in. I take a deep breath, feeling my finger curl around the trigger. I just have to press down, squeeze a little, and the shot will go off. It's not a huge thing. Just shooting a bottle. Not a man. Not a real person. Just a bullet and some glass.

Breathe out. I don't think about it too hard. I press down, squeezing, and the trigger goes down more easily than I'd thought it would.

Too easily, maybe.

The kick startles me, despite Viktor's warning. Thankfully I'd braced myself well, but the jolt of it still sends me rocking back on my heels, the pistol coming up in my hands dangerously close to my nose. I stop it before I can get hit in the face, and it takes me a moment to re-center myself and actually look towards the bottle I'd just shot at.

The top of it is broken. It's not exactly a square hit, but it's something, especially for a first shot.

"You hit it," Viktor says, and there's something almost like a hint of pride in his voice. "With practice, you could be a good shot."

"Thank you." The response is automatic, even though I don't know how I actually feel about that. I like being good at things, and the pride in his voice warms something inside of me, but at the same time, this isn't something that I ever *wanted* to be good at.

"We'll try again," Viktor says, and I take a shaky breath, feeling my hand tremble around the gun.

"I need a second," I tell him quickly. "I need to catch my breath." He doesn't say anything as I turn to face him, and I realize suddenly that he's still very close, less than a hand's breadth between us. It does nothing to slow the racing of my heart or make it easier for me to catch my breath—if anything, I can feel my pulse leap into my throat, my chest tightening as I look up at him.

Viktor's blue eyes are bright in the cold Russian sunshine, his face set in hard lines, but I can see a glimmer of something shining through in those eyes, something softer. Pride, maybe. Desire, possibly, however impossible that seems. I don't know how he could want me, but his gaze is fixed on mine, unwavering. My pulse gallops in my chest as all other thoughts flee my head except for how close he is, how handsome he is, the adrenaline from the shot turning into something else. *Kiss me*, I think out of nowhere, my eyes flicking down to his mouth. I know how good it feels on mine, in other places, and I suddenly want him to kiss me more than almost anything else in the world.

And I don't fucking know why.

Is it being out here in the middle of nowhere, the world beyond us so hazy after everything that's happened that it's hard to remember that it exists at all? Is it the things he's done for me over the past days, the way he's cared for me, so different from the man I thought I knew? Is it the way he's pushed me today, as if he really cares about whether or not I can survive this?

It's as if he *wants* me to be strong. It goes against every paranoid thought I've had, but if it's true, it means he wants more than what we've had before.

It means he wants a partner. A real marriage.

I don't know how that's possible for us. But right now, I don't care. I only care that he's standing close to me and that it's been so long since he's kissed me, and I feel as if my blood is thundering hotly through my veins.

"Viktor," I whisper his name without meaning to, my tongue flicking out over my dry lips, and I see Viktor's gaze drop to my mouth immediately. It feels like it did in our bedroom, when I came home, when he pushed me down to my knees, when he made me want things that I hadn't known I could. When I let myself forget what I *should* want, and simply felt, when I'd let him give me pleasure in the most shameful ways he possibly could.

I shouldn't want him. But I do, in a way that I've never wanted any other man.

Franco hadn't been able to command me. He hadn't even been my equal. He'd been a sniveling child, a man who wanted power given to him because he had none of his own. He hadn't known what to do with a woman like me, one who had been born with a place in the world and a power to hand out.

But Viktor does. Viktor could do things with me—*to* me—that I'd never imagined.

I want him to kiss me.

I want to find out.

"Caterina." Viktor's voice is a hoarse whisper in the cold, and I know there are eyes all around us, his men, possibly even Levin, but I don't care. A thrill runs through me at the sound of my name on his lips, from my chest and out through my body, over every nerve and vein, until I feel like I'm pulsing with it, with want and need, and I can see that same dark heat in his eyes.

He wants me. I don't know how or why, but he does.

I want to ask him to kiss me, want to *beg*, and I won't do it. I won't say *please*, no matter how badly I want to, but I don't think I need to. I can feel myself flushing despite the cold, my heart pounding so loudly that I think he must be able to hear it, and I know he can see it in my eyes. I feel embarrassed at how naked the desire must be, flooding up the way it had in my dream last night. Yet, I'm aching suddenly, my body pulsing with a second heartbeat of need.

How can he do this to me? I shouldn't—

"Caterina—" Viktor says my name again as if he's going to tell me we can't, or get back to the lesson. Then he groans, his eyes darkening as he reaches out, his fingers gripping my chin as he drags my mouth towards his.

"Oh fuck," he growls, and then before I can breathe or think, his mouth is crashing down on mine, hard and rough and everything that I'd needed.

I hadn't thought I could take pleasure in roughness ever again, but maybe this is what I need. All I know is that it feels fucking *good*, fierce and hard as his lips press against mine, his tongue sliding over the seam, pushing inside, demanding entrance into my mouth, and I give it to him. I've never been one for public displays of affection. I feel myself arch towards him, forgetting that there are others here to see, to see me falling into him, needing the hot onslaught of his mouth as it slants over mine and starts to devour me in a way that I hadn't known until right now that I was so desperate for.

I want a touch that feels good, a touch that I actually desire. I want to forget all of the pain, all of the fear. There's still pain, every wound in my body screaming after the exercise and tension, and now the roughness of Viktor dragging me towards him, but I barely feel it. All I can think about is the sensation of my mouth opening for him, the heat of his tongue, the taste of him, and I can feel the longing in his kiss. The same need echoed in the way he's touching me.

It makes no fucking sense, but I can feel the suppressed desire, the nights that he's been wanting me, his hands cupping my face as he holds my lips to his, and then running over my arms, down to my waist and hips, pulling me against him as he groans aloud again, as if he doesn't care who might see or hear either. The sound dances over my skin, firing over every nerve, and I moan, so flushed with heat that it could be Russian summer for all I know and not frigid spring cold. I feel as if I'm burning up from the inside, and I can feel how hard he is, the thick ridge of him pressing against my inner thigh. It reminds me of every night we've spent together, everything he's ever done to me, and suddenly I want it all over again.

I want it *all*.

"Oh god," Viktor groans, his tongue sliding into my mouth again, and I have a sudden vision of him bearing me down to the hard cold ground, yanking down my sweatpants, driving inside of me so that I can feel all of that hard, hot thickness filling me. It makes me feel insane—I've never imagined being fucked in front of anyone else. I've always been a little shy, proper even, not the kind of woman who wildly makes out with anyone in public, not even my husband.

But right now, I'm not sure if I would stop him if he tried.

He can't possibly mean it, I think wildly, even as he's still kissing me. *This is some kind of trick, a trap. How could he want me like this?* It feels almost desperate, the way he's touching me and kissing me, like an obsession, like he was afraid of losing me and never wants to stop touching me again.

But that's not the Viktor I married.

My husband is cold and self-controlled, violent only when necessary, a man who compels fear and obedience. He doesn't have obsessions; he doesn't lose control. That's not him.

I pull back, gasping, stumbling back with the gun still clutched in my hand. For one wild moment, an image of myself lifting it and pointing it at my husband flashes through my head, of me pulling the trigger and firing, the way his skull would open, the way the bullet would end all of this. My marriage, my torment, and probably my life too.

If he's the one who put me through all of this, then he deserves it. But I don't know that that's true.

I don't even know if he had anything to do with his first wife's death.

I don't know *anything* for sure about this man that I've promised the rest of my life to.

"Caterina," Viktor says my name, his face suddenly very still, and I wonder if he can read my mind, if he knows what I'm thinking.

My hand is clenched, white-knuckled around the gun. I could do it. I just don't know if it would be the right thing.

I don't know. I don't know. It's all I think anymore.

Levin clears his throat from behind me, making me jump, and my fingers go loose, the gun falling to the ground. I take several quick steps back, my heart pounding, and Viktor steps forward smoothly, scooping it up off of the ground and looking towards his right-hand man.

"Is it all prepared?" he asks, and Levin nods as I look confusedly between the two men.

"What are you talking about?" My voice is still shaking a little, and I breathe in, trying to make it stop.

Viktor smiles at me, his eyes cold and dark.

"Caterina, my love, I have a surprise for you."

CATERINA

"Caterina, my love, I have a surprise for you."

The world feels as if it spins to a stop for a moment. *A surprise? A surprise?*

"What—" The word spills out of my mouth before I can stop it, and I stare at Viktor in confusion. I don't know whether to be afraid or not, and there's no hint in either of their faces as to what it could be. Levin's face is cold and unreadable, and Viktor's mouth is curled in a cruel smirk, which tells me nothing.

My heart skips a beat in my chest, and I feel my throat constricting, my breathing coming sharp and fast as if I'm on the verge of a panic attack. A dozen horrible scenarios run through my head, and I'm so focused on the possibility of any of those being true that it takes a second for me to register what's actually happening.

A few yards away, the door of the large shed has opened, and two men are being dragged out by some of Viktor's soldiers.

They're so badly beaten and tortured that I don't recognize them at first. The larger one's eyes are swollen shut, his nose broken and lips puffed up, and the smaller man has one eye completely shut, the other bloodshot and his jaw clearly broken. He's making small whimpering noises as the two are dragged towards where Viktor, Levin, and I are standing. When they get closer, it's clear from both their appearance and stench that they've soiled themselves any number of times.

My first reaction is pity, my gut twisting with horror that my husband ordered these things done to other people, other human beings. And then the soldiers throw them down onto the ground, nearly at my feet. The smaller man raises his head just enough to spit despite his broken jaw, a garbled word that sounds very much like *bitch* coming from his torn lips.

I recognize them both then. I know who they are. And every ounce of pity flees, replaced by a wave of hot anger and bitter resentment that threatens to overwhelm me and makes me feel almost dizzy.

I sway on my feet, and suddenly Viktor is at my elbow, steadying me. "Do you like your gift, *printsessa?*" he asks, the smirk on his face transforming into a smile.

"My gift?" I choke out, looking down at the two men kneeling in front of me like I'm some sort of princess or a queen.

Maybe I am. My father's princess, Viktor's queen. It's what I was always meant to be, what I was raised to be. A mafia princess, and now a Bratva leader's wife. I've wanted to believe that my parents would be horrified to know that I'd been given to the Russians, and maybe my mother would have been. But my father would have traded me to achieve his ends even faster than Luca did, and I know that's the truth.

The soldiers have guns trained on their backs, so there's no chance of them trying to escape, even if they could. And there's no point in them even trying to run. They wouldn't get far.

Not in the state they're in.

"I can't believe you didn't kill them," I whisper. It must have taken a great deal of restraint for Viktor not to finish it if, in fact, he had nothing to do with my kidnapping.

Or maybe not. Maybe he didn't care enough to do more than make an example of them. Perhaps the idea of them hurting his wife wasn't enough to inspire the kind of anger that could invoke a killing rage.

Or maybe—

"I kept them alive as a present to you," Viktor says, breaking through my thoughts. I can hear the pleasure in his voice, almost anticipation, like a predator looking forward to his next meal.

"For me?" I choke out, still not quite understanding. "Why would I want them alive?"

"I don't think you want them alive," he says, that smirk returning. "I think you want them fucking dead. And that's why they're kneeling in front of you right now."

"Oh," I whisper, turning my head to look back down at the two men as the pieces start to click into place. I'm beginning to understand now. "You wanted me to get to see them die."

"No." Viktor shakes his head. "I want you to have the opportunity to kill one of them."

I stare at him, shock written on every single one of my features. "What?" I manage to choke out, looking down at the gun still in his hand and then back up at him. "I've never—"

"Oh, I know," Viktor says smoothly. He looks down at the two men with distaste. "You see, despite all of our efforts, we couldn't get a clear picture of who was really responsible for the damage done to you. They're both responsible, of course, but there was an argument between these two as to who *really* wanted to have their—*fun*—with you in that cabin."

Just hearing that sends a shudder through me, one that I know Viktor can't help but see, my chest and throat tightening at the memory. It still feels too fresh, too immediate, and I feel that hot rush of anger again. These two men have taken so much away from me, hurt me so badly, and I know that I should feel that what Viktor has already done to them is enough.

But I don't feel that. If I'm being honest with myself, I don't feel that it's even close.

"Whichever one was the most responsible," Viktor continues, his voice cold and hard, "is my gift to you, for you to take your revenge."

"And the other?" I choke out, my heart hammering in my chest.

"Is for me to kill, so that I can take mine."

A jolt of pure adrenaline crashes through me, and any thought that this might have all been some elaborate plot designed by him flees my mind, if only temporarily. I know that I should hesitate, resist, tell him that I don't want this. That I should cringe at the idea of taking another human being's life.

But these aren't humans. They aren't men.

They're animals, and all I can think about is every single man who's hurt me, who's used me, who's made me a pawn. All of the emotions and pain come rushing back, filling me, bleeding through my veins as I look down at Andrei and Stepan.

I can't change how my father controlled my entire life, making me into nothing more than a tool for his own needs, always a bargaining chip and never just his daughter. I can't undo the times Franco's fist connected with my face or other parts of my body, the feeling of his fingers digging into my flesh, or the cruel words he spit at me. I can't undo the things he did to me, Ana, and other women, too, maybe. I can't even change the fact that Luca, too, the one man I trusted—and still trust, for the most part—went against his better nature and sold me off to a cold and violent man who traffics in other humans for a living.

A man who I can't help but desire, against *my* better nature.

I can't change any of it. I can't go back in time before Andrei and Stepan tortured me in that horrible cabin. I'll carry the scars of that with me forever.

But I can have this. I can take back this power. I can make them pay for what they did, and somehow, in a way, that feels like making everyone else pay too.

It feels as if every terrible thing, every pain, every emotional and physical wound, narrows down to this one opportunity.

This one change for vengeance.

Looking down at the two of them, I don't feel like a princess or a queen anymore. I feel like a vengeful goddess, and holding their lives in my hands feels more heady and powerful than I'd ever thought it could. I don't think Viktor would spare them even if I asked for him to, but it doesn't have to be me who takes their lives.

It doesn't *have* to be, but I think that's what I *want*.

No—I *know* it is.

"Give me the gun." My voice is cold, hard, and clear, and the trembling and frightened emotion of a little while ago completely gone. I sound almost like a different person, someone unafraid. Someone who wouldn't hesitate to take her revenge on the men who hurt her.

Someone stronger than I've ever been before.

"Which one is yours?" Viktor asks, and I swallow hard. I look down at Stepan's face, sneering up at me defiantly despite his broken face, as if he thinks he can intimidate me into backing down. Into sparing his life or begging for Viktor to spare his. As if I would want anything other than death for him.

A bullet to the head seems almost too easy.

"Him." I gesture towards Stepan. "Stepan is the one who was responsible for most of this." His name tastes bitter on my tongue, but it's worth it when Viktor holds the pistol out to me, and I see the defiance start to drain from his face.

When I take the gun from Viktor's hand, the blood drains from it entirely, his skin going chalk-white.

"I'm not the best shot with this yet," I say casually, the weight of the gun settling against my palm. "But I don't think even I can miss from this close range."

The feeling of it in my hand doesn't send a cold chill through me this time. I can't think about anything other than the rage bubbling in my veins, the way I feel hot and angry, letting my emotion drive me for the first time in my life.

I deserve this catharsis. I've had so much taken from me. And the men kneeling in front of me deserve nothing at all.

"No, please!" Stepan starts to beg in garbled vowels, spit and blood bubbling as he chews at his lower lip, his eyes starting to tear as the one open eye goes wide. I realize at that moment that he hadn't expected me to do it, that he'd thought I was too weak. That he'd thought he could sneer at me and spit at me, and I'd still refuse to take the gift of revenge that my husband had offered me.

Well, he's fucking wrong, I think bitterly. And at that moment, I'm

STOLEN BRIDE

more sure than ever that this is what I want, looking down at the sniveling men in front of me.

"It's your choice, whether to do it or not," Viktor says calmly next to me as I look down at the gun. "They'll die either way, but you don't have to be the one to pull the trigger." He pauses, and there's a gravity to his voice when he speaks again that makes me look up at him, my gaze meeting his.

"It will change you, Caterina," he says quietly. "You won't be the same once you pull that trigger. You can't ever go back to being a person who hasn't killed another. It will follow you for the rest of your life. But it doesn't have to be a bad thing. It can make you stronger, just like everything else I've shown you today."

There's a seriousness in his voice that gives me pause, that makes me wonder for the first time who Viktor was before he pulled a trigger for the first time, if he was a softer man, kinder. If there was someone else he could have been if he hadn't done it.

I'm sure he didn't have a choice, though, not really. I do. I can hand him the gun and walk away, go inside, and not have to even so much as witness their deaths. I can let someone else fight this battle for me.

But I've been letting other people fight my battles for way too long. Hell, my best friend was the one who took out my abusive husband. If she could do that, then I can take what Viktor is offering me.

A chance to have my revenge, to take back a piece of myself.

Whether he's doing it as part of a plot to indebt me to him more or out of a genuine desire to give it to me doesn't matter.

The result will be the same. And I want it.

"I wanted to give you the opportunity," Viktor says, his voice deep and dark at my ear. "The choice to take it or not is yours."

I don't have to think twice. I give myself just a moment to savor the look of terror on Stepan's face, to see his mouth start to form the words to beg me again. I hear something that sounds like *please*, and I feel a cruel smile twist my mouth, very much like the one I've seen on Viktor's face in the past.

Maybe this will make me more like him. But I can't bring myself to care.

"Fuck you," I say, very clearly. And then I pull the trigger.

His eyes go wide when he hears me speak, but that's all he has time for. I might have just winged the bottle during my practice, but he's too close for me to miss, the muzzle of my gun nearly pressed to his skin when I pull the trigger. The shot rocks me backward, the acrid scent of gunpowder filling the air, and I watch him topple over as if I'm in a dream, the wound in his forehead blossoming open, blood trailing over his pale skin as he wobbles on his knees and falls.

My own blood is roaring in my ears, and dimly I hear another gunshot right next to me. Andrei falls too, his mouth open as if to beg for his own life, and when I look sideways, I see Viktor standing there, his own smoking gun in his hand as he looks down at the body of the man he just shot. There's not an ounce of remorse on his face, and I know there's none on mine either.

My husband lifts his head slowly, looking at me, and our eyes meet.

I can't hear anything over the pounding in my ears, can't feel anything past the adrenaline buzzing over my skin, can't move from the spot where I feel rooted to the earth. My fingers go nerveless, dropping the gun to the ground for the second time today, but this time Viktor doesn't reach for it.

Instead, he reaches for me.

With one swift movement, he hands off his own gun to Levin and sweeps me off of my feet into his arms, scooping me up bridal-style as he strides away from the bodies, from Levin and his other men, back towards the cabin.

VIKTOR

I know it's fucked up that nothing has ever made me desire my wife more than watching her put a bullet through another man's skull.

But the moment she pulled the trigger, I knew I couldn't wait for another second to have her again. I know that she's tired, sore, still injured, and still healing, but I'm past rational thought.

I need my wife. I need to make her mine again, to possess her and remind her who her body belongs to. To wipe away all the fingerprints those animals left on her and replace them with my own.

It feels good to sweep her into my arms again, to feel the delicate weight of her body as I stride away from my men towards the cabin, leaving the bodies behind for them to clean up.

That's for them to deal with, not me. I am their leader, their *Ussuri*, their *pakhan*, and I've done my part.

Now it's time for me to be something else.

Caterina's husband.

She might think that what we had is over now, but she's wrong.

It's only beginning, and I've never wanted her more than I do at this moment.

I stride through the back door of the cabin, letting it swing shut behind me as I head purposefully towards the hall that leads to my bedroom. I feel Caterina stiffen in my arms, her head tilting back as she looks up at me. "Viktor—" she starts to say, but I shake my head, pushing open the door and heading directly towards the bed.

She gasps when I lay her back on the bed, following her onto the mattress as I bend down, kissing her for the first time since that morning in my loft in Moscow. Her lips are as sweet as I remembered, full and soft, and I feel her hesitate for just a moment, her body very still beneath mine.

And then her arms go around my neck, and she's kissing me back.

My blood is pounding in my veins as I slant my mouth over hers, crushing my lips against her mouth, teeth grazing her lower lip as I press her down into the bed, nudging her legs apart so that I can move between them. I'm already rock-hard, my cock straining against my zipper, aching with the need to be inside of her.

And it's only magnified by the fact that it isn't just me.

I'd thought I'd have protestations to silence and arguments from her to quell. Caterina's hands are against my chest, her fingers gripping the front of my shirt, her lips pressed fiercely against mine. I can feel her panting underneath me, her legs parting to allow me between them, her hips arching up to grind against the thick, hard, fabric-covered ridge of my cock. Her tongue tangles with mine when I push it into her mouth, desperate to taste her, and I groan, an almost unbearable lust rippling through me as she kisses me back.

My wife has never been like this with me—hungry, needy, desperate. But I can feel it almost radiating off of her, adrenaline and need combining into a nearly explosive force that has her arched against me despite the way I know her body must hurt right now. I want to be skin to skin with her, to strip her bare, but I don't think I can wait that long.

I need to be inside of her. I need to feel my wife again, and everything else can come later.

I reach for the waist of her too-big sweatpants, feeling the material bunch in my hand as I drag them down her slender hip, feeling her flesh graze against my knuckles. It sends a blossom of heat through me, making me ache in ways I haven't in years, and I groan against her mouth as I strip them off, feeling her kick them loose.

There's nothing underneath them but her bare skin. I feel my chest constrict with a spasm of need as I feel the soft skin of her inner thigh, bring my fingers higher to the smoothness of her pussy, the skin already flushed and hot and leaking arousal. I can feel it, sticky on my fingers, the softness of the hair there, damp with her need as she spreads her thighs wider, whimpering against my lips.

She wants me, needs me, and it sends a heady dizziness through me that makes me feel as if I can't wait for another second to be inside of her. I know she's not thinking right now, high on a wave of adrenaline and emotion, and I know that, in a way, I'm taking advantage of that. But I can't bring myself to care. She might never be this way with me again, might never be so turned on and wild and careless with me, and I want to enjoy it right now while I can.

I want her, all of her, and this might be the only time I get it.

With one hand, I undo the buckle of my belt, yanking down the zipper of my jeans with a feverish hurry. I hear Caterina moan as I kiss her, feeling the vibration against my mouth. It makes my cock lurch, springing free of my jeans as I wrap my hand around it, feeling the pulse as I surge forward.

Caterina gasps when she feels my cockhead push between her folds, her slick arousal instantly coating the tip with hot wetness that makes me groan with a pleasure that's almost painful.

There's no chance of taking this slowly. I'm well aware of my own size and of how small and delicate Caterina is, but I can't slow down or stop myself. I have to be inside of her, and now.

I thrust forward, hard, my cock sinking in her to the hilt as I feel her stretch around me, her body spasming at the sudden intrusion. She cries out, half pleasure and half pain, her head jerking back and fingers tightening in my shirt as she breaks the kiss, eyes wide as she looks at me.

I hold myself there, cock throbbing deep inside of her, and watch her eyes flick from my taut face down to the shirt that she's gripping tightly, spattered with the blood of the men that we just killed. Something changes in her eyes when she sees that, a wild heat filling her face, and her hands tighten for a fraction of a second before she drags me back down, her chin tipping up as one of her hands goes to the back of my head, her fingers knotting in my hair as she pulls my mouth down to hers.

Fuck. Caterina has never failed to turn me on more than any other woman, but something about her desire, about her *wanting* me, makes me almost crazed with desire, teetering on the edge of what could become an obsession, an addiction. I had a taste of it the night that she was drunk after the gala, and this is so much better, the aftermath of the violence turning into something wild and passionate, a spark threatening to conflagrate here in our bed.

Her legs wrap around my thighs as I start to thrust, hard and fast, her arousal gushing around my cock as I feel her get even wetter for me, her heat searing into my thick length as I sink into her again and again. *I should be more careful,* I think, but I can't slow the pounding rhythm of my hips, and it occurs to me that I'm not sure if she wants me to. Her hips arch up with every thrust, taking me as deeply as I can go again and again, her legs tightening around mine as she cries out against my mouth.

"Fuck, Viktor, I'm going to come—"

The sound of her gasping those words against my lips, her head thrown back as her body starts to convulse, makes me nearly lose it myself then and there. I feel her pussy spasm, rippling down the length of my cock as she pulls me even deeper, squeezing me, and the pleasure is beyond anything I've ever felt before. She's hot and wet and tight, her orgasm crashing through her as she writhes beneath me, her hand tightening in my hair to the point of pain as she throws her head back and moans so loudly that I know anyone in the house could hear—if there was anyone in the cabin.

There better not fucking be.

I want to be the only man who ever hears my wife's cries of pleasure again, the only man to ever know what she sounds like when she comes for the rest of her life. I'll kill any other man who touches her, who so much as *looks* at her.

She's mine.

My princess, my queen. My *printsessa*. My mafia bride.

I'm slamming into her now, fucking her hard and fast, and I can feel my cock swelling to the point of exploding inside of her. I can't stop, can't slow down, and I wrap my hand in her hair, pulling her head back so that I can look into my wife's eyes as I fill her with my cum.

"Fucking come for me again, Caterina," I order, the words a snarl as I slam my cock into her again, and her mouth opens as she cries out, her back arching as I feel her tighten around me again.

"You're mine," I murmur. "My body, my pussy, my fucking wife. And I'll destroy anyone who ever dares touch you again."

She moans, gasping, and I surge forward once more, feeling her envelop me, clenching around me. Then there's nothing but the most exquisite, burning pleasure as I feel the first hot rush of my cum explode from my throbbing cock.

I throw my head back, groaning aloud, hips pumping wildly as I empty myself into her. I feel her nails in my chest, feel her arching, grinding, and I grind against her, wanting to sink into her even more deeply if I were able to. It feels so fucking good, her heat pulsing around me as I come, and I stay buried inside of her until every last drop of cum has spilled inside of her, my cock still throbbing with the aftershocks of my orgasm and her still pulsing with hers.

I slump forward on my forearms, trying not to crush her as I catch my breath. "You're mine," I whisper against the shell of her ear. "And God help any man who tries to say otherwise."

CATERINA

A few minutes earlier

From the moment Viktor scoops me up in his arms and carries me towards the cabin, I know where this is headed.

I just can't quite believe it.

I don't know how he can want me so much. He's seen what my naked body looks like now. He's seen how thin I am, almost to the point of scrawniness. He just watched me kill a man. But I can feel the need practically radiating off of him, burning into my skin as he strides into the cabin and down the hall that I know leads to the bedrooms. My heart is pounding in my chest as I stiffen in his arms, unsure if I want to let this happen or not. If this is something I want.

I know it'll change things between us if I do. I can't claim there's a "before" the kidnapping and "after" if I do this. But I can feel the adrenaline pulsing through me, sparking over my skin like electricity, and I feel as if I'll explode if I don't have some release. If I don't get all of this emotion out somehow.

Emotion—and desire, too. I want to pretend that part of the reason why my heart is racing and my skin is prickling isn't that

STOLEN BRIDE

Viktor is holding me tightly in his arms, against his broad chest, the scent of his sweat and skin filling my nose.

I start to say his name, telling myself that I should protest, that I should come up with a reason to stop this, to tell him to take me back to my own room. But he shakes his head, his face set in taut, stern lines, and something about the look in his eyes makes anything else I might have said die on my lips, my heart pounding so hard that I think he must be able to hear it.

He isn't going to be told no, and something about that thrills me. I know I *should* if only because of the state my body is in. I'm still wounded, still healing, exhausted from the training and the highs and lows of the afternoon. But I know that he's going to carry me to bed and remind me of all the reasons why I shouldn't let him.

And that thrills me and terrifies me all at once.

I can't help but gasp when he lays me back on the bed, leaning over me as he follows me onto the bed, the length of his body stretched over mine. This close, he's even more of an intimidating presence, his darkly handsome face taut and his eyes bright with desire. He *wants* me, I can see it, and I can't understand it. I can't understand why he would want me still after all of this, but it's very clear that he does.

And then he kisses me, hard and firm and demanding, his mouth grinding down onto mine with an eager passion that takes my breath away. I hesitate for a second longer, still and frozen underneath him.

Just let go. Just this once. You can say it was the adrenaline, that you got swept away. Give in, just for a little while.

My arms go around his neck, almost without my meaning for them too, and I'm kissing him back with equal fervor, my mouth hot against his as I pull him down to me. I can feel the quick panting of his breath, the way his mouth slants over mine, his lips crushed against my teeth, his grazing against my lower lip with the hint of a bite that makes me gasp aloud again.

My hands fist in his shirt, gripping the fabric as if I can't get close enough to him, and when he moves between my legs, they part for him, and I feel how hard he is. He's straining against his jeans, hard, long, and thick, and I remember all too well how it felt to be filled by him, stretched and full and fucked in a way that no other man has ever managed. I kiss him back fiercely, arching up to grind against him, my own heat radiating out as I revel in the feeling of him hard and straining for me, his tongue pushing into my mouth desperately, as if all he wants in the world is to taste me.

All I've ever wanted in my life is to be desired, wanted, loved for myself. It's always been nothing but a silly dream because who *I* am, myself, at my core, doesn't matter to anyone. What matters is my station, my family, my name, the power that I can give a man through a marriage alliance, as if we lived centuries ago instead of in the modern world. This moment, with Viktor, makes me almost feel as if he wants me for nothing but myself. Not my beauty, clearly, and maybe not even because of who I am.

It's a fantasy. But it's one that I'm hungry for, desperate for, and I want so badly to give myself over to it that I can't stop myself. I can feel the adrenaline and need and desire coiling together inside of me, ready to explode, making me feel as if I'm coming out of my skin, as if I can't breathe. The only thing I can think of that can salve any of it right now is Viktor inside of me, fucking me, making me feel wanted.

I don't want him to wait, to go slow, even if it hurts. I don't even want him to wait long enough to take off my clothes. Clearly, he has the same idea because his hand is already on the waist of the ridiculous men's sweatpants that I'm wearing, pulling them down, his knuckles grazing my hip in a way that seems to shoot electricity straight between my legs. I feel a gush of warmth there, arousal flooding through me and making me wetter than I've ever been, heat gathering in my core until I feel as if I might burn up from the inside out.

Viktor groans against my mouth as he pulls them off and I kick them free, his fingers sliding up my inner thigh to where I'm bare, my skin damp and hot and flushed. I moan when he touches me there, his fingers grazing over the hair that he once ordered me to shave off, the sticky flesh of my inner thigh. I can hear myself whimpering, almost begging him for more, and I can't stop myself. I feel like I'm floating on a wave of adrenaline and emotion, and I know I shouldn't give in to it, but I don't want to stop.

This can be the only time, I tell myself. *Just this once.* I don't know if I *could* stop now, even if I talked myself into it. My body seems to have a mind of its own. I moan again as Viktor yanks at his belt, undoing the buckle and his zipper with quick, fumbling movements that let me know exactly how desperate he is to be inside of me. I feel it lurch against my inner thigh as it springs free of his jeans, his hand wrapping roughly around himself as he surges forward between my thighs.

I gasp at the feeling of him pushing between my folds, hot and throbbing, and I'm so wet that he slides in instantly, groaning with a sound that's somewhere between pleasure and pain. I know he isn't going to go slow, and I don't want him to. I want to be fucked, to forget everything except for the feeling of him inside of me and the pleasure that I know he can give me, to give myself over to it instead of fighting it. I can feel him forcing his way into my slender body, filling me, and I spasm around him, crying out in that same mixture of pleasure and pain that made him groan a moment ago. I break the kiss, fingers twisting in his shirt as my eyes go wide at the feeling of him impaling me.

He goes very still, every inch of his thick, rigid length buried inside of me, and I look from the taut, straining lines of his face down to where my fingers are curled in the fabric of his shirt. It's spattered with blood—maybe Andrei's, maybe Stepan's, maybe both—and I see that there's blood on my fingers too, around the edges of my nails. It sends a shudder through me, but it's not a shudder of revulsion.

That adrenaline rushes through me again, hot and wild, a reminder of what we just did, of the revenge he offered me and that I took. My hands tighten in his shirt again, my body shaking with the force of the emotion that sweeps over me.

We're bound together now by something deeper than wedding vows, something more than sharing bodies or a bed. I hadn't wanted to take those vows that I said at the altar, but I'd wanted to do what I'd done today. I'd wanted to kill Stepan, and Viktor had given me the means to do it.

I killed someone today, and Viktor was there to witness it. He'd been the reason we had at all.

And something about him fucking me right afterward, taking me straight to bed and letting all of this emotion wash over him, feels more intimate than our wedding night.

I drag him back down, my chin tipping up as I grab the back of his head, my fingers knotting in his hair as I pull his mouth down to mine. I kiss him, hot and hard, tongue in his mouth and teeth in his lower lip, fingers digging into his scalp as I feel him shudder above me. My legs wrap around his thighs as he starts to thrust, hard and fast, and I can feel myself soaking his cock, so wet that he slips in and out with ease, slamming into me as he sinks into me again and again. I can feel that he can't slow down. I arch up with every thrust into me, taking him as deeply as I can, reveling in the slam of his body against mine as my legs tighten around him.

I can feel the orgasm building, tightening inside of me, more demanding and powerful than any climax I've ever felt. I can feel the muscles in my thighs twitching, my back arching, and I can feel it about to sweep over me, take me, drown me in pleasure.

"Fuck, Viktor, I'm going to come—"

I've never said it like that to him before, full of desire and need, giving myself over to it completely. I can feel my body start to convulse as I gasp it against his lips, spasming around him as I pull him deeper and begin to come hard, writhing beneath the weight of his body. He's still thrusting as hard as he can against the clenching grip of my pussy around him as I come. I throw my head back, my hand tightening in his hair, pulling at it, and I moan loudly, not caring who hears. All I care about is how good this feels, about the pleasure rippling through me, driving me wild, making every bad thing disappear for a few minutes.

This kind of desire and pleasure is dangerous. It could make me want it again and again until I lose myself in a man that I can't trust, can't ever be an equal to, and shouldn't love or want. The orgasm rocks my entire body, all the way down to my toes, and as soon as it

STOLEN BRIDE

starts to fade, I want another. I want more. I want to drown in pleasure and forget all the pain.

Viktor is slamming into me, fucking me hard and fast, and I feel him, hard and swollen inside of me, and I know he's close. He's breathless, blue eyes bright with desire, and he wraps his hand in my hair as he pulls my head back so that I'm forced to look up at him, our eyes meeting as I feel him start to throb inside of me with the onslaught of his coming orgasm.

"Fucking come for me again, Caterina," he snarls, slamming into me again hard, and I cry out, my back arching as I feel my body start to obey him, my pussy clenching around him as my entire body tightens, wanting to hold him inside of me for as long as I possibly can.

"You're mine," he murmurs. "My body, my pussy, my fucking wife. And I'll destroy anyone who ever dares touch you again."

The words are electric, sparking over my skin, and I gasp, moaning as he surges forward into me again. I feel myself clenching around him, and then the sound that comes from him is almost animalistic as the first hot rush of his cum bursts inside of me.

Viktor throws his head back, the tendons in his throat taut as he groans aloud, hips pumping into me as he comes hard, spilling into me in waves. My hand presses against his chest, nails digging in, arching and grinding against him as I feel my body convulsing around his, his pleasure and mine twisting together, bursting over us both.

I want him to stay inside of me, to keep feeling this for as long as I possibly can. I don't want it to stop. I feel him slump forward onto his forearms, and he whispers, "You're mine," against the shell of my ear. "And God help any man who tries to say otherwise."

Something about it now thrills me. I'd always hated being possessed, being treated like an object, like a prize. Still, right now, it makes me feel a flush of arousal that I've never felt before, my heart leaping at the sound of his voice growling in my ear.

In the aftermath, I don't know what to do. I don't know whether to scoot out from under him, or push him away, or simply lie there. I'm suddenly very aware of the fact that I'm still wearing the oversized t-shirt pushed up around my hips and nothing else, bare from the waist down, and that Viktor is still fully clothed except for his open jeans.

His hair is falling over his forehead, making him look younger despite the grey at his temples and speckling the stubble on his chin. Despite myself, I reach up, touching his face where the hair is rough and short.

"I've never seen you not clean-shaven before," I say quietly before I can stop myself. "I like it."

"Oh?" Viktor raises an eyebrow. "Is that so?" He pauses, considering. "I suppose you wouldn't have. If you like it—"

A smile twitches at the corners of his mouth, and I'm momentarily taken aback. It's such a small, intimate moment. It feels like something between an ordinary married couple, the kind of thing a husband and wife *should* say to each other. Still, we've never had that kind of relationship. I've never considered for even a second that we would.

And yet, his gaze holds mine, as sweet and intimate as I could have ever hoped for, if I'd dared hope for such a thing.

And then he drops his head, his lips grazing over my neck, a soft caress that takes my breath away for an entirely different reason.

"I should get up," I murmur, turning my face away, but he cups it in his palm instead, turning my eyes back to him.

"Why?" He smiles lazily. "No one will come into the cabin until I tell Levin otherwise. The security is outside, and the others will stay there."

"They must be cold—"

Viktor laughs. "This is nothing. It's a pleasant spring day outside to them." His hands reach for the edge of my shirt as he kisses my neck again, pushing it up towards my waist and higher still, as if he wants to undress me. Alarm bells immediately start going off in my head.

I reach for his hands, pushing them down, and Viktor pauses, looking down at me quizzically.

"Do you not want me to touch you like this?"

The fact that he's asking at all is startling. I blink up at him, my hands still wrapped around his in a bid to keep him from undressing me further. *Do I want that?*

I'm not sure if I do want him to stop, but I know I'm terrified of him seeing me naked under these circumstances, of seeing his desire go away once he gets a look at the body that is supposed to arouse him. All I have to offer a husband is power and beauty—what happens when half of that equation is gone?

"I don't want you to see me naked like this," I blurt out, once again before I can stop myself. I bite down on my lip the instant the words are out of my mouth, wondering what the fuck is wrong with me and why I can't stop saying things to my husband that is more bare and honest than I've ever been with him. I shouldn't trust him, I *can't*, so I shouldn't allow myself to be so vulnerable. I should lock everything up as tightly as I can. Yet, somehow, everything that's happened today seems to be laying me completely bare.

"What?" Viktor seems to look genuinely confused. "Like what?"

I blink at him. "My wounds. The ones that are already starting to scar. I don't look anything like myself—I look sick, and thin, and hurt—I'm not beautiful anymore."

"Caterina." Viktor's eyes widen slightly, and one of his hands pulls free of mine, letting go of my shirt and sweeping down my side. "Didn't you see how much I wanted you just now? How could you think that I wouldn't find you beautiful?"

"I mean, I'm still mostly covered up—" I look away again, wanting suddenly to be anywhere else, to curl up into a ball and disappear. I don't know how to have this conversation with Viktor, a man I've never been able to be myself with, who has never been my husband in anything but the strictest sense. I can't open up to him, besides the things I've already stupidly blurted out.

"Then let me take all of this off, and I'll show you exactly how beautiful I still think you are."

There's something deep and serious in his voice, a caring sincerity that I've never heard before, and it startles me. My eyes fly back to his, and I can feel myself stiffen as his lips go to my neck again, brushing over the lingering bruises where Stepan choked me. His hand is on my waist, not pushing the shirt up yet, just resting there as he kisses me, small brushes of his mouth that make me feel a lump of emotion rising in my throat.

He doesn't ask me if he can keep going, not quite. I don't think it's in a man like Viktor's nature to ask for what he wants. But he goes so slowly that I could stop him if I wanted to, push him away, tell him no. His lips linger on my throat for a long time, brushing over every bruise until they slide down to my collarbone.

His hand comes up then, tugging down the neck of my shirt just enough that he can let his lips drag over the ridge of bone. It sends a shiver down my spine, a gasp slipping from my lips, and his eyes roll up to meet mine, obviously pleased.

"Let me see you, Caterina," he murmurs, his hands returning to the edge of my shirt. "You'll see that my desire for you hasn't changed."

I swallow hard. It's almost as if he's asking my permission, something he's never done before, and I don't know how to tell him yes or no. I feel paralyzed, wanting his touch and at the same time terrified to want it, scared to let him keep going, terrified of the look on his face when he realizes that he can't possibly want me like this after all.

Franco was cruel. Andrei was cruel, Stepan was cruel. My father never physically hurt me, but in his own ways, he was cruel too. How long before Viktor turns cruel to me, too?

What if he already is?

But his hands start to slide the shirt upwards, over my waist and up my ribs, his hands sliding over skin that is bandaged and hovering over still-wounded places, and I can't stop him. I can't open my mouth to say anything, and I know that deep down, I'm hoping that I won't see the disgust on his face that I'm so afraid of.

That this isn't just some elaborate trap.

And I know how foolish I am for that.

Viktor's hands push the shirt up, up, up, until it slides over my breasts, baring my nipples to the chill air of the room, and I feel them tighten before he even touches them. My heart stutters in my chest, and I close my eyes tightly, not wanting to see the look on his face when he finally looks down at me. His body is hovering over mine, hiding the worst of it, and then he pulls the shirt up over my head, leaving me bare beneath him, and him still fully clothed.

"Take your clothes off too, then," I whisper, still not opening my eyes. "I can't be the only one naked." My heart rises up into my throat as I say it, choking me, and I feel like I can't breathe, like I might dissolve at any moment if this goes the wrong way. This isn't what Viktor and I do. It's too romantic, too intimate. I'm feeling things I shouldn't feel, that I don't want to feel, that I *can't* feel, not for him.

"I've never told a beautiful woman no when she asks me to get naked," Viktor says above me in his deep voice, rough around the edges with desire, and for some reason, the thought of another woman telling him to take his clothes off sends a hot pulse of jealousy through me. It's stupid, I shouldn't care, but I suddenly hate the idea of any other woman being beneath him like this, of him wanting someone else, fucking someone else with either the rough, desperate need that he just fucked me with or the soft touches that he'd given me a moment ago.

I can feel him shift above me, feel the fingers of one hand go to the neck of his shirt, and I can feel him pulling it off. I reach up without meaning to, running my hand over the smooth skin of his chest, the fine hair there, and my fingertips skim down the taut skin of his flat stomach, down his abdomen, and I hear his sharp intake of breath. I feel him shift again as he pushes his jeans down his hips, kicks off his shoes. When I feel him kneeling over me again, his voice fills my ears with that rough, silky sound, like fingertips catching on fine material.

"Open your eyes, Caterina."

I know better than to disobey an order from him. I open my eyes slowly, and I see my devastatingly handsome husband straddling my hips, kneeling on the bed over me, his blue gaze fixed on my face and nothing else. It's as if he was waiting for me to open my eyes to look at me as if he wants part of it to be me seeing the expression on his face. I feel my chest tighten, fear skittering over my nerves as he leans forward, pressing his lips against the top of my breast, one of the few unmarred spots of skin.

"You are beautiful," he tells me, his tone full of a sincerity deeper than anything I've ever heard from him before. "Every—" he brushes his lips over my nipple, his breath skating over a spot that he can't touch because of the cut there, just below the curve of my breast. I'm littered with them, and there are more spots that he can't touch or kiss than ones that he can. "Single—" he kisses a bare spot of skin on my ribs, then between my breasts. "Inch."

He rolls his eyes up to look at me then, his hands resting lightly on my waist. "I want to kiss you all over, Caterina, every inch of you, until you see how much every part of your body turns me on. It has since the moment I saw you walk past the room while I was meeting with your father, and it still does."

"You didn't even want to marry me at first. You wanted—"

"Sofia would have been expedient for my position," he says, a hint of irritation entering his tone. "I didn't *want* her. She is extremely beautiful, but I've desired you for a long time, Caterina. But it was clear that your father had no interest in marrying his daughter to the Bratva *pakhan*. He preferred blood."

"And what do you prefer?" My voice sounds hoarse, too, choked with emotion.

"I prefer you naked in my bed over anything else."

I gasp as Viktor presses his mouth to a bare patch of skin on my belly, his fingers skimming over every unhurt part of me, dragging his mouth lower. His hands rest on my inner thighs, missing the bandaged wound and careful of the cuts leading up towards the place where I suddenly want his mouth more than anything. I can't believe he's moving down there, after having just fucked me, his mouth grazes over one hipbone and then the other, and then his fingers are between my thighs, opening my folds, and his lips are on my clit.

"Viktor!" I gasp his name aloud, my body tightening in a way that makes every wounded part of my body sting and ache and burn, but I can't quite bring myself to care. He's looking up at me with a hunger that says clearly that there's nowhere else he wants to be, nothing else that he wants, his tongue flicking out over my sensitive bundle of nerves and making me gasp and twitch.

"I want to find out what touches you like, my lovely bride," he murmurs, the words vibrating against my flesh. "If you like it long and slow—" he drags his tongue over my pussy, flat and soft, rubbing it over my clit as I gasp again, moaning as he presses his tongue against me. "Or quick and fast."

His tongue starts to flick over the hard bud, quick and fluttering. My thighs tighten, another moan escaping from my lips as my toes begin to curl with the bursts of pleasure that rush through me every time his tongue passes over my clit.

"Or circles, maybe?" Viktor's lips curl in a smile as he swirls his tongue around, and I gasp again, my head falling back. His mouth feels warm and wet and soft, his lips pressing against me and his tongue working to send the pleasure rushing over me again and again. It's not until he leans forward, his lips fastening around my clit and his tongue fluttering as he starts to suck, that I make a sound that's very close to a scream.

This is the kind of pleasure that's addictive.

The kind that could make me forget everything I know I'm supposed to feel.

VIKTOR

I hadn't realized how self-conscious Caterina really was or that she'd believed I'd never want her again. It's hard for me to fathom because I want her more than ever despite everything that's been done to her. She's more beautiful than she's ever been to me because I've seen for myself over the past days, and especially today, how strong she is. How resilient.

I hadn't been sure if I'd made the right choice in a bride, but I know now that I did. Caterina is everything that I believed she was and more. And I feel sure that when we leave this place, when I stop Alexei and bring my empire back under my control, she'll be the kind of bride that I can rely on to be at my side.

Seeing her tremble beneath me, her hands grabbing mine when I went to take her shirt off, makes me want to be tender with her, to show her exactly how beautiful I really do find her. All of the ferocity and passionate desire that had burned inside of me when I brought her into the cabin has changed into something gentler, more muted. I still want her, my body aching for more even though I came harder than I had in weeks only a few minutes ago, but now I want something different.

I want to wipe that fear away from her face. I want to feel her go soft and yielding beneath me again, to trust me. I want her to believe me when I say that I find her just as beautiful as I always have. And I know no other way than to show her.

I know, deep down, that these feelings are teetering on the edge of something that I don't dare put a name to. Something that could change things between us forever.

But I don't think too hard about it as I whisper reassurance to her, as I run my lips over the bruises on her throat that those monsters left. Her soft flesh beneath my mouth feels as good as it always has, her sharp collarbone a harsh line that I soften with my tongue. When she asks me to take my clothes off, too, I feel a sudden pulse of desire that feels altogether different than anything I've felt for her before.

Her eyes are tightly shut, her body tense and frightened, and there's a strange intimacy in the moment. I know that she's not asking me to get undressed because she's horny or because she has a deep need to see my naked body. I know it's because she feels vulnerable right now, half-naked with me fully clothed other than my softened cock outside of my jeans, and she can't let me take that next step unless I'm as naked as I plan for her to be.

There was a time when I would have ignored her request, would have taken pleasure in the power of stripping her bare while I remained fully clothed. But not now. Now, I feel something different.

I feel things for Caterina that I never have before. Possessive. Protective, even. I think of the night when I went into her room and watched her sleep, and I know that there's another word that could be used, too.

Obsessive.

Addicted, maybe.

Her eyes stay tightly shut while I strip naked, tossing my clothes onto the floor. Something about the moment feels more intimate than ever before, the world narrowed down to this hard bed in this remote cabin, and it's hard to remember where we are or the circumstances of it.

All I can think about is Caterina.

I tell her to open her eyes when I'm straddling her hips, fully naked at last. I see her dark eyes skim over my body nervously, down my chest to the slightly swollen cock hanging between my thighs. A little of my arousal returned from kissing her and stripping down naked in front of her. The way her gaze lingers on it makes it thicken even more, a pulse of blood swelling it to a half-erection, and I make a noise deep in my throat as I bend forward to kiss her breast.

I whisper to her how beautiful she is, how lovely, kissing every inch of bare, unmarked skin that I can find as I make my way down her body. I've never gone down on a woman after I've just come inside of her, but I don't even think about it as I slide my mouth down her belly, to her hips, down to the part of her that I want to taste.

After all of this, I want to give her pleasure that's only for her. I want to feel her unwind and come apart, let her experience again what it feels like to let go. To not have to think, just for a few moments.

The sounds she makes as I lick her, as I run my tongue over her soft wet flesh, around her clit and over again, testing and teasing, are music to my ears. I know that it won't always be like this between us. It can't be. But for a brief time, at least, we can lose ourselves in this.

I want to help her heal from what was done to her. It's why I gave her Stepan to kill instead of doing it myself as I would have liked to. It's why I pushed her to take her revenge and why I want her to know exactly how beautiful I find her, despite everything.

What's happened to her could have broken a lesser person. I know that it won't break her. It clearly hasn't yet. But I want to do all I can to bring her back from it.

I tighten my mouth around her, sucking, drawing all of that hot, swollen flesh into my mouth. She cries out with an almost anguished sound of pleasure that I'm not sure I've ever heard from her before. I feel her shiver, a rippling spasm passing through her entire body. I press my palms against the inside of her knees, where the flesh is smooth and unbroken, pushing her thighs wider so that I can get access to as much of her as possible. I can feel her tightening, her body on the verge of climax, and I keep going, pushing her towards the edge as she starts to squirm under my hands.

When the climax breaks over her, it's hard and fast, and I feel her convulse, her arousal flooding over my tongue as she bucks against my face, coming harder even than she did on my cock a few minutes ago. I can feel the ripples of her climax, the muscles in her legs tightening. She cries out, again and again, her head tossed back as I keep licking and sucking, swirling my tongue around her clit until she finally pushes at my shoulder, gasping.

"I can't—it's too sensitive—" her hips buck as I give her one final lick, running my tongue over her pulsing clit as I move backward, kissing her inner thigh again before pushing myself up to stretch alongside her.

I can't gather her into my arms the way I would like to; she's still too injured for that. But I can lie there next to her, my hand touching an uninjured space on her upper arm. She's still panting, her eyes closed as she rides out the last aftershocks of pleasure.

When Caterina finally turns her head to meet my eyes, I let her see in my face how beautiful I think she is still, letting my gaze drift down the length of her body and back up again. It's true that she doesn't look like she did when I married her. She's thinner, her skin paler, her body even more fragile than it was back then. But those things can change. And if she's physically scarred from this experience, then it won't matter to me.

"You look gorgeous when you come," I tell her, my fingers stroking that small patch of skin on her upper arm. "And beautiful afterward, all flushed and messy."

Caterina drops her gaze, her cheeks flushing even more, and she reaches for the blanket to cover herself, but I reach out and stop her.

"I want to look at you a little while longer," I tell her, my hand resting on the flat of her belly. She flinches when I touch her there, and I'm unsure why, but I move it anyway, returning it to her arm.

Caterina doesn't say anything, but she doesn't move my hand or try to cover up again either. We lie there in silence for a little while, the only sound in the room our mingled breathing, until finally she sighs and turns to look at me.

"So what happens next?" she asks softly, her lips pressed together.

"We leave to go back to Moscow tomorrow," I tell her, and I can see the flicker of fear in her face. I know she's remembering the kidnapping and what happened to her in the loft. "We won't be there long, though. We'll meet up with the others and then head to a more secure safe house while I work out what to do to deal with Alexei."

"The others?" Caterina echoes, her expression confused. "Who else?"

"The children, the other members of my household that might be in danger," I explain. "And Luca, Sofia—and Ana."

CATERINA

It's all I can do not to panic on the trip back to Moscow.

We're piled into the vehicles that Viktor used to find me, the ones taken from the cabin where I was being held. There are men with guns at every window, watching for anyone who might attack on the way. I'm swathed in another oversized outfit of salvaged men's clothes, my entire body feeling as if it's rattling with every bump and divot and pothole in the uneven forest roads as we make our way back.

Moscow is the second to last place I'd ever want to go back to, right after the cabin where Andrei and Stepan tortured me. The memory of the white-blond man and the needle sliding into my neck is still all too fresh, something that haunts my dreams almost every night. Just the thought of going back there makes my chest feel tight and my throat close up so that it feels hard to breathe.

I can feel Viktor's eyes on me as we travel back, watching me as if he's worried that I might crumble. It's far from the most comfortable trip I've ever been on. Some of the rougher patches make me grip the edge of the seat, my fingers digging into the fabric until I can almost feel my knuckles turn white in an effort not to let on the pain that I'm in.

When we approach the city, I can feel myself starting to tremble. Viktor touches my hand, and it should soothe me, but it doesn't. Even knowing that I'm going to see Sofia and Ana soon doesn't do much to quell the fears churning in my stomach, the memory of what happened the last time I was here. It all feels too fresh, too recent, and I wish that we could be anywhere but here.

I know we will be soon, but it doesn't help at the moment.

We're driven to a huge hotel, gleaming and white and tall in the middle of the city, and the trucks pull up in the front, the armed men surrounding us as Viktor opens the door and helps me out. My heart is racing as he hurries me up the steps into the lobby, and I realize with a start that there's no one else there except for the concierge. No guests milling around, no one checking in, no one at the bar. It's completely empty.

"Is there no one else here?" I whisper, leaning closer to Viktor as he escorts me towards the elevator, his hand urgently at the small of my back.

"I've had it emptied while we're here," he says stiffly, and I feel a small shock ripple through me, a reminder of my husband's power. It's not entirely unfamiliar to me, but I've never seen it enacted so closely before. The idea that this huge hotel is ours alone while we're here seems insane. The emptiness of the elevator and the absolute silence of the hall that we step into when we get off of it only underscores the fact that he's telling the truth.

Viktor takes me down the hall to a room near the end, opening the door and walking in after me. The room is huge and open and sunny, but he draws the blinds immediately, checking the windows before he does.

"We're almost at the top," I blurt out. "Surely no one can get in?"

"You'd be surprised," he says darkly. "I'm sure you want to shower," Viktor adds, nodding towards the attached bathroom. "Let me know if you need help."

It's said in a way that's more casual than sexual, just a normal husband offering to help his recovering wife, and I feel that flash of intimacy again, that feeling that there's something here that could blossom into something more if it had the room to grow.

I just don't know how it ever could.

"A shower sounds good," I manage. It sounds *better* than good, truthfully, it sounds like heaven, and that's only underscored when I walk into the massive attached bathroom, complete with a huge dual-head shower and a soaking tub.

I wish more than anything that I could fill up that tub and sink down into it, but I'm under strict instructions from the doctor not to soak my healing wounds any more than necessary. I'm not even supposed to take showers that are all that long, but I'm going to be testing the limits of that one. I feel filthy after the trip and after days of being in bed with minimal showers and only the limited soap and water at the cabin.

I've never thought of myself as particularly high-maintenance, but I hadn't realized how used to luxuries large and small, or how much I would miss them until they were entirely gone for a while. The heavy stream of water from the showerhead, pulsing against the sore muscles of my back, the scent of expensive lavender shampoo and soap, the steam that wreathes and builds in the heated room until every breath smells like lavender and comfort—they're all things that I had no idea I could miss so much until they were gone.

After I've washed every inch of myself that I can and shampooed my hair twice, I lean against the wall while the deep conditioner soaks into my hair, closing my eyes and enjoying the heat of the foggy shower after so long in the spring chill of the northern Russian forest. I don't know where we're going next, but I hope it's somewhere with a better heating system than that remote cabin.

Victor had said "a more secure safe house," but I don't really know what that means. Another cabin? A house more like his back home? A fucking fortress? I don't have any idea. Of course, my father had had safe houses like any mob boss, but I'd never *been* to one. Despite the conflict between the mafia and the Bratva while my father had been in power, he'd kept us well-insulated from it. My father had been a cruel man and not the most loving father, but I do give him credit for that. He'd made sure that my mother and I were protected.

Up until he couldn't anymore, of course, and my mother had died.

I feel a flash of bitterness at that memory, but I push it away. There's nothing I can do to change it now, just like I can't change any of the things that happened to me. All I can do is try to move forward, even though I don't know what that future looks like now.

A vision of Viktor's face in bed with me yesterday floats in front of my closed eyes, the way he'd looked down at me with that intense desire. It hadn't made any sense to me, but he hadn't seemed to be lying. He hadn't fucked me after he'd seen me naked, hadn't been completely hard, but it hadn't seemed to be from revulsion. He'd seemed to just be focused on my pleasure, something else that is somewhat out of character for him.

I don't know if it makes me feel better or worse that my husband might have a better, kinder side to him than I knew. It makes it harder to understand him and the things he does. And it still doesn't answer the mystery of his first wife—how she died and whether or not he might have something to do with the kidnapping that I endured.

I know better than to trust him. But it doesn't stop me from wishing that I could.

It's not until my fingers start to wrinkle and the water starts to cool that I finally force myself to get out of the shower. I stayed in far longer than I should have, per the doctor's orders, but I needed it. The bathroom is comfortably hot and steamy when I step out, and I wrap a towel around myself and another around my hair, realizing that I have no idea what I'm actually going to wear. I don't want to put the oversized, unwashed clothes back on, but I don't actually have anything else.

Viktor is lying on the king-sized bed when I walk out, shirtless and in only joggers that rest just below his hips, the most casual that I've ever seen him. His eyes skate over me with a sudden heat that startles me. I can't get used to the idea that he could want me, seeing me in stark broad daylight, but as I walk closer to the bed, he makes a motion with his finger, encouraging me to keep going.

"Take the towel off," he says, his voice gruff with that edge of desire that I know how to recognize so easily now. "I want to see you."

"I—"

"Let me see you, Caterina," he says, in a voice that brooks no argument, and I know exactly what he's doing. He's trying to reinforce how he sees me, over and over, until I stop hesitating to let him see me naked, until I don't feel self-conscious anymore. I don't know how long that particular tactic is going to take to work, if it ever does, but I obey him anyway.

I don't *want* to feel like this, like a stranger in my own skin, and if my suddenly thawing husband can help me with that, so much the better.

What I don't want to admit to myself is that if sex between us is going to be the way it was yesterday, I could get used to this.

I could *want* it all of the time.

I tug the corner of the towel loose, letting it fall to the floor. The moment it falls away, I feel the slight chill against my bare skin. I feel my stomach twist, my heart pounding in my chest with a feeling close to panic. But nothing changes in Viktor's face. Nothing negative, anyway. All I see is a growing desire, his eyes heating as he looks at my bare body and skin still flushed from the heat of the shower.

"Come here," he says, beckoning again, and I hesitate.

"The sheets are white—what if—"

"Don't worry. They can be replaced. Come here," he repeats, and I know better than to make my husband ask a third time.

Slowly, I climb onto the bed, my hair still bound up in the smaller towel. As I kneel on the mattress next to him, Viktor reaches up, plucking the towel out of my hair and tossing it aside. The abundance of wet hair that was bound by the towel, now cascades down around my shoulders. He runs his fingers through it, wrapping some of it around his hand as he pulls me down for a kiss.

"I want you again," he murmurs against my lips. "My wife. My bride."

A small thrill of desire runs through me at that, and I can feel the dampness between my thighs, just at the feeling of his hand tight in my hair and the whispered words of desire. I'd never known that some of the things Viktor does to me could turn me on so much, and I suspect there's much more that might if I gave it a chance.

I don't know if I want to, though. I don't know if I want to know how dark my desires could be, given space to explore. And I don't know that I want to give in to Viktor so completely. I have some idea of the things he might want to do to me, the sort of submission he might expect if I gave in to it willingly. I feel a curl of excitement somewhere deep inside of me at the thought.

But I would have to be able to trust him, and I don't know if I can do that. Not yet.

Viktor's hand slides down, pushing his joggers off as he kisses me, and I catch a glimpse of his thick cock lying against his stomach, already hard and ready for me. "I want your mouth," he groans against my lips. "If you can."

I run my tongue over my lower lip, testing the spot where it was split, feeling for soreness. It's not completely healed, but something about his concern for my well-being makes me *want* to do it for him, to take him into my mouth and feel him against my tongue, taste him.

"I don't know how much I can do," I whisper. "But I'll try."

CATERINA

Viktor nods, letting go of my hair and groaning as I reach for him, running my fingers down the length of his shaft as I slide downwards, moving a little bit awkwardly as I try to find a position that doesn't hurt me to lie in. I catch a glimpse of the healing wounds around my wrists, and I can't help but wonder if he notices it when he looks down at my hand encircling his cock, how it can possibly be that it doesn't turn him off. But the throbbing against my palm tells me that he's anything but turned off. There's already pre-cum pearling at the tip, and I rub my thumb over it, feeling the stickiness against my finger as I slide my hand downwards, leaning forward to brush my lips over him.

He groans when I purse my lips over the swollen flesh, running my tongue over the small opening where I can taste him, the pulsing vein that runs along the top of his shaft throbbing against my fingers as I slowly slide down, inch by inch. I can't take him very far into my throat, but I make up for it with my lips and tongue and hand. Rubbing my tongue over that very sensitive spot just beneath the tip of his cock, stroking him firmly as I do, until I hear him groan aloud.

Viktor's hips arch upwards, thrusting into my hand as I touch him, licking and sucking and stroking, feeling him throb and pulse in my grip, enjoying this little bit of power I have over him, to please him exactly the way I know he likes and draw it out for as long as I want.

Or until he gets tired of being teased, that is.

It's a while. He lets it go until he can see me getting tired, his face taut with pleasure as he enjoys the heat of my mouth, my tongue lapping at him, and my hand moving in firm strokes up and down his thick length. Then he reaches for me, pulling me up his body.

"I don't want to be on top—" I protest, as his hands rest on my hips, pulling me over him to straddle him with his cock brushing against my inner thigh.

"I want to see all of you," Viktor insists, his gaze raking over me. "Can you ride me, Caterina? Or does it hurt too much?"

"Slowly, maybe," I hedge, and I wonder if I really want to do this. I see the desire in his eyes, seeing me bare and atop him, and his cock lurches against my thigh, further evidence of how turned on he is by me. Can I be this vulnerable in front of him right now? Can I even manage to do this with my body still healing the way it is?

"If you get tired, we'll switch," Viktor says, his hands stroking my hips, and I nod, suddenly breathless. I don't recognize this man, this isn't the husband I married, and this is a man I could actually fall for. A handsome, caring man, one who is worried about my well-being, who doesn't want to push me further than my limits. I would never have thought that this side of him existed.

I gasp when he angles his cock between my thighs, feeling the swollen head pushing at my folds, ready to impale me. I feel that rush of need, the memory of the pleasure that I feel every time he fucks me, intense and all-consuming, and I know that it's so close. As he starts to thrust upwards, his hands resting on my hips as he slowly pulls me down the length of his cock, I can feel it beginning to flood my veins, sparks dancing over my skin as he fills me, his cock touching every nerve ending I ever knew I had and some that I didn't.

His fingers are pressing against a few cuts on my hips and near the top of my ass, but I can't bring myself to care. Even the bit of pain brings a sharp edge to the pleasure, one that I don't mind. I don't pause too long to think about that, only slide down the rest of the way, letting out a gasping moan when I feel him sink to the hilt, filling me entirely.

His fingers are pressing against a few cuts on my hips and near the top of my ass, but I can't bring myself to care. Even the bit of pain brings a sharp edge to the pleasure, one that I don't mind. I don't pause too long to think about that, only slide down the rest of the way, letting out a gasping moan when I feel him sink to the hilt, filling me entirely.

Viktor groans at that, his fingers tightening on my hips, and I let out a small cry as he starts to move, rolling his hips against me as his face goes taut with pleasure. I know his expressions by now, the ones that tell me how good it feels for him, and in this particular moment, it fuels my own, making me slick and hot and wet for him as I start to tentatively move on my own, sliding up and down the length of his hard cock.

I can tell that I won't be able to do it for long, but it feels so fucking good, better than I could have expected. Even the edge of pain doesn't take away from how good it feels, it only heightens it, and I move faster, even though I know my muscles will pay for it later. I can feel the orgasm starting to build, curling through my body. I gasp as I grind against him, feeling his thick cockhead pressing against that spot just inside of me each time I slide up, sending a dart of electric pleasure through me.

"Oh god," I whisper, my hands pressing against his chest, and Viktor groans, moving with me and matching my rhythm as I get closer and closer to my climax. Part of me wants to hold back, to not give in to the idea that this man can give me so much pleasure, but the rest of me wants it too badly. He feels so good inside of me, filling me up, every inch sending heat blooming over my skin as I slide down. When I take all of him again, he holds me down hard against him, one hand still on my hip as his other slips between my legs, teasing my clit as my thigh muscles start to shake.

"Viktor!" I nearly scream his name as the orgasm hits, my back arching and my fingers digging into his chest. I feel the ripples of it all the way down to my toes, my hips slamming down onto him as I seek out even more pleasure, every bit of it that I can get from him. His fingers are still teasing my clit, rubbing in tight little circles that drive me wild, making me shake as I cry out his name again, a second orgasm hitting right on the heels of the first from the pressure of his fingers combined with the thick stretch of his cock filling me. It feels as if it won't ever end, as if I'll burst apart at the seams, dissolve right here. I'm still trembling when he pulls his hand away and gently turns me, rolling me onto my back on the cool sheets as he stretches out atop me, his cock still firmly embedded deep inside of me.

His thrusts slow then, in long strokes that leave me gasping with each slow movement, and to my surprise, he reaches out, his hand pressing against my face, his thumb against my lower lip. My mouth parts, lips wrapping around his thumb as he speeds up a fraction, thrusting just a little harder, and Viktor groans aloud at the sensation.

"*Fuck*, Caterina—" he thrusts again, holding himself there as my tongue flicks against the rough pad of his thumb, and I feel him throb inside of me. "I'm not going to last much longer."

I nod breathlessly, my hips arching to meet him as he starts to move again, and I can feel the break in his rhythm, the way his body is beginning to tremble and tighten. I *want* him to come in me, I realize; I want to feel the way he quivers and thrusts hard and fast, the hot rush of him when he finally loses control. This man is so in control of every single part of his life, and yet with me, in bed, I see that falter.

His hands are pressed into the mattress on either side of my head, his body tense and straining. A moment later, he throws his head back, rising up to kneel between my legs as he starts to thrust harder, faster. I can *see* him, see the way his abdomen tightens and his mouth parts as he approaches the point of no return, his hands suddenly on my hips again as he groans aloud, cursing in Russian as I feel him harden inside of me even more, that last swollen throbbing before he erupts inside of me.

"*Bladya!*" he shouts, an almost primal groan spilling from his lips as he thrusts into me hard, shuddering as I feel the hot rush of his cum, and his entire body is rigid, each muscle flexed and hard as he bucks against me, coming in waves that feel as if they might never end.

I don't know if I want it to end. It feels good to have him so close, to hear him cry out with pleasure, to know that I can do this to him. That I can *still* do it to him, after everything.

I can feel him on my thighs, hot and sticky when he rolls off of me, panting to lie next to me on the bed. "I just took a shower," I laugh, and Viktor smirks as I look at him.

"I'm sure you won't mind an excuse to use that shower again," he says. "You might as well go ahead and clean up; I need to make a call. But I needed to have you first," he adds, letting his gaze rake over me again with a lascivious expression that tells me he'd be happy to do it again.

It feels so *right*, so normal, and it terrifies me. I don't know what to do with that, with quiet banter in bed with my husband after sex. So I just push myself up from the bed, giving him a quick smile before making my way slowly towards the bathroom.

Small victories, I tell myself. Not all that long ago, I could barely get from my bed to the bathroom to pee, and now I can walk there and shower after having sex with my husband without more than a manageable amount of pain. I know it's something that I need to be thankful for, and I try to focus on that and not all of the fears that I have lingering in my mind.

My second shower is much quicker—I haven't forgotten what the doctor said about lingering in the water. I carefully dry off after, braiding my hair and wrapping another towel around myself as I get ready to go back out and ask Viktor about clothes. I don't know what call he had to make, but surely it can't be so important that I can't hear it, or he would have gone elsewhere to take it.

"No, she doesn't know," Viktor says, his voice carrying as I step outside of the bathroom, and I freeze in place, my heart suddenly pounding in my chest.

"Of course I set it up," he continues, and I feel all of the blood drain from my face.

"She won't find out if I can help it." He pauses, as if listening to whoever is speaking on the other end. "Of course she'll owe me. I rescued her. It doesn't matter. But I'm not going to cash in on it unless I need to. What kind of man do you think I am?"

A monster. That's all that's running through my head. I feel like I'm going to pass out, clutching the side of the door for dear life as the blood pounds in my head, roaring in my ears as the room tilts. *No*, I tell myself firmly. *No, you can't faint. If you do, you'll never get out of here.*

That's what I have to do, get out of here. I feel a sudden rush of nausea burning in my gut, and I spin on my heel and rush towards the toilet, heedless of any pain in my headlong attempt to get to it before I vomit all over the floor. Every muscle in my body revolts as I bend over it, retching up what little food I have in my system as I clutch my stomach, heaving, again and again, tears streaming down my face.

The thought of what I just did with Viktor is almost enough to make me throw up all over again. *How could I have been so stupid?* I'd been right all along—he'd set up my kidnapping to break me, and then staged a rescue to make me feel indebted to him, to mold me into a wife who would be more pliable, more willing to give in to him and even care for him, believing that he'd shown me a different side of himself.

When in fact, he was really the monster I'd believed all along. No, worse, because I'd never thought that he'd do something so horrible. I'd had suspicions about what might have happened to his first wife. However, I hadn't thought he'd go to the kinds of lengths that involved having his own wife kidnapped, brutalized, her body ruined, and mind nearly broken, only to pretend to be the hero.

Nausea rises up again, and I bend over the toilet once more, my thoughts racing as I heave all over again, clutching the porcelain.

I have to get out of here. I can hear Viktor's voice faintly from the bedroom, and I push myself to my feet, grabbing for the clothes that I'd left in a pile on the floor from my earlier shower. As quickly as I can, I slip back into the oversized sweatpants and t-shirt and the boots that are a size too big, stuffing my feet into them and lacing them as tightly as I can.

Fuck, what am I going to do? I might be able to get out of the hotel, but what about after that? I don't have any money. The credit card that Viktor gave me after our marriage was in my clutch back in the loft before I was kidnapped. I couldn't get away with using one of his, and besides, he's *in* the bedroom. I can't steal anything right out from under his nose.

And then, as I hover indecisively in the middle of the bathroom, I hear the sound of the door to the room opening and then shutting heavily.

Now. If you're going to do anything, it has to be now.

I slip out of the bathroom, looking around frantically to make sure Viktor has really left. I have no idea if he's taken his things with him, but I see a pair of jeans left on the bed, and I go straight for that, shoving my hands in the pockets to see if I can find his wallet.

Nothing. I take a deep, shaky breath, trying to think. His heavy jacket is on the back of the chair, and I check that next, searching every pocket and coming up empty-handed.

Until I reach into the pocket just inside and feel the slender leather shape of my husband's wallet.

Fingers trembling, I pull it out. I know better than to try to use one of his credit cards, but when I check the pocket again, just behind the wallet, there's a money clip. When I pull it out, I see a thick fold of cash, and I swallow hard, my mouth suddenly dry.

Stealing from the Bratva is a dangerous thing. I know that as well as anyone. I don't think that being Viktor's wife will save me from those consequences—it clearly hasn't saved me from suffering in other ways. But I don't see an alternative.

I take the money and try to get the fuck out of Moscow. Back home, maybe, or somewhere else, somewhere far enough that my husband can't find me, if there is a place like that. Or I stay here, knowing that my husband had me tortured, that he let those men hurt me in ways that won't ever heal, and then pretended to be my savior. I stay here, knowing that for the rest of my life, I'll have to sleep beside him, fuck him, raise his children and be his wife—a wife to a monster worse than any man I've ever known.

Worse even than Andrei or Stepan, because Viktor is pretending to care about me.

I clutch the money in my fist, shoving it into the waistband of my sweatpants and pulling the drawstring tighter. I know I'll have to slip past security, and I don't even know how I'm going to get that far, but all I can do is put one foot in front of the other and get as far as I can. If I'm caught, will it really be so much worse than living the rest of my life knowing what Viktor did?

I don't think so.

There's a tall, bulky man posted outside of my door, and I nearly dart back inside, fear clogging my throat and making it hard to speak.

"What are you doing out here, Mrs. Andreyva?" the guard asks, his eyes narrowing. I take a deep breath, trying to sound sure, like the wife of the *pakhan* and not a guilty girl trying to escape her brutal husband.

"Viktor asked me to meet him downstairs," I say, lifting my chin. "I'm already running late. I took too long in the shower."

The last sentence has the desired effect—I might not be the beauty I once was, but I clearly have enough left to make a man lose his train of thought a little at the idea of me in the shower. He looks caught off guard, as if he's trying very hard not to let me see the thoughts that crossed his mind just now.

The guard blinks, recovering after a second, and clears his throat. "Mr. Andreyev said nothing to me about you leaving your room, Mrs. Andreyva."

"I don't think he needs to tell you his private information, not when he's already given me instructions," I say haughtily, forcing myself not to let my voice crack. "I think he trusts me to be able to give his security appropriate information."

The guard frowns, reaching for his walkie, and I feel myself get dizzy with fear again. "I should check with him—"

"If you want to be responsible for making me late, be my guest," I tell him sharply. "But I'm letting Viktor know it was your fault I was standing here in the hallway, so soon after being injured, and not on my way down to sit with him and have lunch."

That does it. The guard goes slightly pale around the edges, and he nods. "I'm sorry, Mrs. Andreyva," he says almost contritely. "I'll be here to keep watch for you when you return."

I manage to hold back my sigh of relief until I turn and hurry towards the elevator, my heart in my throat, my heavy damp braid bouncing against my shoulder as I try not to look as if I'm literally running for my life. I can hardly breathe by the time I dart inside of it, the guards posted on either side having been able to see my discussion with the security just outside my door. I slam the button for the service floor in hopes that I can avoid more security altogether. There might be some of Viktor's men posted down there, but it's possible that they left that alone, figuring that anyone who might try to sneak in would be stopped by the guards on every floor. *There's fucking enough of them,* I think bitterly.

An hour ago, I might have been grateful for them. But I don't know what danger is real anymore and what's contrived, whether there's really a greater problem that means that everyone needs to be at the other safe house, or whether it's all a lie created by Viktor to cover up the fact that he plotted to break me.

I hadn't thought having my suspicions confirmed would hurt so much. I have to blink back tears as the elevator goes down, fighting back the urge to simply lean my head against the side of the elevator and burst into tears. Maybe it wouldn't have, before yesterday, but now all I can think of is the way Viktor had whispered to me that I was beautiful, the way he'd kissed me as he slid down my body, the gentle touches then and only just an hour or so ago, in bed together. The way he'd made me let down my guard, be more vulnerable with him, start to open up because of the way he'd cared for me while I was recovering, how afraid he'd seemed to be of losing me. The revenge that he'd helped me take.

Knowing that it was all a lie, just an elaborate setup, makes me feel sick and heartbroken all at once. I can't let myself go far enough to think that I'd been falling in love with him, but some part of me *had* opened up. I'd allowed a sliver of light to peek in, to wonder if there was a part of my husband that might be worth loving, and that door had just slammed shut in my face so hard that it had practically broken my nose.

When the elevator door opens to the service floor, I don't immediately see any signs of guards. I slip out, breathless as I look for a back door, any way out of the hotel that might get me past Viktor's security. There are bellhop and room service carts lined up against one wall, and I dart behind them, hiding myself from view as well as I can while I try to scope out where to go next.

There's a double door on the far wall, one that I suspect would take me out to the street. I can't be sure, but it's my best shot. If there's security on the other side when I burst out of it, I'm fucked, but I can't see any other way out.

I hear the sound of muted voices, and I duck further behind the carts, shrinking backward and trying to be as small and still as I can while they pass by. It's three of Viktor's men, and I hold my breath, heart racing as they walk past, chatting about lunch. They're so casual that it's almost startling, but they pass by without so much as noticing a glimpse of me. I sag against the wall when they get into the elevator and I hear the chime of it going up.

It's now or never. I know there's a chance, too, that the door might be alarmed—but I have to give it a shot. I don't have a better plan, and I don't have time to come up with one.

I touch the waistband of my sweatpants to reassure myself that the money clip is still there, and then I take a deep breath and bolt towards the double doors.

The entire way there, in the few moments that it takes me to run for the doors, I'm certain a hand is going to grab me and pull me back, or a voice is going to shout that they see me, but no one does. I shove the doors open with both hands, heart pounding, waiting for the shriek of an alarm or the startled faces of guards on the other side.

But neither of those things happens. This particular door is both unalarmed and unguarded. I burst out into the chilly, overcast Moscow day, my pulse racing so fast that I feel as if I might pass out again, rooted to the spot on the sidewalk just outside the hotel.

Go! My mind screams at me. *Get the fuck out of here before someone sees you!*

I don't know which way to go to get to a bus station or a train or an airport. I don't speak Russian. I don't think I have enough money for a flight, but I'm not certain, and a bus isn't going to take me far enough, fast enough. A train seems like the best bet, but I know exactly how I look, and I'm not even sure I'll get as far as buying a ticket if I can find it at all.

There's a fifty-fifty shot of going in the right direction. I can go left or right, and I force myself to turn left, making myself choose without any real idea if it's correct. All I know is that I need to get away from the hotel, no matter what direction I go in.

I can feel the blisters forming on my heels and pinky toes from the too-big boots within a block, but I don't slow down. I don't stop. I keep going, turning down streets that look like large, main ones until I feel as if I've put enough blocks between the hotel and me to stop and ask a passing stranger which way the train station is.

He looks at me suspiciously and says something in Russian that I don't understand that sounds more than a little irritated. But all Russian sounds that way if I'm being honest.

"Only English," I say, pointing at myself. "Train. Train station. Go? Train—" I mimic whatever I can think of—a train whistle, wheels rolling—and the man looks at me as if I'm a complete idiot. With my bruised face, wet hair, and oversized clothing, I probably look fucking homeless.

The irony isn't lost on me. I'm one of the richest women in the world by virtue of my own inheritance and my husband's wealth, and yet I'm on the street in a country where I don't speak the language, looking desperately poor and begging for directions.

The man shakes his head, looking disgusted, and keeps pedaling down the street. I have to ask two more passersby before I finally find a woman who speaks heavily-accented English and is able to point me in the direction of the train station.

Fortunately, I'm not too far off. I turn down the street she pointed out, hoping that I haven't been so noticeable that it will be easy for

Viktor to ask about a dark-haired woman in oversized clothing trying to find a way out of Moscow.

With any luck, I'll be on a train before he can figure it out, even if I have. And if I'm paying with cash, it will be much harder for him to find me.

My entire body hurts by the time I make it to the train station, every inch of me on fire with pain. Still, I force myself to limp into the ticketing area, trying to stand up straight and look more like a woman who should be traveling on her own, and not the injured, escaped bride of a Russian mobster.

"I need a ticket out of Moscow," I tell the woman at the counter.

She raises an eyebrow. "Where to?"

"Just whichever one is leaving next." I pause, realizing how desperate that sounds, and regroup. "I just felt like being a little spontaneous today, that's all. A vacation to a random spot. Doesn't that sound like fun?"

That's exactly the kind of bougie nonsense that will probably catch her off guard, and it does exactly that. I see a pinched expression cross her face as she taps on a keyboard, as if she's thinking about how much *she* would like to take a random vacation, in the middle of the week, to anywhere she might feel like going on a whim.

She gives me the price, and I hand her the wad of cash, with no real idea of what the equivalencies of Russian money are. She raises her eyebrow again, and for a terrifying moment, I think she's going to question me, accuse me of stealing the money, call security. I see a flicker of something pass over her face, and she opens her mouth.

And then her eyes settle on my face for a second, looking at me. Not just glancing, but really *seeing* me, and I know what she's looking at—the bruises on my face, purple and yellowing, the fingermarks healing on my throat. She looks back down at the wad of cash and peels off a few bills, handing me back the rest.

"Your name?" she asks brusquely, and I let out a sigh of relief.

With that sort of innate understanding that all women have, I know that I've gotten lucky. If it had been a man at the counter, he'd have probably called security on me. But this woman saw my bruised face, the suspicious wad of money, and my uncertainty about where I was going. She saw a battered woman running from a man.

She's incorrectly assumed, of course, that it's Viktor who did it. But in a way, he did. And I'm not about to correct her.

"Irene Boltskaya," I say, making up a fake name on the fly.

"ID?"

My breath catches in my throat.

"I lost it," I say lamely. "On the way here. Is it really necessary if I'm paying with cash?"

Her eyes flick over my face again.

"Usually, yes," she says. "But today, I'll let it go. You seem to be in a hurry, Ms. Boltskaya."

"Just eager for some relaxation." I shove the money clip back onto my waistband, trying not to think about how difficult it will be once I get off of the train to go any further without some kind of identification. *I'll worry about that when it happens,* I tell myself. The first thing is to get out of Moscow. Once that's accomplished, I can concern myself with trying to get ahold of Luca, maybe, and telling him what Viktor has done. I know he'll protect me if he can. It will cause the war that I've tried so hard to prevent, but I'm not sure if I can care about that anymore.

Viktor has gone too far this time. And I can't stay with a man who would do those things to me.

The next train leaves in less than an hour. Too long for my comfort, but there's nothing I can do about it. I take the ticket and thank the woman behind the counter and hurry towards the waiting area, sitting in the furthest corner and keeping my head down in an effort to be as hard to spot as possible. If Viktor or any of his men get this far before I leave, I'm hoping that they simply won't recognize me. I take my hair out of the braid as well, running my fingers through it so that it's thick and curly around my face, obscuring my features.

Every footstep and voice sends a dart of panic through me until I feel as if I'm constantly on the verge of an anxiety attack, but the minute's tick by. When I hear my train number called for boarding—

or at least I think so, based on the number I hear and the people standing up to head towards the track—I let out a small sigh. *Just a few more minutes,* I tell myself. *A few more, and I'll be on the train. He won't catch me then. There'll be nothing to trace me. That woman won't tell him anything.*

Of course, I know what means Viktor has at his disposal to make people talk. But I force myself not to think about it as I get into line, keeping my head down as it moves slowly forwards towards the train sitting on the tracks.

My escape. Just feet away, and now inches, closer and closer, until I can smell the heat from the metal.

And then, just as I'm a few steps away from handing my ticket over, a hard, rough hand clamps onto my arm and spins me around.

The face looking down at me isn't Viktor's. But it's pale and blue-eyed, the hand gloved and squeezing my arm almost painfully, and I know without a doubt that it's one of his men.

"Mrs. Andreyva, it's time to come back home."

CATERINA

The ride to the new safe house is colder and tenser than any drive I've been on before. A heavy air of foreboding hangs between Viktor and me, and I don't dare even sneak a look at his face. The look on it when his men brought me back to the hotel was terrifying enough.

I should have known better than to think I could escape him. They'd tracked me down just as easily and quickly as I'd feared, giving my description out until they found the people I'd talked to trying to locate the train station. Everyone was very eager to help, from what Viktor had coldly told me. *I bet they were,* I think darkly again, looking out of the tinted bulletproof window of the armored vehicle taking us to the next safe house. The car feels like a jail cell, and I'm sure the house won't be any different. Viktor will have me under lock and key now, closely observed. He said as much in a few words.

We have a veritable train of armored cars—the rest of our household, as well as Luca, Sofia, and Ana, in others. I didn't see any of them when I was brought back to the hotel. Viktor kept me locked in our room for the day that remained before we left. He hadn't come back to our room either, instead, leaving two men at the door with strict instructions that I was not to leave for any reason and that they were not to move, "not even if the fucking hotel burned down around their ears."

I'm sure they would have happily stood and burned to death rather than face whatever punishment Viktor would mete out for leaving me or letting me out of the room. I didn't bother trying.

I'd had my one escape attempt, and it had failed. I knew better than to try again. There was no point, anyway. Viktor had made sure the windows were locked and that anything I could possibly use to facilitate an escape—for instance, money—wasn't left in the room. He'd taken every single possession out of the room except for a change of clothes that he'd had purchased for me, something that he'd made abundantly clear he didn't think I deserved any longer.

I would have almost felt bad, seeing what was in the crisp shopping bag sitting atop the bed, if I hadn't known what Viktor had done. There had been a pair of soft, silky underwear and a matching wireless bra, things that would make me feel completely dressed while still not chafing my healing skin. On top of that, there had been a light wool sweater dress made of fine soft cashmere with elbow-length sleeves and a midi-length skirt with a scooped neckline. This dress would cover almost all of my wounds while being soft and forgiving, in a lovely pale blue color that I know Viktor loves.

It's the kind of outfit that said he had put some thought into it— and it was undoubtedly expensive. Before I knew the truth about what he had done, it would have been one more thing to chip away at the walls I'd put up to protect myself from him.

Looking at it then only made me feel sick. But I'd known I'd have to put it on anyway.

"There's only the one set of clothing," he'd said coldly, standing at the door with his ice-blue eyes fixed on me. "I'd had more purchased for you, but perhaps I'll make you earn it." A cruel smile had curved his lips then, his eyes colder than I'd ever seen them, glittering like hard jewels in his taut face. "Perhaps I'll lock you in a room naked, so there's no chance of you going anywhere until you learn to behave. But don't worry, Caterina. There's plenty of punishment before that for you."

And then he'd left, the threat clearly hanging in the air.

Remembering it makes me shiver. I'm sitting as far on one side of the car as I can, putting as much space between us as I can manage. I'm acutely aware of the man sitting in front of me in the passenger's seat and the ones behind us, all armed. I could try to throw myself out of the car, but the doors are locked, and I'm pretty sure I can't even engage mine if I tried.

I wouldn't get that far before someone stopped me, anyway.

I'd thought I was a prisoner in my marriage before, but now it's very, very real.

Terrified is putting how I feel mildly. I don't think Viktor would treat me as roughly as he does someone like, say, Andrei and Stepan, but I still can't get their broken and bloodied faces out of my mind. I've angered him terribly, and I know that he's going to punish me for it.

I just don't know how.

Deep down, I can't regret trying to run, either. Whatever happens to me now, if I hadn't, I would always have wondered if I might have succeeded, if only I'd tried. I'd done everything in my power to get away and escape Viktor, and I'd failed. Even the sympathetic woman at the train counter hadn't been enough to keep them from finding me. I'd had the one chance, and it hadn't been enough.

Now I have to live with that.

I just don't know what that will mean for me.

The armored car comes around a bend, and then suddenly, I see our destination looming ahead of us as the forest splits open. We've been going up the mountains for some time, and what I see ahead nearly takes my breath away, even knowing that it's about to be my prison.

I hadn't been wrong when I'd wondered if the next safe house would be a fortress. It's exactly that, a massive chalet-style home with towers that look as if they're aspiring to pierce the clouds wreathing the tops of the mountains and a huge, solid barricade all around it. I can see from our vantage point that it's a considerably sized estate, if guarded to the teeth, but I doubt I'll get a chance to explore much of it.

Viktor's threat to keep me locked naked in a room somewhere suddenly feels much more immediate. It seems dramatic to think of him locking me in a tower garret like Cinderella, but I'm not so sure that it is anymore. He's a man who I'm certain can come up with creative forms of punishment, and I'm certain that he believes that I've earned exactly that.

As we approach, the heavy gate opens. I see the soldiers standing there, wearing black clothing, Kevlar, and heavily armed. There are others along the wall surrounding the estate, and as the cars crawl through the gate, I catch a glimpse of their set, hard, emotionless faces.

These aren't men that I can cajole into letting me out. They aren't men I can trick with a story of Viktor having given me different instructions than what they were told. Viktor will be very clear with them. And even if I could, it doesn't matter. I'm somewhere in the Russian mountains with no transportation and not even suitable clothing for trying to get away. I'm sure any vehicle I could take is locked up tight in some inaccessible garage.

I'm trapped here. There's no way around it and no other options for me. Once again, I simply have to survive as I've been doing all this time.

There are more guards at the front of the house, which is as beautiful as I expected. It's almost castle-like, made of stone with balconies and heavy doors and architecture as lovely as it is forbidding. It's exactly where I would expect a Russian mob boss to bring his captive bride.

Viktor isn't often a predictable man, and all of this seems a little on the nose for him. But then again, clearly, I didn't know my husband as well as I thought I did.

The door to the armored car opens, and I step out, the air chilly even through the cashmere of my dress. Viktor exited first, and he's standing there, his gaze even colder as he takes my elbow, his fingers digging in as he leads me towards the house. The days of him touching me gently, being cautious of my healing injuries, are clearly past.

I twist my head around and see the others exiting the cars. I catch a glimpse of Sofia, standing next to Luca and whispering something to him, her bump starting to show under the shape of the sweater she's wearing. I feel a leap of excitement seeing her, my best friend that I haven't seen in what feels like months, but Viktor is already pulling me towards the front doors, not giving me a moment to greet anyone.

I catch a glimpse of Anika and Yelena getting out of one of the other cars, flanked by Sasha and Olga, and Max climbing out of another. I don't see Ana, and I feel a sudden flare of panic, wondering if Viktor left her behind as some kind of beginning to my punishment. I know she won't be safe in Manhattan, not if there's been a mutiny with Viktor's business. Several of Viktor's brigadiers hate her because she'd spied on them to find out information for Sofia, and without Viktor and Luca there to enforce the treaty, she'll be at their mercy.

"Where's Ana?" I ask, trying to keep my voice from trembling as Viktor escorts me into the house, his grip on my elbow verging on painful. "You didn't leave her behind, did you? You—"

"She's in one of the cars," he says sharply. "But you have other things to worry about right now."

A wave of relief washes over me, so intense that my knees feel weak for a moment. "Viktor, I want to see Sofia. I haven't seen either of my friends since—"

"There will be time for that if you don't anger me more than you already have," Viktor says tightly. "But for now, you're going to come with me. And we're going to *discuss* your disobedience."

The tone of his voice tells me that *discussing* isn't necessarily what's going to happen. I feel my heart stutter in my chest, my blood running cold as fear wraps icy fingers around my spine, sending a shiver through me as Viktor escorts me towards a winding iron staircase. I catch a glimpse of a huge living room with a roaring fire already built and several other rooms with closed doors, but there's no time to look for very long. Viktor is already hustling me up the staircase, behind me, so that there's no chance of me turning and running.

Not that there's anywhere for me to go. There's no point in trying to run. My chances of escape are long gone, and I know it.

"The master suite is to the left," Viktor says, nodding towards a set of heavy mahogany double doors. "We're the only ones on this floor. Guests are on the floor above us."

Lovely, no one will be able to hear me scream, I think dryly as I push the doors open. They swing open to reveal a bedroom that would have taken my breath away under different circumstances. The floor is gleaming hardwood, swathed in expensive-looking rugs, with a massive four-poster bed draped in velvet swags along the canopy. There's a dark wine-colored duvet on it, with a mound of pillows and a thick fur throw along the end, with a nailhead leather bench at the foot of the bed.

The furnishings are all dark wood, from the side tables to the heavy wardrobe on one side of the room. There's a stone fireplace on the opposite end, with a fire already built in it, with velvet and leather wing chairs arranged in front and a wooden table with a tray containing a bottle of champagne and two flutes. I almost snort aloud when I see that, as unladylike as I'm sure Viktor would find it. Whoever put that there was clearly trying to make this a romantic setting for the *pakhan* and his wife, but this isn't a honeymoon suite.

I'm pretty sure it's about to be a torture chamber.

Viktor closes the doors behind us with a heavy *thud*, the click of the lock sending a chill over my skin. I stand in the center of the room uncertainly, my back to him, my fingers trembling despite the warmth. I know he's waiting for me to turn around, but I'm going to make him command me. I'm going to make him drag every single bit of obedience out of me, because fuck it. If I'm already in trouble, I might as well go all the fucking way.

I don't think meekness is going to save me now.

"Turn around, Caterina," Viktor finally barks, his voice cold and harsh. I don't hesitate, but I obey slowly, turning until I'm looking at my husband, my leather flats scraping against the wooden floor. He doesn't look like the man who pretended to care for me so tenderly in the cabin safe house. He's not wearing jeans and a rolled-up flannel now, his hair loose and messy around his face. There's no kindness in his eyes. He's dressed the way he always did back home, in an expensive, tailored suit with the jacket off and no tie, his hair styled back smoothly, his face expressionless. The only emotion I see is in his eyes, and the anger is evident there, as well as how hard he's working to hold it back. That terrifies me most of all because I have no idea if he intends to unleash all of that carefully controlled rage on me or keep some of his control.

"Eyes down," he barks, taking a step towards me and then another. "It's time you learn your place, Caterina, and how a wife should behave with her husband. You've lost every privilege that you've ever had with me. In time, perhaps, you can earn them back."

I drop my gaze instantly, biting my lower lip. I don't want to let him see my fear, but I can feel my panic rising bit by bit as he speaks. I don't think Viktor will hurt me the way Andrei and Stepan did, but he can hurt me in other ways—and even then, I'm not entirely certain that he won't. It's become clear that I know this man even less than I thought I did, and I'm terrified of what more there is to find out.

"Very good," he says, his voice curling around me like smoke, thick and seductive and deadly. "You're obeying. That's a good start. This will be easier on you if you obey."

That shouldn't send a thrill through me. It shouldn't make my fingers tingle for reasons that have nothing to do with the fear quivering in my stomach. It shouldn't make my heart speed up a little, my pulse leaping into my throat. I shouldn't want to hear Viktor tell me to *obey*, but something dark and deviant inside of me thrills to the sound of my husband's thickly accented voice ordering me, here in the rich trappings of our bedroom in this secluded Russian castle.

"Let's see if you can obey this well in all things. On your knees, Caterina. On your knees for your master."

Master. He's never called himself that before, and I feel that dark thrill again, something foreign sparking in my blood and making my cheeks flush. Nothing about that should turn me on, but as I sink to my knees, feeling the thick tapestry of the rug through the thin cashmere of my dress, my heart speeds up another notch.

"Very good." Viktor steps closer, and I can see when I look up from under my lashes that he's undoing the cuffs of his shirtsleeves, slowly and methodically. My pulse beats against my throat as he starts to roll up those sleeves, just as slowly, until the crisp white fabric is above his elbows.

He clasps his hands in front of himself, looking down at me. "Do you know what's going to happen now, Caterina?"

"No," I whisper, and that's somewhat true. I know he's going to punish me, but I have no idea how or in what way. I don't want to speak any of my darkest fears aloud and give him ideas if he hasn't thought of them already.

"You're going to be punished for running away." His voice is rich, almost seductive, as if this is a pleasure for him. *What am I thinking?* Of course it's a pleasure for him. He's taken pleasure in punishing me before when he spanked me at my home after he'd thought I'd run off with the girls. I wonder if this will be better or worse, if he'll be more or less angry that I ran off on my own, instead of with his children as he'd thought.

From the look on his face when his men dragged me back, I don't think he's going to be less angry. Maybe just as angry but in a different way.

"What do you think your punishment should be?" Viktor asks casually, still looking down at me. "What kind of punishment is appropriate for a wayward wife who humiliates her husband in front of all of his men?"

"I'm sure I don't know," I say quietly, trying to keep any hint of defiance out of my voice. I want to yell at him, accuse him, tell him that he's a fucking monster, but I don't dare make this worse than it's already going to be. My hands are trembling, knotted in my lap, and although it takes everything in me to speak to him in a way that might mollify him just a little, I know that's my best chance of making it out of this in one piece.

"I meant it when I said I might lock you in a room naked," Viktor says thoughtfully. "Many men would do far worse. I could give you to my men for a night since you're so eager to leave my side. I'm sure once they were done with you, you'd be grateful to return to my tender mercies. Or I could keep you in one of the towers, caged even, like the pretty bird that you are." He reaches down, brushing a strand of hair away from my face. I shiver when his fingers touch my cheek. I don't want the touch to send electricity over my skin. I don't want the shudder to be one of pleasure or for his touch to make my heart beat faster in my chest for reasons that have nothing to do with fear.

I also don't want to think about the way he touched my face in his bedroom in the cabin, how he kissed me softly and whispered to me how beautiful I was. I don't want to think about the way he'd cupped my cheek in the hotel room before I'd overheard his phone call, how he'd looked at me as if I was the most beautiful thing in the world and made me wonder, just for a moment, if there could be more for us.

Clearly, I'd been wrong. I'd been so wrong. And now his touch makes my stomach curdle.

"We'll start with something simpler I think, since you've obeyed so well today." Viktor runs his fingers through my hair, gently at first, until his hand slides around the back of my head and I feel them twist, knotting in the thick locks and pulling my head back so that I'm looking up at him.

I let out a small whimper of pain despite myself. His hand is tight in my hair, holding my head in place, and his gaze rakes over my face, over the still-healing bruises and pause on my lips, then back up to my eyes.

"I meant what I said, you know," he says quietly. "You are very beautiful, Caterina. My beautiful bride. And I don't intend to mar that beauty the way those beasts did, if you're afraid of that. But I will punish you nonetheless."

He reaches down then, undoing his belt with one hand, and I know what's coming next. He starts to undo his zipper, but then he pauses, his hand going still.

"I was going to fuck your mouth for my own pleasure," he says thoughtfully. "But I don't think a disobedient wife has earned the right to suck her husband's cock, even as a punishment. So we'll start with something else instead." Viktor takes a step back. "Stand up and strip for me, Caterina. All the way. Every bit, until you're bare."

Somehow that's worse than being forced to suck him off. I don't want to touch him in any way, not anymore—or at least that's what I'm telling myself, despite the traitorous shivers of arousal that I can feel crawling across my skin. But he knows how I feel about my body, about my appearance now. And he knows how vulnerable it will make me feel to strip down for him.

But I know I have no choice.

Slowly, I get to my feet, keeping my eyes down. I kick off my leather flats, pushing them away, and Viktor clears his throat.

"Look at me while you do it," he instructs. "I want to see your face."

It just keeps getting worse. I look up at him, trying with every bit of self-control I have not to let him see the anger in my eyes, the resentment. I try to look meek, repentant even, a woman who knows she was wrong. It's the only way I'm going to survive this. That's all this is anymore, just like it was with Franco, a game of survival. And no matter how much that breaks my heart or how sick it makes me to know that Viktor turned out to be no better, I have to get through this.

In a way, he's worse because Franco was never this diabolical. He was never capable of planning such a complete and utter deception.

I thought I'd married a monster before.

But Viktor is so much worse.

I raise my eyes to my husband's icy gaze, meeting them without so much as a flinch.

And then I bend down, reaching for the hem of my dress.

CATERINA

*E*very inch of clothing that I remove is excruciating.

Not physically. Something like undressing isn't really painful anymore, thankfully. But as I pull my dress over my head, I can feel his eyes raking over me in a way that isn't sweet or caring anymore. It feels as if he's flaying my flesh from my bones with his gaze, taking me apart, taking whatever dignity I had left. I can feel the weight of his gaze, the anger in it, the cruelty, and as I let the dress fall to the floor and stand there in the rose-colored silk underwear that he purchased me, I can feel myself starting to shiver.

And yet, underneath it all, I feel a glimmer of heat. There's lust in his gaze, too, even if it's a cruel lust. And something deep within me wants to know what he'll do next, how far he'll push me, what he'll make me feel. I hadn't forgotten the shock of arousal I'd felt when he'd bent me over my bed and spanked me, the way I'd felt horrified and humiliated and terribly turned on all at once, confused more than anything else. I hadn't forgotten how it felt when I went back to him, and he took me in every possible way, forcing an orgasm from me as he fucked me hard and took my ass for the first time.

If this were a different sort of night, I would feel the urge to fight back, to be defiant, to bait him. But I've gone too far, and I'm afraid of what might happen if I do. I'm afraid of *him*.

My husband. A man with all the power in the world over me.

"All of it," Viktor says clearly, his voice thickly accented and harsh. "Don't make me ask a third time, Caterina. Or it will be so much worse for you."

I nod, my throat suddenly tight. I reach for the clasp of the silky wireless bra, feeling my nipples stiffen under the silk despite myself as I undo it. I don't want him to see even a hint of arousal, but something about undressing under his harsh gaze while he remains fully clothed sparks something in me, flushing my skin as I slide the straps down my arms. I tell myself that it's just the heat of the fire, that it's built too high, but I know that's not the truth.

I know as I let the bra fall to the floor that even if I were given the chance to leave this room, I'm not entirely sure that I would.

Slipping my fingers under the edges of the silk panties, I push them down my hips, grateful to have them off if only so that he doesn't get a chance to see the way the silk has started to cling damply to my folds, the rose silk darkening at the space between my thighs.

I don't want him to know that this is turning me on—not yet, anyway. At some point, I know he'll find out regardless. And that shameful thought sends another flush of heat over my skin, turning my cheeks red for a reason that I know has nothing to do with the heat of the fire.

"Very good," Viktor says approvingly, his eyes skating over me as if he were appraising art or something else that he wanted to possess. Something that would belong to him.

I already do.

"Go to the bed," he instructs, his voice sharp. "Grab on to the bedpost at the foot of it, and bend over at the waist, Caterina. Keep your legs together for now."

My pulse leaps in my throat. I know what comes now. I can hear the clink of his belt buckle as he undoes it, and I want to believe that he's just getting ready to fuck me, but I know that's not the case. In just a moment, I'm going to feel the heat of that belt across my ass, and the thought should be absolutely horrifying.

It shouldn't make me feel a pulse of heat between my thighs or an answering wetness that threatens to drip onto my thighs, making my knees tremble with anticipation. *What kind of woman* wants *her husband to spank her? What kind of woman* wants *to be disciplined?* I hadn't been as sheltered as some mafia daughters. I'd gone to college. I knew about sex, what men liked, and even some things that I would have considered kinky. But nothing could have prepared me for wrapping my hands around the cool mahogany of a bedpost in my husband's bedroom, bending over naked for him to punish me with a belt, and feeling a flutter of what I know beyond a shadow of a doubt is anticipation deep in my belly.

"Beautiful," Viktor whispers. I hear the snap of the leather as he folds the belt in half, and then I can feel him standing very close to me, his hand hovering over the curve of my ass. He strokes the belt over that curve, the cool leather a shock against my flushed skin, and I hear the noise he makes deep in his throat. "You're so lovely when you submit to me, Caterina. When you know that your place is here, obeying me. Giving in to me."

I'm not going to give in to you, I want to snap, gritting my teeth. But my body already is. I know that with the first crack of that belt, there's going to be pain, but there's also going to be pleasure. I can feel the gathering heat between my thighs, the need, the way I'm already starting to ache to be touched. This is almost fucking *foreplay*, and I hate myself as much as I hate him for that being the case.

I despise and desire my husband in almost equal measure, it seems. And there doesn't seem to be anything that I can do to change that, either. No matter what despicable things he does.

He runs the belt over the curve of my other ass cheek, down to the top of my thigh, and a shudder ripples through me. A gasp slips from my mouth when I feel the leather move away from my skin, and I know any second now I'm going to feel the first lash.

"Twenty, I think," Viktor says, his voice rougher around the edges than before. I can hear the desire there, thickening the accented syllables, and I swallow hard.

"Count them out loud, Caterina," he orders, and then before I can so much as draw a breath, the belt comes down across my ass.

"One!" I gasp out, my fingers clutching the bedpost, my body jerking backward with the force of the blow. I feel heat blossoming across my skin, pain radiating out from the stripe that the belt made across my pale flesh. I hear Viktor's grunt as he brings it down again, this time across the other side, and I cry out. "Two!"

"Very good, my little *printsessa*. See? You can be obedient when you need to be." Viktor brings down the belt again.

"Three." I can feel a sob rising in my throat, my ass aching already from the stinging, burning pain, but between my legs is a throbbing heat, my thighs sticky with desire. If Viktor decided in the next second to grab my hips and fuck me here and now, I know I'd come in a matter of moments. "Four!" I cry out as he brings it down again, and I can hear his breathing behind me, heavy and full of the same lust radiating through me.

He brings the belt down in alternating strokes, across my cheeks, down to the sit-spot where my ass meets my thighs, and I gasp out each one, my fingers so tight around the bedpost that my knuckles turn white. Each crack of the belt against my skin is a new and more intense pain, but it's immediately followed by a burst of pleasure, an aching need that makes me want to whimper and sob and beg. I can *feel* my clit, swollen and pulsing, and I want Viktor to touch me there, to brush his finger over it, run his tongue over the place where I need it the most. A memory of him doing exactly that in the cabin sends another shudder through me, and I hear Viktor's dark chuckle behind me as he brings down the fifteenth stroke of the belt.

"You don't have to pretend that this doesn't turn you on, my little *printsessa*," he says, dark humor in his tone. "I know how wet you are. If I touched your pretty pussy right now, you'd be dripping for me, exactly the way you are when I fuck you with my hard Bratva cock. You claim to despise me so much, to be above such a thing, but I've made you beg for it." He chuckles again, bringing down the belt, and I nearly scream as it comes down across a prior lash, my nails digging into the wood of the bedpost. "I made you beg to come with my cock in your ass, *printsessa*, so don't feel that you need to pretend that this doesn't make you fucking soaking wet."

I let out a small sob, my head bending forward as he brings down the next. "Seventeen," I moan, squeezing the bedpost. *Only three more. I can do this.* I feel as if I'm going to collapse from the pain and explode from need all at once, my entire body wound taut with the competing sensations.

"Eighteen. Nineteen!" I bite my lip as Viktor brings down the belt in two quick successive strokes, and then he steps closer, running the leather of the belt over the rising welts on my cheeks. It feels cool against my flaming skin, and Viktor brushes it over my other cheek before stepping back.

"I don't think there's an inch of bare skin here left for me to whip," he says, his voice deepening. "So I have something better in mind. Spread your legs, Caterina."

"What?" I wrench my head around, my eyes opening wide with fear as I look at him. I'm pretty sure I know exactly what he means, and I don't want it. *I don't, right?* I can't want that. The sudden throb of heat between my legs at the thought means nothing.

"Don't make me ask twice, *printsessa*," Viktor says darkly. "Or I'll add five strokes."

I gasp, sliding my feet apart instantly. Just the thought of *one* stroke where I know he intends to land it is almost too much. I can't imagine more. *Five more? Impossible.*

I spread my legs until he commands me to stop, and my head drops forward, my cheeks flaming with embarrassment. I know how exposed I am; I can feel my folds parting, every inch of me exposed to him, from the tight hole between my cheeks down to my aching, pulsing clit. I know he can see the glistening on my thighs, the wetness gathered where I want his cock, and it's all I can do not to beg him to fuck me here and now. I need it, I want it, and only the last remaining shreds of my pride keep me from telling him exactly that.

"Arch your back," Viktor instructs, and I blush more deeply than ever before as I force myself to obey. The pose pushes my ass out, gives him an even better view of everything that's entirely on display for him. Everything that belongs to him, whether I like it or not.

I don't like it. I don't.

"Such a beautiful pussy." Viktor's voice is a deep, lustful growl. "Such a shame that I can't pleasure her the way she deserves. But *you* don't deserve it, my lovely bride. You don't deserve the orgasms I could give you. Not with the way you've behaved. But perhaps, if you're very good—" he steps forward, his hand resting on my inner thigh, so close to where the heat is radiating off of me in waves. "Perhaps in time, you can earn those privileges back."

I swallow hard, forcing myself not to beg. Not to tell him how much I want it.

Viktor steps back, and I hear him snap the belt. "Last one, *printsessa*. Call it out unless you want more."

Chills ripple over my skin, and I moan, knowing what's coming next. My only warning is the *swish* of cool air against my swollen, overheated flesh, and then the pain that blossoms from between my legs as the belt connects with my soft, sensitive folds, the end of it snapping against my hard clit, threatens to bring me to my knees.

It also brings me so close to coming that I scream with the mingled pain and pleasure, my entire body shaking as I cling to the bedpost for dear life.

I'm still trembling when I see Viktor toss the belt onto the bed, his hand resting on one of my red, welted cheeks as he looks down at me.

"You took those blows very well, *printsessa*." His voice is smooth, almost pleased. He makes a small, soothing circle on my cheek with his hand, his voice softer now. "I'll never hurt you, Caterina. Not like those animals who kidnapped you did."

A burst of resentment blossoms through me, cutting through the fog of arousal and need. I want to scream at him that he can't call them animals or claim that he wouldn't hurt me like that, not when he set the whole fucking thing up. But I don't because I'm barely standing under my own power after his punishment, and I can't take anymore right now. I would either collapse or combust, and I can't bear the thought of either. So instead, I look directly ahead, still holding the position he instructed me to until he tells me otherwise, and listen to him speak.

"You are still my wife, Caterina," Viktor says, some of the dark severity returning to his voice. "There are certain things that I expect from you. There will be consequences if you try to leave me, disobey me, or embarrass me. There *must* be, for my household to run the way it's intended. How can I expect my staff or my men to obey me if my own wife will not? How can I expect them to be content when you are given everything, and you still try to run from me?" He's quiet for a moment. "What I'm doing is for your own protection, Caterina."

Another rush of resentment and anger runs through me, leaving me quivering under his touch. "I could protect myself," I hiss. "Wasn't that the point of those lessons? Or was that all just another sham?"

I bite my lip then, forcing myself not to say anything else, not to make it worse. I can feel Viktor's hand tensing, pressing against the welts.

"I see your sharp tongue is back." He steps forward, reaching for my chin and turning my face so that I'm looking at him. I meet his gaze, giving him just a hint of the defiance that I want to throw in his face so badly. "You'll endure one of my punishments every night, Caterina, until you learn to submit to me. The sooner you come to terms with that, the happier your life with me will be."

He lets go of my jaw with a jerk, stepping backward. "You can stand up and dress now," he says casually, reaching for his belt to thread it through his pants. "I'm sure you want to talk to your friends."

"Am I allowed to go downstairs, then?" It's difficult to pry my fingers away from the bedpost. My hands and back feel stiff, and I turn away from him, unable to meet his eyes as I gather my clothes up from the floor. I know it could have been so much worse, but I'm burning with resentment as much as unfulfilled need.

Viktor steps up behind me as I reach for my underwear, his hand going to my ass. I freeze in place as his hand slips between my cheeks, across my drenched folds, and I gasp as he slips a finger inside of me, a shock of pleasure rushing over me that makes me feel even more humiliated than before.

I want him to stop. I want him to keep going. I *want*, and I don't know how to untangle all of it.

He chuckles darkly, pulling his finger free and reaching out with his other hand to tip my chin up so that I'm forced to watch as he licks my arousal from his finger. "Delicious," he says with a smirk. "You're so very wet for me. You must need to come so badly." His hand tightens on my jaw. "Is that true, *printsessa*? Do you need me to make you come?"

I swallow hard. I know what the penalty will be for lying to him, but I can't bring myself to admit it. I can't tell him that the spanking made me want him to fuck me, to debase me even more, to make me beg and writhe and scream for him even while I hate him with every fiber of my being.

"No," I whisper, and Viktor laughs, slapping my welted ass and making me cry out.

"I'll remember you lied when it comes time for your punishment tonight." He strides towards the door, twisting the knob and making me grab my dress and hold it in front of myself, just in case someone happens to be walking by. "Enjoy sitting down at dinner tonight," he says, his lips twisting in a cruel smile. "I'll see you then, *printsessa*."

And then he walks out, leaving me there.

CATERINA

Sofia and Ana are in the large living room when I come downstairs, sitting by the roaring fire on the sofa with a tea service in front of them. They're talking quietly when I walk in, trying not to make it evident from the way I'm walking that Viktor just whipped me thoroughly with his belt. It's bad enough that I can feel the silk of my panties clinging between my thighs, wet and cool against my flushed skin.

"Caterina!" Sofia leaps up from the sofa, setting her cup down and coming around to embrace me gently. I want to sink into her arms and sob, but I manage to avoid doing that, hugging her back instead and then coming to sit next to her as she pours me a cup of tea, forcing myself not to wince. Fortunately, the sofa is very soft, making it easier to sit down normally, but I'm dreading dinner.

Ana is sitting on her other side, her feet tucked up underneath her. I can see her wheelchair folded up next to the sofa, and my chest tightens. I'd hoped that things had gotten easier for her while I was gone, but that doesn't seem to be the case.

I open my mouth to say something, but I'm interrupted by a knock at the door. A pretty girl who looks to be in her early twenties walks in, dressed in a black and white uniform. It's not revealing at all, but it looks exactly like others that I glimpsed walking in, and I can only guess that she must be part of the staff. I wonder bitterly if she's one of the girls Viktor has bought, someone like Sasha maybe, that he gave the option of a different kind of job.

"More tea?" the girl asks sweetly, and Sofia nods.

"Thank you, and extra honey and cream as well." She picks up the tea tray, handing it to the blonde girl. "Thank you," Sofia says again, and the girl gives a quick nod, her eyes down as she carries it out.

My stomach twists with nausea again. I have no real reason to think the girl is anything other than ordinary household staff, but Viktor has made it so that I can't help but think the worst of him. After all, why shouldn't I?

"Are you okay?" Sofia asks gently, her hand covering mine. "Luca told me some of what happened to you. I'm absolutely horrified. But he also said you're recovering well?"

The sudden insane urge to tell her the truth grips me, what I'd overheard, how certain I am that Viktor staged the entire kidnapping to break me, to make me submit to him, then pretended to care for me and nurse me back to health to earn my loyalty. But I stop just short of actually starting to say the words. I don't know if she'll believe me if I tell her. There was a time when I would have felt that I could tell her anything, but she isn't just my friend. She's also Luca's wife, and she has concerns of her own, her own family to manage, and her own place in the hierarchy. I can't endanger her by telling her something that could cause so many problems. If she believes me, she might tell Luca—and there's no telling what could come after that. Luca might say that the treaty is more important than saving me from a man who would do such a thing, despite his promises to protect me if Viktor turned out to be dangerous—a thing that could strain their relationship. Or he might break the bargain, and the fallout from that would be severe, too.

I'd been ready to go to Luca when I'd thought that I might be able to escape. But I know that it's no longer an option. We're all under his roof, in his safe house that's practically a fortress, and it's not safe for any of us.

What Viktor did will remain between the two of us, no matter how much I want it to be otherwise. No matter how much I want to be free.

"I'm getting better," I manage. "Viktor kept me in the other safe house long enough to let me recover as much as I could before moving me here."

"I know how hard it is," Ana says softly from the other side of Sofia. "I still don't feel like myself, even though the doctors all say the injuries are healing well. I can't make myself try to walk—" she stops, her voice cracking a little. "You're braver than I am, Cat," she finishes with a small smile. "But then again, you always were brave."

"We all are," I say firmly. "All three of us." I glance at Sofia, remembering how she was responsible for Franco's death. She'd saved herself and Ana and maybe even me too, when she'd faced him down and shot him.

Sofia bites her lip, her hand going to touch her stomach as the blonde girl brings in another tea tray and pours three cups before slipping away. I can see the way she breathes in when her hand smooths over the small bump, and I can tell how frightened she is, even though she's doing a good job of hiding it.

"Viktor and Luca will fix this," Sofia says confidently. "Liam is coming as well, as soon as he locks down what's happening in Boston and has enough men ready there to keep Alexei from moving in. They won't let anything happen to us." Her hand stays on her stomach, and I know that the *us* encompasses her future son or daughter.

My chest tightens as I think of the baby I might have had. I have no idea if I'd been pregnant when I was kidnapped, but there's no way that any child could have survived what was done to me. Just the thought makes me feel hollow, and I keep my hands planted firmly in my lap, even as I want to let them stray to my stomach. I don't want to give anyone the wrong idea, and I don't want to explain. I know that it sounds crazy that I was so sure that I might be pregnant, when there hadn't been any real signs. It had just been a feeling, and I know that doesn't mean anything at all.

One thing has become very clear to me: feelings have no place in my life anymore.

We all chat for a while longer, the conversation shifting to more normal things—or as normal as we can manage, given the state of our lives. Sofia talks about her violin practice, a hint of wistfulness in her voice as she mentions a performance that was coming up, one that she'll almost certainly miss now. She talks about her doctor's appointment just before they left and how she and Luca agreed not to find out the sex of the baby until he or she actually arrived. "He wants it to be a surprise," she says, smoothing her hands over her jeans. "And I think that's a nice idea."

"Have you talked about names?"

"A little." Sofia laughs. "He's very sure that it's a boy, so he insists on Giovanni, for my father, if it's a boy. Which I think is very sweet."

"It is sweet," Ana says softly, and I can hear a hint of wistfulness in her voice, too. I hadn't forgotten what she said when the three of us went shopping for my wedding dress, how badly she wants love, and how sure she is that she'll never find it now.

"How are you doing?" I ask her, leaning forward. "How are—things?" It's hard to know what words to use when I talk about what happened to her. I don't know if the guilt will ever entirely go away, that it was my husband who was responsible for it. And I don't know if she'll ever fully recover. She's still thin to the point of waifishness, as much as she was when she was a ballerina, if not more. I know from what Sofia told me that she *could* walk again but that she can't bring herself to try. Her doctors have been pushing her, from what I'd heard just before I left for Moscow with Viktor, but to no avail.

Ana has decided that she's broken beyond repair, and no one, not doctors or friends, can convince her otherwise.

If Franco wasn't already dead, I'd kill him again myself, I think bitterly, looking at Ana's pale face. After all, I've already killed one man.

I wonder what Sofia or Ana would think if they knew. Sofia has done it too, pulled a trigger, and watched a man who deserved to die get his just deserts at her hand. Ana hasn't, but I know she was glad that Franco was dead.

I don't think either one of them would judge me for it—they might even praise me—but at the same time, I can't bring myself to say it out loud. As glad as I am that I killed Stepan, and as good as that revenge felt, it's colored now by the fact that Viktor had a hand in it. Stepan was a pawn, and that takes some of the satisfaction out of it.

Viktor was the one who should have died for that, not Stepan—or maybe both of them. Stepan might have been the tool, but Viktor was the one who ordered it. And that makes me feel a deep bitterness that twists my stomach and makes me feel nauseous, a nausea that climbs my stomach and slides up into my throat, until—

"Oh god." I jump up, clapping my hand over my mouth and running for the nearest bathroom. At first, I'm unsure where it is, and I have a horrid feeling that I'm going to vomit all over the gleaming hardwood floor, where everyone will see. I press my hand tighter against my mouth, looking wildly around, and then I see a small door that I hope leads to a downstairs bathroom and not some kind of linen closet or something.

It does, and I only just make it to the toilet in time to fall to my knees and heave into it, clutching the sides as the tea and minimal amount of food that I've eaten all come rushing up. I squeeze my eyes shut, feeling the hot tears slide down my cheeks, and I wonder, not for the first time, how I'm going to endure this. How I'm going to go on.

Maybe I should have jumped off that balcony on my wedding night and saved myself so much pain.

If Sofia and Ana notice how quiet I am until dinnertime, they don't mention it. We all change before dinner, and Viktor, thankfully, isn't upstairs in our room. I don't know at first *what* I'm going to change into, since the cashmere dress I'm wearing is the only item of clothing I have. When I go back upstairs and look in the wardrobe and the closet, I'm shocked to see that sometime either before we arrived or since I've been upstairs, it's been fully stocked with clothing of various styles in my size—jeans and t-shirts, workout clothes, bras and panties, casual dresses and more elegant ones. I pick out a black knee-length dress with a gold metallic collar, even though I know Viktor doesn't like me in black. Especially now, as thin and pale as I am, I know he'll hate it.

Good, I think viciously. *Let him hate it.* Maybe it will make my punishment later worse, but I can't bring myself to care. Any small act of defiance that I can manage is all I can think of to make this even the slightest bit tolerable. He wants me to submit to him, but all I want to do is show him that I'm still not broken, despite what he did to me. Despite what I know, he still plans to do.

I slip on a pair of black heels and add gold jewelry, sweeping my dark hair up into a bun at the back of my head, another thing that I know Viktor doesn't care for. He prefers my hair in a chignon or loose, but I'm going to show him that there are still decisions I can make for myself.

I might be his wife, but I'm not his possession. And I'll die before I let him hear me beg again.

VIKTOR

*D*inner is a tense affair.

Caterina comes down in a black dress that found its way into her wardrobe somehow—I instructed the staff not to purchase anything black for her, but it's clear that someone along the way didn't pay attention. It makes her look gaunt and pale, and I can see from the defiant glint in her eyes that she dressed that way on purpose.

That's okay, I think with a savage pleasure as she walks to the dinner table. It'll make punishing her later all that much more enjoyable. She'll learn to bend to me, or she'll suffer the consequences. Either will bring me pleasure and peace—eventually.

Yet again, the little stunt that she pulled in Moscow has changed things between us. I'd thought that they might change for the better when she'd been recovering in the cabin. I hadn't realized until I'd thought I might lose her how much I cared. I'd felt that same fear and dread that I'd felt with Vera come rushing back, all of the old guilt and hurt eating at me until all I could think of was nursing Caterina back to health until she was strong enough to learn the things she might need to defend herself and to take the revenge I'd offered her.

But then, for some reason that I can't fathom, she'd decided to try to run. Despite everything I'd done for her, all the ways I'd tried to show her the feelings that were growing, the things I'd done to show her that she was still beautiful and desirable to me, she'd thrown it all away in a desperate bid to steal from me and try to leave Moscow.

I still can't fathom what she was thinking. The money she'd taken from me wouldn't have lasted long, and she doesn't speak Russian. Without identification or contacts, she wouldn't have been able to get out of Russia. She might have had some harebrained plan to contact Luca, but I'd bet anything that she wouldn't even have remembered the number to call him at.

It had been a ridiculous, barely-baked, impossible plan. It had, frankly, been the plan of a desperate woman. For the life of me, I can't come up with a reason why Caterina would be so desperate to escape me that she would have done such a massively foolish thing—especially with the danger that she'd already escaped once still out there.

At this point, I don't even care what the why of it is. All I want to do is make sure that it won't happen again, that Caterina is made aware of her duties as my wife, and that she learns her place. That she learns to obey me. I don't have time for a disobedient wife that I have to watch like a hawk—not again. I married Caterina first and foremost because she understood this life and because I had believed she would understand the role she was meant to inhabit.

Since it seems that she doesn't, I intend to make certain that she grasps those things very soon.

It brings me some pleasure to see her sitting gingerly in the chair at the table, clearly uncomfortable on her sore ass. It also gives me an uncomfortable half-erection every time she shifts in place, and I remember our session earlier. The vision of Caterina bent over and grasping the bedpost, her upturned ass welted and red isn't one I'll forget soon. Neither will I forget the sight of her legs spread and pussy dripping, her body responding despite itself, or the sound of her cry when I whipped that same drenched pussy with my belt for the first time.

I intend to punish her similarly later. But for now, her discomfort is distracting me from other, less pleasurable matters at hand.

Namely, what to do about my traitorous former brigadier, and the mutiny he's enacted.

Liam will be arriving tomorrow, and Luca and I will meet with him then to decide what needs to be done. Until then, I can distract myself with my disobedient, wayward bride and the ways I plan to bring her to heel.

Caterina is almost entirely silent at the dinner table, and she stayed close-lipped all the way upstairs to our bedroom once we retire for the night, after wine in the living room with the others in front of the fire.

"It's much more pleasant to be here than the cabin, don't you think?" I ask conversationally as I close the bedroom door, striding towards the wardrobe and taking off my cufflinks. "A cook that can make us decent food again, good wine, better company." I give her a terse smile, one that she doesn't return. "Proper clothing." I let my gaze rake over her, the smile turning lascivious. "Although I think now, wife, I would prefer you with less clothing." I flick my hand at her. "All of it, off. Now."

Caterina blinks at me. "You can't mean to—"

The smile never leaves my face, though it doesn't quite meet my eyes. "I told you, every night until you learn to submit to me. That begins tonight. Take that awful dress off. I don't want to see it on you again."

Caterina's chin tilts up. "I like it, actually."

"I don't give a shit what you like, *printsessa*," I tell her flatly, my voice cold. "I married you for a reason—your bloodline and your knowledge of this life. I thought that would make you an easy wife, one who would fit in without much trouble, but it seems I was wrong. If I have to break you to make you into the woman that I need, then that's what I'll do."

Something crumples in her face at that, her skin paling slightly and the defiance draining out of her eyes. I don't understand her reaction, but I push my confusion away. *It doesn't matter.* I'm not here to worry about my wife's feelings; I'm here to ensure that she doesn't continue to make my life more difficult than she already has.

Things are going to be different between us now. Just not the way I had hoped.

"Strip," I order her again, my expression taut. "I don't like repeating myself, Caterina. You know that."

I see her jaw tighten, but she starts to obey, slowly. She kicks off her heels, and I retreat back towards the bed, watching her as she slowly unzips the back of her dress, pushing it off of her shoulders and down her hips, leaving her in only the black panties that she'd worn underneath.

"You didn't wear a bra to dinner?" I make a *tsk*ing sound with my tongue, shaking my head. "That's hardly appropriate for the *pakhan*'s wife, don't you think?"

"They're uncomfortable while I'm still healing," Caterina protests, shrugging. "And I don't really need one." She gestures to her small breasts, and I let my gaze drag across them, savoring the sight of the small, perfect shapes and her pink nipples, already hardening despite the warmth of the room.

I know why that is, of course. She wants me, even though she doesn't want to admit it. The things I do to her turn her on, but she's too embarrassed to say it aloud, to give in.

Before I'm done with her, though, she'll beg for it. Maybe not tonight, maybe not for some time, but my wife will be begging for me to fuck her before I'm finished allocating out all of the punishment that I have planned for her.

"Take them off." I motion to her panties. "That'll be an additional punishment for making me ask yet again."

Caterina flushes, her cheeks turning a particularly lovely shade of pink as she obeys, hooking her thumbs under the edges and pushing them down her slender hips. I see the hint of dark hair as the panties slide down, and I give her a tight, forbidding smile.

"Go into the bathroom." I gesture towards the adjoining door. "Now."

Caterina follows my gaze down to her thick pubic hair and back up, clearly remembering what I'd ordered her to do back home, just before everything went to shit.

"Viktor—"

"Caterina." My voice drops an octave, dark and threatening. "If I have to continue repeating my orders, your punishment will be much worse than what I had originally intended for you tonight. Now go. I'll be right behind you. Into the bathroom."

Her cheeks are flaming red, but she obeys this time, turning and walking in the direction I've instructed. Following, I'm treated to a lovely view of her perfect, pert ass, striped red from her spanking earlier, the welts bright against her pale flesh.

I gesture towards the granite countertop. "Can you sit on the edge yourself, or do I need to pick you up?"

I see another flare of defiance in her eyes, and I almost expect her to argue again. *Go ahead,* I think, narrowing my eyes at her. All it will do is give me yet another reason to dish out punishment, something that I'm more than happy to do.

She pushes herself up on the countertop, wincing a little as her ass meets the cold granite. Her thighs are pressed tightly together, something that I don't intend to allow for very long.

"Spread your legs," I tell her sharply. "As wide as you can, and stay that way."

Caterina flushes even more red than she was before, if that were possible. Still, she dutifully obeys this time, spreading her thighs until she's splayed open for me. I finally tell her curtly that that's enough. I take a moment to enjoy the view—her pussy is as lovely as the rest of her, shades of pink darkening where the blood is rushing to her skin, her lips already plumping with arousal despite herself. I force myself not to grin—my wife likes me telling her what to do, forcing her to display herself for me, pushing her past her limits. Her body tells the truth, even if she won't.

But one thing that's become abundantly clear to me during her little escape attempt in Moscow is that my wife is a woman whose word can't be trusted.

I reach for the far end of the sink, where I've left a can of shaving gel, clippers, and a razor. Caterina's eyes go wide as I turn the clippers on, intending to cut down the length of her pubic hair before I shave her—every inch of her pussy—bare. Myself.

"Viktor, you're not going to—"

"Oh, I am," I assure her. "I told you I wanted this bare. You didn't do it yourself, so now you'll endure the embarrassment of having me do it for you. And you won't breathe a word of complaint."

Caterina's lips go very thin, pressed together tightly, and I see her breathing quicken, her chest rising and falling as I bring the buzzing clippers very close to her spread pussy, all of it bare and open for me to see exactly what I'm doing.

She gasps when the buzzing touches her folds, her hands clenching the edge of the countertop as the clippers cut through the hair. "Who's going to clean up the hair?" she asks through gritted teeth as I slide them up one side.

"The maids, of course, in the morning," I tell her with a tight smile. "Who else?"

"Viktor!" She gasps my name. "You can't—they'll think—"

"They won't think. That's not their job." I give her one more swipe with the clippers, the hair short enough now for me to take the razor to it with ease. "As for your own personal embarrassment about it, you should have thought about that before you disobeyed me and ran away from me. You undercut *my* authority in front of all of my men, Caterina. You defied *me*, embarrassed *me*. Do you understand? I can't allow that. And now you're going to reap the consequences."

Caterina gasps again when I touch her with the shaving gel, spreading it over her hair as I turn on the tap, rinsing off the razor once before bringing it towards her pussy. She makes a small noise in the back of her throat when I make the first slow swipe, moving closer so that she can almost feel the heat of my breath against her inner thigh, spreading her folds with my thumbs as I inspect my work after each pass. I go as slowly as I can, wanting to draw out her humiliation, enjoying her discomfort. It's not turning her on as much as some of the things that I do to her, but I can see the gathering dampness, the way she twitches each time I touch her. She's aroused, and I intend to make that arousal much more unbearable for her as the night goes on.

When she's entirely bare, I stand up, reaching for a washcloth and running it under hot water. Caterina starts to close her legs, and I slap the inside of her thigh with one hand, hard.

"Not until I tell you that you can," I say sharply, wringing out the washcloth and coming to stand between her spread thighs again, running the warm cloth over her sensitive skin as I wash away any remaining trace of shaving gel or hair.

Caterina looks mortified, her cheeks burning red, and she won't meet my eyes, not even when I finally stand back and tell her that she can get off of the counter.

"Go and take up that same position on the bed," I tell her. "Back against the pillows. Unless you want another spanking?"

Caterina looks thoroughly alarmed at that, shaking her head as she slides down from the countertop. I see her sneak one glance at her newly shaved pussy in the mirror before slinking towards the door, slipping through it, and back into the bedroom.

To my surprise, when I walk back in, she's obeyed me perfectly. She's leaning back against the pillows, her thighs splayed open, feet flat on the bed. I walk around to the foot of it, sitting casually on the bench there as I look at her bare, flushed pussy, and take note of the glistening folds, the way I can see her clit poking out, red and swelling from arousal even though she hasn't touched herself yet.

"You were so wet earlier, after your punishment." I raise an eyebrow. "You must have needed to come very badly. That's a reward you'll have to earn. But perhaps you can have a little pleasure after enduring all of that."

Caterina blinks at me as if unsure of what I have planned. She's right to be suspicious, of course. Everything I have planned for her is intended to be a torment.

"Touch yourself," I tell her, one side of my mouth curling up in a half-smile. "However you would like to be touched. I want to watch you get that pussy dripping for me. But—" I raise a finger, narrowing my eyes at her. "You're not allowed to come. If you do, you'll regret it for days, I promise you that."

Caterina's lips part, her eyes widening, and I know she wants to argue. I know that pleasuring herself in front of me is the last thing in the world she wants to do. But she also knows that dragging it out and making me ask again will only make things worse for her in the end.

Slowly, her hand drifts down, her throat twitching as she swallows hard.

I watch her as much for my own pleasure as anything else. I enjoy having a woman on display, watching her touch herself in her unique way, and the idea of watching Caterina like this has always aroused me, fiercely. I just haven't had an opportunity yet to torture her in exactly this way.

Now I do.

Her fingers slide over her folds, drifting slowly down, tracing the edges of her swelling flesh. I can see the edges darkening, the skin growing puffy and aroused as she touches herself, avoiding her clit. I know why—she doesn't want to lose control, to get really and truly turned on, the way she would if she touched herself in earnest.

"Don't hold back," I tell her sternly. "Touch yourself the way you would if you were alone. I can tell the difference."

Caterina bites her lower lip, and then her fingers slide slowly, reluctantly up towards the swollen red bud between her folds, the spot that I know she wants so desperately to touch.

She can't hold back the moan that slips from her mouth as her fingers brush over it. Her head tilts back slightly, her lips parting, and her fingers move faster as if she can't help herself.

It's intoxicating, watching her. Her hand twitches, wanting to stop, wanting to continue, and I can see the arousal leaking from her pussy, coating her folds, making me wish that I could taste her. If she behaves well enough, maybe I will.

Not tonight, but soon. I imagine torturing her with my tongue, bringing her to the edge again and again, and then backing off, seeing her squirm and hearing her whimper and beg.

The idea of it is exquisite.

Her hand goes still suddenly, her chest heaving, and I smile at her, letting it spread slowly across my face. "Good girl," I tell her, watching her fingers tremble as she pulls them away from her clit. "Wait for it to ease up, and then start again. Do that over and over until I tell you to stop."

Caterina's teeth sink into her lower lip, and I know she's biting back a retort, some cutting comment that would tell me exactly what she thinks of my instructions. But she waits a few seconds, as instructed, and then her fingers start to move over her clit again.

I see her lose a little more control with each ebb and flow of her pleasure. Her head starts to tilt back, her mouth opening, her hand moving in quick, sharp circles that tells me how much she wants it. Her pussy is drenched, and I can see her clenching, wanting to be filled.

She won't get that tonight, at least not the way that she wants it.

"Stop." I stand up smoothly, and she pulls her hand away, her eyes wide and her chest heaving, small panting breaths slipping out. "Lie down," I tell her, striding towards the side of the bed. "Hands above your head."

There's a flicker of fear in her eyes, but I ignore it. The time for catering to her fears is passed. Tonight is going to remind her of exactly what she owes me.

It takes only a few moments to bind her to the bed. I hear her gasp when I secure her right wrist to the headboard, feel her try to squirm away. "Don't bother," I tell her sharply. "You know your punishment will happen whether you like it or not, Caterina."

Her mouth drops open, and all I can think about is how much I want to fill it with my throbbing cock—although right now, I don't entirely trust her not to bite it off. I've been achingly hard the entire time that I watched her play with herself, and right now, there's nothing that I want to do more than come. I want to be inside of her, somewhere, thrusting until I feel that few moments of blissful, perfect release.

Unfortunately, I have other priorities right now.

Slowly, I undo my belt buckle, watching her dark eyes flick to it and widen. "Your ass took the punishment today, but tonight I have other plans for you." With my belt hanging open, I walk to the foot of the bed, repeating the process of binding her to the bed with first one foot and then the other, until she's spread-eagled on the bed, her naked body bare to me.

I'll have to be more precise with her this way. I meant it today when I said I wouldn't hurt her, and I have no intention of reopening the wounds those animals left on her or causing her more damage. But I also intend for the spaces of bare, unharmed flesh that she has remaining to be marked by my belt so that she can remember exactly who it is that possesses her.

Caterina breathes in sharply when I pull my belt out of the loops, folding it in half. I reach out with one hand, stroking her breast, and her head drops back, her breath coming in small quick pants as she closes her eyes, swallowing hard. My cock throbs in response—even littered with healing cuts and bruises, my wife is an astonishingly gorgeous woman. I want her as much as I ever have—as much as I did on our wedding night, as much as I did back at the cabin.

Holding the belt in one hand, I bring it down on an unmarked space of flesh on her breast, the leather cracking close to her nipple, grazing it.

Caterina cries out, her head tilting back.

"Beg, and it might stop," I tell her darkly. "But until you do, your body is mine to do with as I please."

Her head turns towards me, her face full of some unreadable emotion, and she curls her upper lip, her eyes narrowing.

"I won't beg you any more than I did them. But then again, that's not what you wanted, was it?"

CATERINA

From the look on Viktor's face, you would have thought that what I just said didn't make any sense to him at all. As if I'd spoken in a foreign language.

Which doesn't make any sense to *me*.

My breast stings where the belt struck it, so precisely, that it didn't graze a single healing wound on the left side of my chest, but brushed against my nipple, which is stiff and hard, a sharp, almost pleasurable bolt of sensation still stinging there, after the strike of the belt.

I'm panting from what Viktor made me do earlier, humiliated from him shaving me, and altogether worn out from all of the paces he's put me through. I know the evening isn't close to done yet, and I close my eyes briefly, wondering if I should simply give up and beg him for mercy. Maybe then he'd let me be, at least.

But my pride won't let me. Not yet. Hopefully, not ever.

Viktor brings the belt down on my other breast, this time squarely on my nipple, and I yelp and cry out, pulling against the bindings on my wrists. Being tied down to the bed like this terrifies me and arouses me all at once. The idea of being helpless makes me feel panicked, but at the same time, being spread open for Viktor, lying here at his mercy, sends a rush of heat through me. He could do anything he liked to me, and seeing the *very* visible bulge in his suit trousers, I wish he would do something other than punish me.

I wish he would fuck me.

And I hate myself for wanting it.

The next strike of the belt comes on my inner thigh, again missing anything that isn't unhurt flesh. He makes precise strokes on the inside and outside of my thighs, and I jerk and cry out with each one. But the cries aren't just yelps of pain, each one ends on a gasp or a moan as the pleasure follows the sharp bite of the belt, and I grit my teeth, wanting to hold it back. But I can't seem to stay silent.

The only thing I can stop myself from doing is the one thing Viktor wants.

Although he did it earlier, I'm entirely unprepared for the belt striking my pussy. It comes down hard, and I scream, my face flushing hot as I think that surely someone in the house must have heard.

"Five," Viktor says. "What I threatened earlier, since you wore that awful dress to dinner. On purpose—I know you did. Count them, Caterina."

My mouth falls open. It was hard enough to count the strikes on my ass; I don't know how I'll even speak to count these. But Viktor narrows his eyes, and I know what he's going to say next.

"Don't make me ask again," he says coolly. "What was that one, *printsessa*?"

"One," I whisper, and then the belt comes down again.

"Two!" I scream, pain and pleasure blossoming through my groin and thighs. He doesn't pause, coming down a third time, and I realize with a dawning horror that my body is responding—and that I'm not going to be able to stop it.

I can't call out the fourth. When the belt strikes my clit, the pain transmutes into something else, a pleasure so sharp and brilliant that I see stars behind my eyes. I scream, dragging on the bindings on my wrists as I feel an orgasm like nothing else sweep over my body, twisting it and making me writhe on the sheets, tears burning in my eyes from the intensity of it. Mid-climax, Viktor brings down the fifth lash, and my throbbing, sensitive clit takes the brunt of the blow, the sensory overload so intense that I can barely stand it.

I can't breathe, I can't think, I can't do anything except writhe and gasp with the last aftershocks of pleasure, my body trembling so hard that I can't stop it. Vaguely, I see Viktor ripping open the fly of his pants, his heavy erection gripped in his fist as he moves towards me, stroking hard and fast.

"You came without permission, *printsessa*," he says darkly. "You haven't earned being fucked like a proper wife again, or even sucking my cock on your knees like you're meant to. So take this instead."

His hand is a blur, jerking himself so roughly that it must hurt, and the groan that comes from his lips sounds almost painful as he points the swollen head at my face. I'm not ready for the rush of heat that explodes from him in a matter of seconds, his cum shooting out and coating my forehead, my nose, my lips. I taste the saltiness on my tongue, the heat coating my skin. I gasp, some of it dripping into my mouth as he shoots over my skin, again and again, finally shoving the tip against my lips and cheek as he wipes the last of it on my skin, his hips thrusting as the last drops slip out.

I can hear him panting. I half-expect him to untie me, but he doesn't. He shoves himself back into his pants, glaring down at me with an expression that's almost menacing, and then he turns on his heel, stalking away.

He leaves me there, tied to the bed, drenched with his cum.

And yet, after what he just did, I'm so exhausted that I can hardly bring myself to care. My eyes droop closed, and in a matter of seconds, I've passed out completely.

* * *

WHEN I WAKE UP, I'm alone in bed. My eyes flutter open, and when I go to rub them, I realize I've been untied—I'm laying on my side, and my hand is free. My face feels clean too, soft and smooth, without any trace of what Viktor left there last night before he left the bedroom.

Which means sometime during the night, while I was passed out, someone came and cleaned me up.

That thought is almost as humiliating as anything else that happened last night—maybe even more so. I have no idea who it could have been. The idea of Viktor coming back in and cleaning me up himself seems ludicrous, but the thought of it being anyone else is horrifying.

Slowly, I pull myself out of bed, blinking as I see a note on the bedside table. It's written in Viktor's sharp and slanted handwriting, and I peer at it, noticing that it's still early in the morning.

I expect you to be downstairs for breakfast. I have a meeting shortly after when Liam Macgregor arrives. Don't do anything to embarrass me.

I crumple the paper up in my fist angrily, throwing it across the room. Gritting my teeth, I stand up, wincing as every muscle in my body protests as I walk towards the bathroom to shower. I want to wash everything Viktor did to me last night off, but the aches and pains remind me that I'm in no shape yet to be doing all of the things that we've been doing these past days, both before and after I discovered the truth.

Although—I still can't get the look on his face last night completely out of my head. He'd looked so startled and confused, as if nothing that I'd said made sense. Maybe it was just a ploy again, a way to throw me off, but in that brief moment, he'd looked so unguarded.

I shake my head, shrugging it off. It doesn't mean anything, most likely, and I don't have the energy to analyze it any longer. I barely have enough to get myself through the day.

The shower, at least, helps a little. I stand under the hot water for as long as I can manage without being late, letting it stream over my skin until I feel warm and pink and clean, and then I towel off gingerly, trying not to look too closely at the welts on my breasts and thighs where the belt struck me. It's only made my body all the more a minefield of things to make me feel as if the skin I inhabit isn't mine anymore. I turn away from the mirror as quickly as I can, wrapping my hair up in a small towel before heading back into the bedroom to dress.

Don't embarrass me. I'm sure that extends to my choice of clothing. If I had my way, I'd put on a pair of leggings and an oversized sweatshirt, clothing that's loose and comfortable and won't chafe any of the healing or newly bruised places on my body. But I know that isn't going to please Viktor, so I settle for something else in the array of clothing that appeared in the wardrobe—another wool sweater dress, this one in a deep cranberry color that I know he'll like. I quickly braid my hair, slipping on my leather flats and taking a deep breath before making my way downstairs.

Sofia and Ana are already at the breakfast table, a spread of pastries and dishes of eggs and other breakfast foods between them on the table. They both look up as I walk in, Sofia giving me an encouraging smile.

"How are you feeling?" She gets up to grab a plate for me, and I shake my head quickly.

"I can get it. You don't have to get up." I reach for the plate, my stomach twisting at the idea of eating anything at all, but I know I haven't had enough recently. Viktor is going to start getting upset at me for that too if I'm not careful—he'll want me to put on weight, look more like the woman that he married. For all my defiance, after last night, I don't know how much more of his "discipline" I can take.

I put a croissant and a few spoonfuls of eggs onto the plate to start, slipping into a seat next to Ana as I pick up a fork, poking at the food as I try to convince myself to take a bite.

Sofia glances over her shoulder, as if to make sure that no one else is coming into the dining room and then leans forward a little, her voice low. "How are things with you and Viktor, Cat? I mean really? You can talk to me, you know. You did a lot for me when I was trying to come to terms with my relationship with Luca. I want to be here for you, too, if you need it."

I want to tell her the truth so badly. But I know that's not an option. There's nothing she could do, even if she wanted to, and it will only make things worse. I can't make things worse for myself—I just don't have the ability to bear it. I've been as strong as I can manage, and now I have to simply survive until something gives.

"It's fine," I say quietly.

"Are you sure?" Sofia's eyes narrow in concern. "Cat, you don't have to hide things from me—"

"I didn't expect our marriage to be all sunshine and roses. It was always a marriage of convenience. One that I didn't want, either," I remind her. "It's as good as it's going to be."

"You know—" Sofia takes a breath as if she's worried that I might not like what she's going to say next. "I never thought I would be happy with Luca. I didn't think I could even bear to marry him, let alone fall in love with him. The things you told me about it being a choice helped a lot. I thought I hated him, that he was a monster—"

"Do you know what Viktor's business is?" I cut her off, a sudden bubble of resentment welling up in my chest and clogging my throat. I can't tell her about what Viktor's done, but the truth is that there's so much more than that. Even if he really were the man who had cared for me in the cabin, the one who had whispered sweet things to me and told me how beautiful I was, it *still* wouldn't matter because he would still be a man who sells human beings, who traffics women and gives them over to other men for pleasure. I can't love him, no matter what different sides there could be to him.

Sofia frowns. "No. But all men in this line of work do some things that—"

"He traffics women." I blurt it out, my fork gripped tightly in my hand. "Sex trafficking. That's what my husband does. He brings women in from Russia—and maybe other places, who knows—and he sells them to the highest bidder."

I hear a small gasp from Ana, and Sofia's face pales a little. She swallows hard, looking down at her plate for a moment.

"Have you talked to him about it?" she asks quietly. "Have you asked him why he does it?"

I shrug. "He said something about it being a better life for them, that they would be impoverished or working in brothels in Russia, that this way they live a life of pampered luxury with men who pay hundreds of thousands or even millions of dollars for them. I guess that's how he justifies it."

"And do you think it can be justified?" Sofia looks at me, her face very still. "Or is that why you're so unhappy?"

"I don't think so, no." I bite my lower lip. "I'm supposed to give him an heir, a son to inherit all of this. I'm supposed to raise two daughters who love their father but don't know that he sells other men's daughters." I glance at Sofia's stomach, pushing away the thought of what the doctor had said, that I would likely be unable to have children now. "You had a hard time thinking about giving Luca a son, too."

"I came to terms with it," Sofia says quietly. "It's a difficult life, and not always a black and white one. There's a lot of moral grey area in the men we marry. There are things that Luca does that I don't always agree with. But I know that he's a good man who will do his best to raise his children to be good too, to have a moral code. It's the best I can ask for, and I—I love him." She lets out a sigh. "It's not always easy. But it is worth it, and that's what I decided, in the end. That's what I chose."

I let out a small, short laugh. "I remember telling you that. I don't know if it's the same, though." In fact, I know it's not, not after what Viktor did to me. But I can't say that out loud to her.

"You're not always going to agree with your husband, not in this life that we lead," Sofia says quietly. "But if you can separate the man from the things that he does, maybe you could be happier."

"Maybe." I don't know what else to say because even if I could separate Viktor from his business, love the man and not the things he does, I can't erase the things he's done to *me*. And that makes it impossible to fix anything else.

"I wish I could find love with anyone at all," Ana says suddenly, her voice small and soft. "I don't think I ever will, now." Her fingers tap at the edge of the table, a nervous tic next to her full plate of food. "I don't even remember what I used to be like anymore." She looks up at Sofia then, her face paler than I ever remember seeing it. "That girl who took you into an underground club and talked back to a Bratva man? It's like she was someone else. I barely even remember what it felt like to dance—and that wasn't all that long ago."

The table is very quiet, and Sofia reaches out, touching her best friend's hand, her own eyes glistening. "It will get better, Ana, I promise," she whispers. "Things will turn around."

Ana smiles tightly, her lips pressing together. "I don't see how," she says softly.

And then, just as quickly, she clears her throat, looking over at me with an apologetic smile. "I'm sorry, Cat. We were talking about you. I didn't mean to steal the conversation."

"It's okay." I touch her hand too, not saying the thing that comes immediately to mind, which is that I'm glad for the distraction from talking about my life. It's too complicated, too difficult, and I don't want to discuss it any longer. There's no point when I can't tell the whole story.

The sound of footsteps interrupts anything else I might have said, and the three of us look up to see Viktor and Luca, both sharply dressed and stern-looking, walking into the dining room. "Liam will be here shortly," Viktor says, his gaze sweeping over the table without quite meeting mine. "If you ladies would like to join us to greet him."

"I've never actually met Liam," Ana says quietly as Sofia comes around to help her back into her wheelchair.

"He's nicer than a lot of the other mob bosses," Sofia says with a laugh. "Funnier, gentler. He wasn't meant to inherit. He had an older brother, so he wasn't raised to be the heir."

"What happened to him?" Ana asks curiously.

Sofia shrugs. "No one knows. He was in Ireland, Luca said, but no one could contact him or find him. I guess there was an effort made after Conor was executed, but there wasn't time to leave a hole in the Boston leadership. It could have caused problems that would have been so much worse. So they made a choice to simply have Liam take over."

Executed. The word sends a shiver down my spine, and I try to hide my expression as I follow Sofia and Ana out of the dining room. It brings back the memory of the cold metal of a gun against my palm, the kick of it as I fired, the squeeze of the trigger, and the way a man's forehead opened in front of me, his life extinguished in a second.

I've executed a man. One who was following Viktor's orders.

It should have been Viktor kneeling in front of me, begging for mercy.

I can barely keep myself from trembling when I go to stand next to him as we wait for Liam. He doesn't look at me, barely acknowledging my presence, but I want to scream at him.

I think I just want to scream, in general.

The front door opens, and three bodyguards walk in, stepping to the side as Liam enters. I've met him before once or twice—he's young, in his late twenties, I think. He has messy dark hair that makes him look more youthful and a clean-shaven face and a habit of perpetually smirking, as if everything in life is just a little funny, no matter how dark. The most serious I've ever seen him was at Franco's funeral.

Luca and Viktor both step forward, greeting him and then saying something in a low tone that I don't quite catch. Liam murmurs something in response and then steps past them, greeting me first, as he should, since he's a guest in Viktor's home. I'm impressed with how well he keeps up with the conventions, but the Irish are as traditional as any other mob family, with their own rules and rituals.

"Caterina." He squeezes my hand, his expression kind. "I heard what happened. I'm so sorry. I'm glad that the men responsible were given justice."

"Thank you," I say quietly, avoiding his eyes. I can't say out loud, the way I want to, that the man who was really responsible is standing right there, or that I'm so sick of being reminded of the fact that my body is now littered with reminders of a trauma that I can't ever escape.

He lets go of my hand, moving to greet Sofia next. "How is the baby?" he asks. Sofia barely has a moment to tell him that she and the baby are both doing well before he suddenly glances at Ana, a look of surprise crossing his face.

"Ah, but I've never met this lovely lass before." He smiles a sudden, broad grin that shows his perfect teeth and seems to light his face up, making him look even more jovial than usual. "Your name?"

Ana doesn't say anything for a full beat. Her blue eyes are locked onto his face, her mouth opening slightly as if she's gone completely speechless. Sofia's mouth is twitching, and after another moment passes, she hisses under her breath, "Ana!"

"Oh!" Ana blinks. "Anastasia Ivanova. I'm sorry. I'm not quite myself these days."

"Ms. Ivanova." Liam reaches for her hand, raising it to his lips. "I've only just met you, but I can tell that whether you are yourself today or not, whoever you are is one of the most lovely lasses I've ever had the pleasure of meeting."

Sofia and I both stare at him in unison, looking at the two of them. The entire room has gone still, and Liam is still holding her hand, longer than would be considered strictly appropriate for a greeting.

He seems to realize it, too, because he steps back quickly, letting go of her hand and letting it fall back into her lap. Ana has gone even paler than usual, and Liam clears his throat, looking at Luca and Viktor. "Well then," he says, in his lightly accented voice. "Shall we retire for our meeting, lads?"

Viktor raises an eyebrow at the casual address, but just nods. The three men walk away towards the study, and Sofia and I turn towards Ana instantly, both of us trying hard not to laugh.

"What on earth was *that*?" Sofia blurts out, looking at her friend. "I've never seen you look at a man that way in your life!"

"What do you mean?" Ana asks defensively, her hands knotting together in her lap. "He's handsome, that's all. It startled me."

"I've *seen* you look at handsome men before," Sofia says insistently. "A *lot* of them, if you remember. But I've never seen you give one actual fucking *doe eyes* before."

"I was not," Ana says, shaking her head. "He was very good-looking and very polite." She swallows hard, looking away. "I wouldn't let myself have an interest in him anyway. Someone like him couldn't possibly be attracted to me." She clears her throat, blinking rapidly. "Not anymore."

Sofia opens her mouth to say something, but Ana is already wheeling away, her hands clenching the sides of her wheelchair so hard that her knuckles are white.

"We've got to find a way to help her," Sofia says quietly. "She can't keep going on like this. It's going to kill her."

My chest tightens at that, but I can't think of anything to say. I feel as if it's my responsibility, in a way, to help her. It was my husband who did this to her, after all.

But I can't even help myself these days.

I don't know what I could possibly do for Ana.

CATERINA

The next few days almost run together, until the only way that I really can tell them apart is by mealtimes, which are as tense and awkward as one might expect. The only levity is seeing Liam watching Ana across the table, his gaze bright and interested, but it's always marred by the way Ana quickly looks away, clearly unable to believe that a man like Liam could take an interest in her.

I don't know if Sofia has tried to talk to her, but I can't. Each night with Viktor has been a new kind of punishment, him taking out his anger on my body, refusing to fuck me and taking his pleasure in other ways, doing his best to make me beg, and me refusing to give in. It's sapping every bit of energy that I have until I want to scream at him all of the things that go through my head every day, all of the angry, horrible things that I want to say to him.

But I don't. I keep my mouth shut, except for when he drags the sounds of pleasure from me that I don't want to make, or the times I call out the blows as he spanks me, twisting my body up into a tangle of resentment and desire and pain and pleasure that makes me feel more and more confused every day.

What's worse is seeing Luca and Sofia together. They're so obviously in love that it hurts, and every time I see them together, it makes me feel more miserable than ever about the turn my own marriage has taken.

Like, for instance, when I come downstairs a few days after we arrived at the safe house and catch a glimpse of them standing by the large window in the living room, oblivious to anyone else who might walk by. Sofia is standing there with her hand on her small but visible bump, and Luca reaches out, his hand covering hers as he leans down to kiss her. I freeze in place, knowing that this is something too intimate for me to be watching, but unable to look away anyway. The way he kisses her is the sweetest thing I've ever seen, a light brush of lips, his hand caressing her jaw as his mouth moves gently over hers. It's clear from the way they're looking at each other that everything else has disappeared, that for them, they're the only two people in the entire world at that moment.

And then he bends down, pressing his lips against Sofia's stomach as her hand goes to his hair, and I can't watch anymore.

I turn on my heel, fleeing towards the back door and the gardens, my eyes burning. I'm not really supposed to leave the house—or at least, Viktor hasn't given me explicit permission to, which means there's a decent chance that he'll be angry at me for doing it.

But I don't care. I need to be out of this house, to breathe fresh air, and I burst out of the back door past the security, into the gorgeous gardens behind the main house. The path is smooth stone, and I run down it into the thick of the beautifully landscaped flowers and shrubs, feeling tears start to run down my face.

I'd thought, at the very least, that Viktor and I could have a cordial marriage. One where I had the child he demanded—preferably through scientific means—raised his two daughters who desperately needed a mother. I hadn't wanted to marry him, but I'd been prepared to make the best of it.

But now—

I haven't seen Anika or Yelena since we arrived here. They've been kept in their rooms mostly, with Olga and Sasha. I don't think that's a coincidence. I press my hand to my stomach, thinking of Luca kissing Sofia's stomach, and my chest tightens until I feel as if I can't breathe.

The child I might have had was all I'd had to hope for, someone to love me without reservations, someone that I could pour everything into without feeling as if I were wrong in some way for loving them. I can't shake the feeling that I'd been pregnant before Andrei and Stepan, and now, if the doctor is to be believed, I'll never have that baby at all.

I don't know why Viktor hasn't tossed me aside when I can't even give him the one thing he married me for, and he clearly doesn't want me mothering his daughters any longer.

What purpose do I have here? What can I do for him, beyond being a vehicle for his anger and resentment, something to punish and break? *If that's all I am to him anymore, I can't bear it,* I think, my arms wrapping around my midsection as I start to cry harder. I can't take much more. I'm exhausted, wounded, hurt inside and out, and all I want to do is collapse and—

"Caterina."

I hear Viktor's voice behind me, and I stiffen immediately, my entire body going rigid as I try to decide whether to turn and look at him or not, what the right choice is. If I do, I don't know what I'll see in his face, but if he demands that I go back into the house, I don't know what I'll do. I can't right now, I can't go back in—

"Caterina, look at me."

His voice doesn't sound angry—almost concerned? That makes no sense, not any more than the look on his face last night, but it's enough to make me slowly turn, my hands trembling where they're pressed against my body.

Viktor is standing there, worry written across his face, and it shocks me into absolute stillness. He walks towards me, his mouth tightening, and I wince back, although I can't seem to move.

"One of the guards said he saw you run out here." Viktor takes another step towards me, almost touching me now, and I feel as if I can't breathe. "Are you alright?"

He sounds as if he cares. He sounds as if it matters. I feel like I'm going to scream, so many emotions that I can't name them all bubbling up and feeling as if they're going to tear me apart from the inside out.

"No," I blurt out before I can stop myself. "But why do you fucking care?"

Viktor blinks, as if taken aback. "You're my wife, Caterina, I—"

"Stop fucking pretending as if that matters to you!" I scream it before I can bite my tongue, my whole body starting to shake. "Stop pretending as if you give a shit about me, or what happens to me, or anything else!"

Viktor stares at me. "I'm not pretending, Caterina. Your well-being matters to me more than I knew, more than—"

"All of that was a lie!" I clench my hands into fists, feeling my nails bite into my palms, the words rushing out now that I've begun. "After what you've been doing to me since we came here, how could I possibly believe—"

"That's different. You tried to run from me. I had to make an example, to show you what would happen if you didn't listen, to convince you to obey me—" Viktor trails off. "I'm angry at you, Caterina, and yes, perhaps I've taken that out on you in some ways. But above all else, I want to protect and care for you. You are my wife. What can I say to convince you of that?"

"You can't," I bite out, the tears of grief replaced with hot, angry tears burning in my eyes and searing their way down my cheeks. "Nothing you can say could convince me otherwise."

Viktor pauses, his blue gaze darkening, intent on mine. I see a shudder go through him, as if he's trying to resist something, to stop himself.

And then he takes one stride towards me, a hand going into my hair and pulling my head back, his body turning mine and pushing me back into a stand of trees surrounded by a canopy of flowers.

"Then I'll show you," he growls.

And his mouth crashes down onto mine.

CATERINA

I should have shoved him off of me, screamed at him, hit him, anything. I should have kicked him in the balls, maybe.

Anything other than what I did, which was let him kiss me, violently and passionately, in a way that I'm not sure he's ever kissed me, not even when he was pretending to give a shit back at the cabin.

I hate this man. The thought runs through my head, but not enough to break through the sudden heat that blooms inside of me, flaring through my veins and searing my nerves, awakening every sensation that I've felt in the past days that I didn't want to feel.

His lips are firm and hard and hot on mine, his hands gripping my waist as he backs me against one of the trees, and it feels like a different Viktor than the one who looked so coldly at me in the hotel room after his men brought me back, who ordered me to bend over for his belt, who tied me up and left me with his cum splattered across my face. This feels more like the Viktor that I woke up to bathing me in the cabin, the one who stayed by my side, who fed me eggs, and helped me dress. I'd believed that man was a lie, but what I can't understand is why he would pretend now. There's no reason for it, no purpose.

STOLEN BRIDE

And this doesn't feel like pretending. I can feel how hard he is, rigid against my thigh, pressing through the wool of his suit pants and my dress. A surge of lust washes over me at the thought of him inside of me, the thing my body has craved despite myself for days now.

"I need you," he pants against my mouth, barely breaking the kiss to speak, one hand coming up to squeeze one of my breasts. It hurts, my flesh still bruised and sore from the older wounds, and from the night he whipped me with the belt, but there's pleasure there too, compounded by his thumb grazing over my hardening nipple. His mouth presses hard against mine again, his teeth nipping at my lower lip as he surges against me, and I gasp, unable to stop the raging tide of desire that threatens to sweep over me.

I shouldn't let him do this. I shouldn't give any part of myself to him. I should fight, resist, but I can't bring myself to. My body is throbbing, aching, desperate for him. I gasp as his mouth goes to my throat, teeth nipping at the sensitive flesh there and then licking those same spots with his tongue, gentleness after the pain.

He grinds against me, groaning, his teeth sinking in harder as his hand slides down to my hip, and I don't know why he's waiting. He could take me whenever he pleases, but it almost feels as if he's giving me a chance to push him away, to tell him no.

And what happens then? He'll punish me again tonight, probably. I don't believe that this glimpse of the other side of Viktor, real or not, will last. And this is the Viktor I want, the one that I have trouble resisting, the one who makes me want to do exactly what Sofia suggested and look the other way so that I can have what I want.

The man who cared for me, if only briefly. The man who kissed every part of me and told me I was beautiful.

A man I could love, if not for—

"Fuck," Viktor groans, grinding against me. He glances up, briefly, towards the house and backs me further into the stands of trees, so that we're shielded from anyone who might look out here. "I can't wait, Caterina. I need—"

He doesn't finish the sentence, and I half-expect him to turn me around, bend me over and fuck me hard and fast, taking his pleasure and leaving. But instead, he kisses me again, his mouth hard and solid against mine, his tongue piercing my mouth and tangling with mine, and then to my surprise, he drops to his knees.

Just like that night in the loft in Moscow, when I'd let down my guard for a moment and let myself want him. Let myself have that pleasure with him, just for a little while.

And look at everything that happened after that.

"Viktor—" I mean to say his name firmly, but it comes out in a choked whisper instead, a plea instead of a command, and his hands are sliding up my thighs, pushing up my dress, reaching for the black panties clinging to my hips beneath it. I can hear the words in my head, telling him to stop, not to bother pretending again, telling him that I can't ever believe him, forgive him, love him, want him.

But that last is a lie. I do want him. I want what he's doing now, his hand sliding up my thigh, lifting my leg so that my heel rests on his shoulder, his other hand between my legs, tracing the outline of my pussy that's already drenched for him, wet since his mouth first crashed down onto mine.

When his mouth touches me, I cry out. I can't help it. He's been edging me as a punishment for days, teasing me and trying to make me beg, and in the end, I didn't have to at all. There's a small victory in that, in Viktor's mouth devouring me as if he's starving and I'm the first meal he's had in weeks, his tongue running over my folds and up to my clit. When he flicks his stiff tongue over it, moving in quick, small motions that feel like electric shocks of pleasure racing over my skin, I gasp aloud, the sensation so intense after days of deprivation that I can hardly bear it.

"Viktor!" When I say his name again, it's a cry of pleasure, and I know I'm lost then, my hands tangling in his hair as I feel him slide his fingers between my folds, one and then a second thrusting into me, curling as he begins to stroke inside of me in time with each lash and circle of his tongue around my clit.

I can feel him pushing me closer to the edge. My head tips back against the tree, my breath coming hard and fast, and my fingers tighten in his hair, my thighs tensing as I feel the delicious knot of need in my stomach starting to come unfurled, my entire body trembling as I hover on the edge. I'm almost terrified to come because I can feel the intensity of it, how it will crash over me, sweeping me away. I'm afraid of what I'll feel or do afterward, but I can't stop it, hurtling towards the edge as Viktor sucks my clit into his mouth, his fingers thrusting hard and fast in the rhythm that he knows I like.

"Oh god!" I almost scream when the orgasm hits me, crashing over me like a tidal wave of pleasure. Viktor doesn't stop for even a second, his mouth and fingers continuing in a relentless rhythm that carries me through it even as my legs start to shake, the quivers spreading through every part of my body as I convulse, coming hard on his tongue. My fingers tighten in his hair until I think it must hurt, but if it does, he doesn't give even the slightest sign. He holds me there with his other hand, supporting the leg braced against his shoulder as he pins me back against the tree, his tongue lapping up the arousal that gushes into his mouth as I come harder than I think I ever have before. It feels as if it goes on forever. When I finally gasp out his name again, my thighs tensing as my clit goes from throbbing with pleasure to oversensitive, Viktor finally pulls back, his mouth glistening with my arousal.

He stands up abruptly, one hand going to his belt as he surges forward, kissing me hard on the mouth. I can taste myself on his lips, but I'm still shuddering with the aftermath of desire, arousal still pulsing through me despite how hard I just came, and I don't even care. In a way, it's arousing in and of itself, a reminder of the pleasure he just brought me. I remember vividly the day he ate me out like that in the cabin, licking me to a sharp, intense orgasm even though he'd come in me only moments before.

"I can't wait any longer," Viktor pants, and I don't know if he's saying it to himself or me, but it doesn't matter. He's picking me up, lifting me so that my legs go around his waist, my skirt around my hips. I feel the soft wool of my dress catching on the rough bark of the tree as he yanks his zipper down, freeing his rigid cock and thrusting into me in one swift motion that takes my breath away.

I'm so wet that he slides in effortlessly, sinking into me to the hilt, and I moan aloud as the pleasure bursts over me, his cock filling me completely. His body presses against mine, pinning me to the tree, his hips moving in fast, hard thrusts that make me gasp as he buries his face into my neck, groaning. The sound vibrates over my skin, sending a shiver of pleasure through me. I clutch his upper arms, feeling the muscles flex as he thrusts into me again, hard, holding himself there for a moment as he shudders.

"You feel so good," he groans, his lips pressing against my throat, dragging up to my jaw. "You feel so—*fuck!* So fucking good—"

His hand grabs my chin, turning my mouth to his as he kisses me again, hard and possessive, his tongue thrusting into my mouth as his cock thrusts into me again, and his forehead presses against mine, his breath coming in short bursts.

"You drive me mad," he whispers, shuddering. "You—*fuck*. I can't do it again. I can't."

What is he talking about? It's on the tip of my tongue to ask, but I don't have a chance because his next hard thrust takes my breath away. He pulls out almost to the tip and then slams back into me again, impaling me against the tree, and then does it again, long and slow, until I'm shuddering against him, on the precipice of yet another climax.

"That's it, princess," he whispers. "Come for me again. Come on my fucking cock. Give me that."

I don't want to give him anything. I *don't*. But my body has other ideas. I'm already clenching around him, throbbing, my head tipped back as he breaks the kiss again and presses his lips to my throat, and I can't stop it. Every inch of his cock sends a burning wildfire of sensation through me, a pleasure like nothing else I've ever felt. I can't remember all the reasons why I hate this violent, cruel, treacherous, brutally handsome man that I've married.

I can't remember all the reasons why he's a monster and not a man.

All I know is that at this moment, he's someone different. And I want him, despite every single reason why I know that I shouldn't.

My hands go into his hair, digging into his scalp, dragging his mouth back to mine as I cry out, a sound that's almost a scream as my climax crashes over me again. I buck against him, legs wrapped around his waist, pulling him in deeper, tighter, wanting every inch inside of me as I come hard. I can feel my arousal flooding over him, soaking my thighs and his cock, my hands pressed tightly to the back of his head as I bite down on his lower lip, tasting blood.

Viktor groans aloud, slamming into me hard. The orgasm seems to keep going, the pleasure cresting and falling as I suck at the spot on his lip that I bit, the metallic taste of copper filling my mouth. I want to hurt him suddenly, punish him the way he punished me, and I dig my nails into the back of his neck hard, my teeth sinking into his lip again as he thrusts into me fast and hard.

He throws his head back with a roar, dragging his lip out of my grasp, and my nails dig in harder as I feel his hips shudder against me, his whole body convulsing with a spasm of pure pleasure. I feel him swell and harden even more, heat flooding me as he starts to come.

"*Bladya!*" he snarls in Russian, and then his eyes fly open, locking with mine as I feel the hot rush of his cum inside of me, filling me, marking me as his.

As if I've been anything else since the day I met him.

As if I could ever stop.

As if I ever had a choice.

CATERINA

I hardly even notice the sticky heat of him on my thighs when he slips out of me and sets me down. What I notice is his forehead pressed against mine, the way his hands are still on my waist, gripping me as if he doesn't want to let me go. He's still panting, his breathing coming hard and fast, and when I breathe in, I can smell the scent of his sweat and flushed skin. It sends another shiver of desire over me, and I hate myself for it.

I hate everything that just happened and want it, with equal measure. But the way he's holding me now in the aftermath hurts a thousand times more.

"What are you doing?" I whisper, closing my eyes tightly against the burning that I feel behind my eyelids again, desperate not to cry. Not here, not with him.

"I don't know what you mean," Viktor murmurs, his hands tightening on my waist.

At that moment, I feel something break inside of me.

I wrench away from him, using every bit of strength I have to twist out of his grasp. "You can stop pretending," I whisper, my voice shaking. "I know, okay? You don't have to keep doing this. It hurts more than when you're cruel."

"Know what?" Viktor sounds confused, and I whirl around, anger bubbling up hot and thick.

"Oh, fucking *stop!*" I glare at him. "I heard you. I thought I was just being paranoid when I thought you might have set it all up. But then I heard the phone call in the hotel room, and I knew."

"Set what up?" Viktor frowns, and I don't know whether to scream or slap him. I hadn't thought that I'd married such a good actor, and right now, I hate him more than I could have ever thought was possible.

"My kidnapping," I hiss through gritted teeth. "You set it up. You had them kidnap me from the loft in Moscow. You had Andrei and Stepan torture me. You faked the rescue. It was all you, all along."

"*What?*" A look of absolute horror passes over Viktor's face. "Why in the hell would I do that?"

I blink, swallowing hard. "To break me," I whisper. "To teach me a lesson because I fought you so hard on everything. Because I wasn't the wife you thought you were getting. Because I was angry about your business. So you had me kidnapped to teach me a lesson, and then pretended to rescue me and nurse me back to health, let me kill Stepan so I would feel indebted to you, so I would obey you and be the kind of wife you wanted, afterward."

"*Christ.*" Viktor curses under his breath in Russian. "Clearly, it didn't work, if that's what I'd tried," he says grimly. "But *fuck*, Caterina, how the fuck could you think that? What kind of monster do you think I am?"

I stare at him, feeling a sudden whirlpool of emotion opening up inside of me, threatening to suck me down and drown me. He looks so genuinely horrified by everything I've just said, but I can't fathom how to believe him. How to not think that this is just another act, another lie, another manipulation.

"Are you saying that's not what happened?"

"*No*," Viktor breathes. He crosses the space between us in two strides, reaching for me and pulling me into his arms. I tense up instantly, but he doesn't let go. "I could never have thought of such a thing in a thousand years, Caterina. I wouldn't do that to any woman, let alone my *wife*." He tips my chin up, his blue eyes fixed on mine. "Alexei was behind your kidnapping, Caterina. I don't know who he hired yet, but I will. I'll find out who he's working with, who took you from that loft, and I'll make them regret every second they've ever lived from the time they came out of their mothers' wombs." He shakes his head. "I had no idea how I felt about you until I took your body out of that cabin, Caterina. I thought you were going to die. I thought I had lost you, and every moment between then and when you finally woke up was as much torture as anything I did to either of those animals who hurt you."

I feel like I can't breathe. I can hear the sincerity in his words, washing over me, wrapping around all my fears and doubts and hurt and anger and threatening to make it all dissolve. I want to cling to them, if only because it felt so certain, so right to hate him. After all, this is a man who does other things that I hate, so why not hate all of him? Why not believe that he could do something so revolting?

But here he is, looking down into my eyes with an expression that comes very close to an emotion I'm terrified to put a name to, his hands clutching me, that fear of loss that he's talking about written over every inch of his face.

"I couldn't lose you, Caterina. Not like—like—"

His first wife. I pull away, wrapping my arms tightly around myself again, my heart pounding. "Your first wife," I whisper. "No one ever said what happened to her. Only that she died. I thought maybe—"

Viktor goes entirely silent, his face paling as what I'm saying, and not saying, sinks in. "You think *I* killed her?" he manages finally, his voice hoarse with disbelief. "You think I killed Vera?"

"Or had her killed," I whisper. "Maybe she was a difficult wife too, maybe—"

"She was." Viktor runs a hand through his hair, shaking his head. "But I didn't fucking have her killed, or god forbid, kill her myself!" He turns away, his shoulders tensing and then whirls back to face me. "I fucking loved her!"

I stare at him. "You did?"

"Yes." Viktor swallows hard. "It was a love match. We were wild about each other. I loved her, and I wanted her, and she was everything to me. I couldn't believe that she loved me back, this woman who was so gorgeous, who every other man wanted as badly as I did."

I blink, swallowing hard. I've never heard him talk about his first wife quite so plainly. It shouldn't hurt to hear him talk about another woman like this. It shouldn't make me feel jealous, but I can feel my gut twisting with bitter, acrid envy that I can't shake.

Viktor sinks onto a bench, rubbing a hand over his mouth. "Sit down, Caterina," he says finally. "I'll tell you what happened."

"I'll stand," I say tightly, and he shrugs tiredly.

"Have it your way," he says, his voice exhausted and hoarse suddenly.

"She got pregnant almost immediately," he says, after a moment's silence. "She was so sure it was a son. My heir. She spent every second in the latter half of her pregnancy making the house perfect, decorating it the way you saw it when you moved in, fussing over every detail. She had names picked out, a nursery decorated for a boy. And when it wasn't, when she gave birth to Anika, she didn't even want to hold her. She didn't believe me when I said that it was fine, that we'd have more children." Viktor lets out a long sigh. "I loved Anika from the moment I set eyes on her, but Vera couldn't, not completely. She wouldn't even redo the nursery. She cared for Anika, but there was always some distance. It was like Anika was her own personal failure. Things changed between us after that."

"And Yelena?" I frown, feeling myself soften towards him just a little. I can't imagine not loving a child that I bore, girl or boy, and my heart breaks for Anika, wondering if she knew how her mother felt, if she ever realized that she was a disappointment.

"Yelena came along after a while, although it took much longer than Vera wanted for her to get pregnant again. Sex was a chore by then, and all she could talk about was giving me a son, as if that mattered more than a happy wife, than having the woman that I loved and not this other person that seemed to have taken her place." He sighs. "It got worse after Yelena. She wouldn't nurse her. We fought—fights like we'd never had before. I said things that I should never have said to her, things that I'll always regret."

There's a long moment of quiet, and I can see that regret in his face when he speaks again.

"I made her fuck me that night, before she was ready for it again. I'll regret that for the rest of my life, too." His jaw clenches as if he's remembering something terrible. "She was never the same after that. She was happy, bright, bubbly, and beautiful when I married her. All she cared about was love, about laughing and having adventures and sharing a life with me. After that—she became obsessed with her body, with being thin and beautiful like the women other men wanted, terrified of getting older, of losing her figure to children. She became sadder and sadder with each month that passed, each month that she didn't get pregnant."

"That must have been hard," I whisper, and I don't know if I mean for him or for Vera—or maybe both.

"It was," Viktor says quietly. "I wish I had known how hard it was for her. I wish I had known which night was the last one we would spend together. I wish that I'd done that last night differently." His jaw tightens, and he looks up at me, some fathomless grief that I've never seen before in his eyes. "Do you know what the last thing she ever said to me was?"

"Of course not," I whisper, my chest tightening despite myself at the look on his face. "But you can tell me if you want to."

"She whispered to me, right before she fell asleep, that maybe we'd made a son. And then the next morning, I got up before she woke and left for a month on a business trip to Russia." He takes a deep breath. "The day I came back, I went straight to the office. And when I came home—"

He swallows hard. "I saw the bloody water first, all over the floor. And then I saw her in the bathtub, her arms slit open from wrist to elbow on both sides, straight down. It wasn't a cry for help. She wanted to die. She *meant* to die. And she meant for me to find her like that."

His voice shakes then, breaking, and I want to go to him. I want to reach for him, hold him, comfort him, but I don't. I feel frozen in place, watching my husband recount a story different from anything I had imagined. And I can feel my heart breaking for him—and for her too, the other woman who had loved this man and been destroyed by him.

"I screamed her name for what felt like forever. I tried to wake her up. I felt like I'd gone insane until the staff found me and called Levin, and he came and took me away from her and had it taken care of." Viktor pauses, and something shifts in his face, his eyes hardening as he looks up at me.

"I didn't find out the rest of it until the next morning when I went back into the bathroom. Everything had been cleaned, but they'd missed one thing."

There's a long silence, and I can almost hear the beating of my own heart.

"What?"

Viktor looks up at me, pain and anger in his cold blue gaze. "A pregnancy test," he says simply. "My wife was pregnant when she killed herself." He pauses. "And she knew."

It takes a moment for what he's said to sink in. I can't find the words to say, my heart stopping in my chest. I can feel the pieces clicking together, the reasons why Viktor is the way that he is, the reasons for how he's always been during our marriage. Why he treated me the way he did back home.

The pain that he's never shared with me before.

I open my mouth to say something, anything. But before I can, we're both startled nearly out of our skin by the rattle of gunfire.

It's coming from inside the house.

Viktor leaps to his feet instantly. "Stay here," he orders, turning to rush towards the house, but I can't obey. All I can think about is Sofia and Ana, Anika and Yelena, Olga and Sasha, all in that house, where I can hear the gunfire like a bad dream.

I run after him without thinking, my heart pounding, blood rushing in my ears. I see his expression as I catch up to him, but he doesn't tell me to stay again. He's laser-focused on whatever is happening inside, and I can see the back door ajar, the security there gone, probably rushed in to deal with whatever is happening.

I burst in after him, my throat closing up as I smell the acrid scent of gunpowder. I hear shrieking, the sound of a woman screaming, and another shout, and more gunfire as Viktor pushes me aside, shouting at me to stay put again as he runs towards the living room.

"Luca! Liam! Levin!" I hear him shouting names as I lean against the wall, panic flooding me, and I hear the sound of Sofia's voice, loud and frightened, and then a scream that makes my blood run cold.

"Anika!"

Someone shouts her name, and there's a rattle of gunfire again, and a man's voice loud above everything else, the words a flood of Russian that I don't understand.

Another shot and a high, thin scream.

A child's scream.

And then silence.

I rip myself away from the wall, rushing towards the living room. My only thought is what's happened to Anika. *She's alright*, I tell myself, feeling my stomach twist with nausea, fear chilling my blood until I feel as if my veins have turned to ice.

I skid to a stop in the doorway, gripping the side of it as my knees go weak.

The living room is a war zone, bodies everywhere that I don't recognize, and a few that I do from Viktor's security. The rest of his men are standing with their weapons drawn, along with Luca, Liam, and Levin, all of them with guns in hand as they look down at the remains of the intruders.

But my focus isn't on any of them. Not even on Sofia, pale-faced and holding her belly as she crouches near Ana, shielding her.

All I can see is Viktor, kneeling next to the sofa, bent over a small, unmoving shape on the bloodied rug.

Anika.

. . .

VIKTOR AND CATERINA's *story concludes in the final installment of their trilogy,* **Beloved Bride. You can purchase it here. Want an exclusive bonus scene of Stolen Bride? Sign up for my mailing list here.**